O9-BRY-497

MEN
MADE FOR
WAR

J. R. GATHINGS

MEN
MADE FOR
WAR

ADJUTANT PRESS
Wilmington, Delaware

© Copyright, 2002, By J. R. Gathings

All rights reserved. No part of this book may be used or repro-
duced in any manner whatsoever without written permission
except in the case of brief quotations embodied in critical articles
and reviews. For information address: Adjutant Press, P.O. Box
8221, Wilmington, Delaware 19803.

Selected historical background material was drawn from:
Stanton, Shelby L. *The Rise and Fall of an American Army:
U.S. Ground Forces in Vietnam, 1965–1973*. Novato, California:
Predidio Press, 1985.

Cover by Didona Design, Ardmore, PA. Cover image was taken
from: Channon, James B. (Compiler) *The First Three Years: A
Pictorial History of the 173D Airborne Brigade*. Published by the
Brigade Information Office.

The quotation facing page one is from: Guy E. Bowerman,
The Compensations of War (Austin: University of Texas Press,
1983), p. 164. Used by permission.

ISBN 0-9717686-0-9

Library of Congress Control Number: 2002094058

Printed in the United States of America
By ADJUTANT PRESS

To
All those who came home too soon

The old life was gone forever and each succeeding day and each succeeding horror drove the peaceful part farther behind us till at last it was gone completely from our ken.

Here we were, men made for war, men born to war, men whose life is filled from beginning to end with war and we felt secretly in our hearts that there could be no other life.

An American Soldier
France, 1918

Chapter I

WAR HONORS ITS DEAD. But what about those who lost their lives and kept on living?

Such men are all around us—brave men who squandered life's chances in a valley of death ten thousand days ago and ten thousand miles away, now playing out their empty lives like a pair of deuces high.

Those of us who made it home from the Team were no exception. But then, what else would you expect from a Long Range Recon Team? We lived war to the fullest, and found ourselves totally lost trying to live without it.

Long Range Recon Teams conducted reconnaissance and surveillance activities in the Viet Cong and NVA's backyard to collect information about Charlie's movements, strengths, and tendencies. Why would someone volunteer to be a LRRP, as they called us? It wasn't only about collecting information. It had more to do with coping at the most basic level—about the exhilaration of uncontrolled fear and, at the same time, the thrill of the chase. We lived and died together every day as a Team, and only two of us came back to live the hollow life of a survivor.

On the Team, at first, there was Z, the Moon Dog, and me. Cap'n Buck came later.

The Moon Dog was a ghetto dude all the way. He kept to himself and didn't say much. He was really out of place as a LRRP. If we had been operating in downtown Saigon the Moon Dog would have been right in his element, but the jungle was a different way of life for him. Still, he learned his craft and never let us down.

1

As for Ezekiel Chandler—Z as we called him—he was the best scout in the Brigade. At first glance he wasn't particularly imposing, but he possessed amazing power, stamina, and agility. His expertise as a woodsman and soldier were unparalleled. While the rest of us were armed with Russian-made AK-47's, Z carried a Swedish K with a silencer. He also toted a concealed .32 automatic pistol and a mountain climber's ice axe. The jungle was home to him. Z was uncanny in his ability to match wits with the Viet Cong. To Z, the VC weren't really the enemy. He considered them as fellow members of a noble brotherhood of warriors.

Before Cap'n Buck came along, the Moon Dog, and I were usually sent out on recon with Z as a three-man team. One day we were trailing an NVA platoon in the western mountains of Vietnam. This enemy platoon was moving along the edge of a small river. The three of us stayed abreast of them from the other side of the river. In the afternoon the enemy platoon crossed over to our side of the river and doubled back in our direction. We concealed ourselves by getting behind a big boulder at the river's edge. We waded out into the river as the NVA platoon passed by along the river bank on the other side of the boulder.

There would have been no problem if the NVA unit had continued moving down stream. They wouldn't have spotted us behind the boulder, and we could have resumed our surveillance once they passed by. Unfortunately, they decided to stop on the other side of the boulder and set up camp for the night. They still hadn't seen us, and Z signaled for us to stay tight. After dark we could wade across the river and find cover on the other side.

We heard the NVA soldiers joking and making their camp preparations on the other side of the boulder from us. They started some camp fires and began clicking away with their radio, sending a message to their headquarters in code. The three of us were okay until a couple of the NVA soldiers decided to cool off in the river. You should have seen the surprised look on the faces of the two soldiers when they came up for air and saw three Americans standing behind the boulder at river's edge gazing at them. Z had screwed the silencer on his Swedish K. Without hesitation he cut the two swimmers down with it. Immediately we hightailed it across the river as fast as we could. When the rest of the NVA platoon saw what was happening they grabbed their rifles and opened fire on us as we dove behind rocks on the other side. We slithered into the jungle with bullets bouncing everywhere. It was recon by fire. They couldn't see us, so it would have been luck if they had managed to hit one of us. It sure gets your attention when that much lead is whistling past your ear. They gave chase, but we made it to our rendezvous point on the other side of the ridge for a helicopter pickup.

At that point we had been out in the boonies for over a week, and we were tired. We were looking forward to getting back to Base Camp to rest up for a day or two. Our plans changed when the chopper pilot heard over the radio that a helicopter crew had been shot down south of Cheo Reo. Right away he changed directions and headed his copter for the crash area. Instead of spending the night at Base, we were embarking on a rescue mission.

The terrain was so rugged that the chopper couldn't land near the crash site. They dropped us off in the valley below, and we started up the mountain on foot to reach the wreckage. We grabbed onto roots and tree stalks to pull ourselves up the steep mountainside.

When we found the fuselage it was lying on its side, caved in. There were no signs of the crew, except for one unlucky crewman who had died on impact and was still trapped in the tangled wreckage. Apparently the VC had taken the rest of the crash victims as prisoners. We knew we had to locate and free the captured crew before they were taken back to a prisoner camp.

The Moon Dog stayed behind at the wreckage site while Z and I headed off in search of the captured crew. When darkness set in we pulled in close to each other and moved very slowly and carefully, tripping and falling from time to time in spite of ourselves.

We came across a well-used trail leading down the mountainside. We didn't know which way to go on the trail, so we waited for someone to come along that we could follow. After a couple of hours three women passed us carrying bags of rice. We started off down the trail after them, staying a short distance behind.

Z's plan was to follow these three women right into the Viet Cong camp, in hopes that the captured helicopter crewmen were being held prisoner there. Things took an unexpected turn when five VC soldiers passed us heading back up the mountain. This created a dilemma for us. Who was more likely to lead us to the prisoners—the soldiers or the three women? We had to split up. Z continued following the women, and I headed back up the hill behind the VC soldiers.

I had to be very careful to move only when the VC were moving so I wouldn't be detected. About an hour later, the VC soldiers turned onto a little trail in the direction of the helicopter crash site.

After a while I lost the trail of the VC squad. I had no choice but to sit down right where I was. I dared not move since I had no idea where the VC soldiers were in the darkness. I sat there in silence for the next few hours, nodding off occasionally even though I was trying hard to stay awake.

At dawn I was awakened by four rifle muzzles thrust into my face. The enemy patrol had doubled back and surprised me.

They rousted me and pushed me along to the crash site. Getting captured is the worst possible thing that can happen to a GI. Now it had happened to me.

Suddenly there came the crack of two rifle shots. They were from the Moon Dog. Still at his post guarding the crash site, he had seen what was happening to me. The Moon Dog's two shots zapped two of the guards. I whipped out my knife and took care of one of the two remaining. But the fourth VC soldier wheeled and poked his rifle at my head. His intention to pull the trigger was interrupted by the command of *"LOI TU-CHOI!"* from above us on the hill. The fifth VC soldier had outflanked the Moon Dog and now held him hostage. He was shoved down the hill to join me. The Moon

Dog and I were blindfolded and forced to lie face down in the dirt, with our hands lashed tightly behind us.

Our two captors were enraged that we had just killed three of their comrades. Obviously their plans were to execute us. First they took their frustrations out on us by pummeling us with their rifle butts.

Fortunately, they did little more than crack a few ribs before there were two "putt" sounds, some thuds, and all was silent. Z had come to our rescue. Having lost the trail of the three women, Z had doubled back to see how we were faring.

Z shrugged off our elation at being saved. We had to stay focused on the mission at hand. By that time the chopper crew had been captured for sixteen hours, and Z was afraid we were losing our window of opportunity to free them before they were moved away to a POW camp. Z reasoned that if one of the three of us was captured the VC would take their new prisoner to wherever the helicopter crew was being held prisoner. It was a crazy plan, but it was our only hope of finding the helicopter crew before they were moved out of the area. The Moon Dog and I had just had a taste of captivity and were pretty banged up, so Z was the logical volunteer to be taken prisoner.

Z pulled his little pearl-handled .32 automatic pistol out of its leg holster and handed it to me. I taped it in the small of his back. Then Z switched places with the body of the dead airman in the wreckage. The Moon Dog and I hid the airman's body and then moved uphill above the crash site and spread out so we would be in a position to follow Z no matter which direction they took him.

We expected the VC, having heard the gunfire at dawn and with no word from the patrol sent out the night before, to send out another patrol to investigate. It was a couple of hours before the new VC patrol finally showed up. They had never seen a helicopter up close, and they couldn't resist taking a peek inside the wreckage.

Z had to moan a little to clue them in that he was still alive. They dragged him out of the wreckage and began arguing about what to do with him. Since they usually killed wounded Americans on the spot, they had to buy into the idea that Z had now regained consciousness and was healthy enough to be taken prisoner. This was a tense moment, and the Moon Dog and I were ready to open up on the VC if it looked like Z would be harmed. We breathed easier when they tied Z up and blindfolded him. Now it was up to us to follow Z and his captors to their hideout without being spotted.

The VC headed down the mountain in the same direction the women had gone the night before. About two-thirds of the way down, we ran into another puzzling situation. The VC patrol, with Z as their prisoner, vanished. They couldn't have been more than forty feet ahead of us when they disappeared.

We decided they must have gone down in a tunnel. The Moon Dog and I spread out to look for a tunnel opening. I finally found a trap door by accident when two women climbed out of it and went off into the jungle.

Since Z and the American helicopter crew were underground, their rescue would be much more difficult. Where in the tunnel system were the prisoners located? How big was the tunnel complex? How many other exits were there? How many VC were inside?

I radioed a status report back to Headquarters. They responded that reinforcing troops would be inserted the next morning. Unfortunately, things didn't wait that long to start happening. In the middle of the night the VC brought their prisoners out of the hatch and started to move them to a new location. There were twelve to fifteen VC soldiers escorting Z and the chopper crewmen.

When the Moon Dog and I caught up to the rear of their column, we began to eliminate their rear security guards. We did this by taking out the last man in their column and trading places with him. Then bumping off the next man, and the next.

We had neutralized four guards in this manner when the Moon Dog tripped and fell down. The radio he was carrying bounced off his shoulder and slid out into plain view. Two of the remaining VC guards quickly grabbed me, and a third put a rifle to the Moon Dog's head. The only lucky thing that happened was that the front half of the column didn't hear the scuffle and continued to march off down the trail away from us.

Before the guards who were holding us could alert the other guards in front about the situation, there was a "BANG BANG" from what sounded like a cap pistol. It was Z's .32. He had ripped the gun down off his back and, with his hands still tied behind him and firing backwards, shot the two guards who were holding me. At the same time an orange flash from the Moon Dog's rifle subdued the VC soldier who he had been wrestling with. Immediately the Moon Dog charged ahead, blazing away with automatic weapons fire to keep the front half of the column away from the American prisoners. I cut Z's hands free and then freed the other three American prisoners.

I stayed on the mountain with the Moon Dog to hold the VC at bay while Z led the freed airmen down the mountain to a clearing where a helicopter could land to pick them up. As the Moon Dog and I heard the chopper take off we broke contact with the VC in the dark and slipped down to the clearing for the second pickup. When the Brigade's rifle companies surrounded the area later that morning they found a huge rice cache in the tunnel system, but little else. As usual, Charlie had picked the area clean and vanished.

Thinking back on those times in the war I marvel that we ever survived. When I look at the old snapshots I can't believe how skinny and naive and young I was then. I was just a boy, really. And I was sent over there to do a man's job with no idea of what war was all about. Audie Murphy may have said war was hell, but his movie sure romanticized it for me. I was convinced that duty to my country outweighed any of the other moral concerns.

There are so many times now when I think of some incident over there, and I'd give anything to have it back so I could do it differently. Then there are times when I wouldn't change a thing. I had to come to terms with life's toughest dilemmas, and I somehow managed to do it. For that I can be grateful.

I couldn't have done it without the support of Z and the Moon Dog, and especially Cap'n Buck. I'll have to admit I had the wrong idea about First Lieutenant Paul Rogers when I first met him. We were accustomed to having a green Second Looey, right out of ROTC, as our officer. Here he was, soon to be a captain, but with no combat experience, sticking his square jaw and stocky frame into our tent at Base Camp just before our jump at Junction City. And right away he started assuming command like we were a stateside unit. I pegged him for a rank rider who would hang around the Base Camp brown-nosing the field grades while sending us out into the boonies. Then he'd accept all the glory for the Team's accomplishments so he could become a company commander and move up the career ladder. Z warmed up to him quicker than I did. It took a while for Cap'n Buck to gain my trust and confidence.

Our outfit, the 173rd Airborne Brigade, had been occupied for several weeks with search and destroy missions in the Iron Triangle. Except for uncovering several tunnels, we encountered only minor enemy activity in that area. Then they pulled us back into Base Camp and told us we'd be jumping that night. Operation Junction City. It turned out to be the only official American combat jump of the War. The Sky Soldiers at Bien Hoa were high as kites. A combat blast was the dream all paratroopers lived for.

Z, the Moon Dog, and I were getting our gear squared away for the jump when this First Looey with a new Ranger tab and jump wings walked into our tent and announced he'd just been assigned commander over the LRRP teams. Like all the new guys, he still had a pale face. He put on a good front for someone I knew didn't know anything yet. I couldn't wait for him to screw up and maybe get himself put out of action so we could try someone new again.

Cap'n Buck gave us the usual pep talk about him having to learn from us, but at the same time he was in charge and would take that responsibility, and he assured us he would win our confidence and respect.

At that point, Z couldn't resist having some fun with our new officer. Z pitched Cap'n Buck a K-bar and sheath.

"Here, I took this off the last lieutenant's body. He don't need it no more, but you will."

"Thanks, Guys," Cap'n Buck answered. "You're all heart. I've only been here twenty minutes, and you're already looking out for me!"

He got out his flint and set about honing the blade. But Z wasn't finished.

"Moon Dog, show the lieutenant how to use one of them gut splitters," Z called out.

The Moon Dog stood up, grinning from ear to ear under his aviator's sunglasses. He whipped out his K-bar and did about ten tricks with it, flipping it from side to side, around the back, over and under, all sorts of ways. Suddenly, in one motion, he wheeled and rocketed that knife toward the far end of the tent, sticking it right in the tent post. Z and I gave him a round of whistles and applause. The Moon Dog was something else with a knife. One time he gigged an NVA soldier in the neck with his k-bar from twenty feet away.

When Cap'n Buck saw that he said, "Whooee! I'm sure glad you're on my side. Where're you from, Armstrong?"

"Cleveland."

"Remind me not to go near your neighborhood when I get back to the States!"

The Moon Dog cracked a big smile. "This blade works anywhere in the world, Sir. Not just Cleveland."

"Okay, that does it," said Cap'n Buck. "Anytime I'm out in the boonies with you, you're on point for my own protection!"

Six hours before the Brigade's big jump, our Team was to do a night jump behind the lines to check out the area and make sure the Second Infantry Battalion didn't run into any surprises when they hit the silk the next morning.

We would be jumping from a chopper at night into unfamiliar, possibly hostile, terrain. Cap'n Buck looked to be a cherry jumper, and I questioned whether he was up to a night jump, much less what might be waiting for us down on the ground.

We jumped at 0200 hours, right after the B-52 prep of the area. Cap'n Buck and the Moon Dog survived the landing without any broken bones, which was a good start. We scooped up our gear and closed into a tight security circle to bury the chutes. That done, we cautiously moved north toward the tree line, with Z at the point.

We had not had a lot of experience at moving around in unfamiliar terrain in the dark. Every time Z paused, the three of us bumped into him. We weren't yet the well-oiled machine we melded into a few months later.

As it turned out, the night movement didn't last long. We slid along the tree line until we came to the beginning of a trail. Within minutes Z felt a trip wire about ankle high. Disarming it in the dark took some time. Down the trail a short ways was another wire, and then another. It was obviously too dangerous to continue moving around at night. So, we moved perpendicular to the trail for several meters and took up a night position in a jungle thicket.

Being Cap'n Buck's first night out in the bush, we had to catch him a few times from rustling too much, or scratching too loudly, or swatting at mosquitoes. We didn't hear any enemy movement during the night, but there was no way of telling, with those trip wires out, whether the VC were in the neighborhood or not.

At first light we started moving through the wood line parallel to the open field to our south, which was the Second Battalion's drop zone. We zigzagged our way deeper into the jungle, trying to stir up any enemy activity. Cap'n Buck was thrashing around a little more than the rest of us would prefer. We'd have to tape up all his jingles when we got back to Base Camp.

The fact that we didn't detect any enemy activity made Z uneasy. Who had put out those trip-wired booby traps?— the VC themselves, or some of their civilian sympathizers? Were the trip wires intended to kill any dumb Americans who might happen to pass by, or were they an early warning signal for a VC force lurking farther back in the jungle?

Cap'n Buck finally motioned for us to circle back toward the clearing. When we reached the edge of the tree line, we sat down back-to-back to have a whisper conference. It was nearly 0800, and the Second Battalion was waiting for word to make the jump.

"Everything looks clear. I'm going to tell them to come on," said Cap'n Buck.

From our position we could see across the fields to the Montagnard hamlet of Prek Klok.

"Wait," Z said. "The Montagnards ain't out in the fields yet."

"So what?"

"That could be a signal to the VC that there's trouble. I judge we ought to wait a while."

This was a real test for Cap'n Buck. Everyone, from General Deane on down, was waiting for his signal to kick off the biggest operation to that point in the War. A green First Lieutenant wouldn't want to hold up the works without a good reason. On the other hand, he needed to build trust with his new Team members.

"Okay," he whispered. He turned to me because I was carrying the radio. "Send the 'Hold' code."

The next twenty minutes seemed like all day. We sat there sweating, tension mounting, not saying a word. Finally, the straw hats started bobbing out of the hamlet and spreading out into the fields to work. This was the all-clear signal to the VC and NVA.

"Send the 'Go' code," Cap'n Buck said.

Thirty minutes later we witnessed a spectacular sight. Hundreds of tiny specks popped out of C-130 aircraft and were pushed abruptly horizontal by the prop blast before their chutes caught wind and floated the Sky Soldiers lazily to earth.

Suddenly the show was interrupted by the putt putt putt of mortars being launched from inside the tree line about a hundred meters from us. Immediately Z, the Moon Dog, and I dashed toward the sound, with Cap'n Buck bringing up the rear. There was no time for fancy maneuvers. The VC would probably risk one or two more volleys and then disappear before our artillery could get a bead on them. If we didn't get there in time there might be nothing left to catch except American 105 rounds pelting us. We heard the second volley go out when we were about forty meters away. At about twenty-five meters, Z motioned for us to spread out on line. Just then a smoke round from one of our artillery batteries crashed in nearby. Our artillery guys were already zeroing in on the mortar position. We charged the position head on, our automatic weapons blazing. The VC, caught up in their efforts to get off a third volley, were totally surprised to find Americans on top of them so fast. Their mouths dropped open in astonishment, but we closed them up permanently. When their rear security guard jumped up and opened fire on us from our left, Cap'n Buck nailed him without hesitation. We breathed a sigh of relief that Cap'n Buck had gotten his first kill so soon. This would be a real confidence builder for him. I also chuckled to myself as Cap'n Buck pumped half-a-dozen rounds into that poor VC. New guys always make absolutely sure the first time!

Within seconds we had a body count of five. The Moon Dog and Z fanned out from the position and took up a defensive posture in case of counterattack. I grabbed the handset of the Prick 25 radio.

"CHECK FIRE! CHECK FIRE! Mortar position has been neutralized. Friendlies in the area. CHECK FIRE. Do you copy? Over."

"Roger. Please identify. Over."

"This is Scout Two. We're popping smoke. Identify color. Over."

The command Huey buzzed overhead.

"Roger, Scout Two. We see yellow smoke. Over."

"That's confirm. Over."

"Roger, Scout Two. Hold position until relieved. Over." Z waded through the bodies to Cap'n Buck, who was looking a bit queasy while studying the black, twisted form of his first kill.

"Breakfast time, Sir," Z said nonchalantly.

Chapter II

FOR THE NEXT SEVERAL days the Brigade performed patrolling in place operations to make sure nothing came in or out of the horseshoe while the 11th Armored Cav drove toward us from the south. The LRRP teams were placed out along the Cambodian border to give early warning in case the NVA moved a large force down against the flank of the Brigade's position. There were a few minor sightings of suspected VC or NVA, but booby traps were the biggest problem.

One booby trap cost the Team dearly. We were moving cautiously down a trail when the Moon Dog's foot went down square into a well-camouflaged punji pit. The punji stakes came right up through his foot. He stumbled and twitched around a bit, looking down in horror as the blood started oozing up around the punji stakes sticking out through the top of his boot. I could see the pain setting in on his face. Before he could scream, Z covered his mouth and whispered for him to be quiet because there might be Cong in the area. The Moon Dog's reflex action was to try to pull his leg out of the hole, but Z held his knee down firmly and whispered for him not to move until we made sure there was no grenade under his foot. Big beads of sweat were popping out on the Moon Dog's face, and we knew he was in unbelievable pain. His whole body was shaking, and he was whimpering quietly, but somehow he was able to suppress the screams. He was one gutsy dude. Z motioned for Cap'n Buck and me to keep back. He held the Moon Dog's foot down with one hand while with his other hand he felt down

13

in the pit below the stakes. As expected, there was a tripped grenade in the bottom of the pit. Z was going to try to hold the grenade's arming spoon down tight while he pulled the Moon Dog's leg out, but the Moon Dog wouldn't let Z risk himself to do that. The Moon Dog motioned for the three of us to back way away from him. For a moment I thought he was going to pull up his leg and blow himself up. Instead he squatted down and reached down in the hole himself to try to get the grenade out. It took him three tries before he could get himself down low enough to get a grip on the grenade, and all the while he was about ready to bust with pain. Finally the Moon Dog slid the grenade out, and we were about to breathe a little easier. Then he had more bad luck. The arming spoon popped off the grenade, making it impossible to disarm. The Moon Dog's only option was to heave it away. Unfortunately, the grenade hit a tree and ricocheted right back onto the trail. There were only a couple of seconds left before it was due to go off, so we couldn't get there to help. The Moon Dog's right leg was still pinned by the punji stakes. All he could do was pull his left leg over to shield his head and body from the blast. There was a loud BOOM. Smoke and dirt billowed up. We ran over and saw that the shrapnel had chewed him up severely in both legs.

Z grabbed the Moon Dog by the armpits and yanked his leg out of the hole with one big heave. Immediately Z hefted the Moon Dog up across his shoulders in a fireman's carry, and away we went. We hopped off the trail to avoid additional booby traps and plunged downhill through the dense underbrush. I was carrying the radio, and while we were crashing down the hill, I grabbed the mike and shouted, "BLACKJACK! BLACKJACK!" That was our emergency rendezvous signal, and I was praying one of our choppers was within range to hear it. Moving that fast through virgin jungle, there was no way to see all the obstacles ahead of us, and each of us went tumbling a time or two. We tried to help Z with the Moon Dog, but he waved us off. We finally swung back on the trail and kept jogging as quickly as we could down it. Around a bend, we ran face to face into three VC. We zapped all three of them without breaking stride.

When we came out into a clearing at the bottom of the hill, I was relieved to hear the clack clack clack of a chopper coming in for us. My legs were burning so badly from oxygen debt I didn't think I could make it another step. I don't know how Z did it, carrying the Moon Dog all that way. When Z reached the chopper, he spun around and slid the Moon Dog backwards onto the floor, and we got out of there.

The Moon Dog was only out of action for about a month. With him not out there with us I felt like I was missing part of myself. The Moon Dog was the Team's first major casualty. We would all get our turns before it was over.

The remaining three of us on the Team continued our recon assignment in support of the Brigade. A week later some strange things began to happen. We came across a pair of fresh graves. When we dug them up, they had both been killed by artillery fire. One was wearing the black pajamas of a VC soldier, but the other body was dressed in civilian clothes. It was unusual to see a soldier and a civilian buried side by side. Then came the mystery of the disappearing trail. We worked our way down one major trail that abruptly stopped. Strangely, it didn't connect up to anything. The next day we cut over and picked up another trail. It suddenly dead-ended out in the middle of nowhere, too. Both trails appeared to have been well-used recently, and then they stopped for no reason. Z studied the map and realized we were very near to the point where the other trail had vanished. We decided to forge through the jungle to the spot where the other trail had also ended. The distance between the trails was approximately eighty meters.

For two hours we moved very carefully through the jungle without finding anything unusual. When we knelt down for a short break, Z beckoned us over to where he was. He was smelling a faint, musty draft wafting out from where he was kneeling. Under a vine-covered, rocky outcropping, we found a small air shaft.

In all likelihood we were standing on top of a tunnel system. Cap'n Buck wanted to call in reinforcements right away, but Z talked him into waiting until we could size up the situation a bit more. The way the paths leading to the entrances were hidden could mean the NVA had abandoned the tunnel when the Americans came into the area. Perhaps they were hoping the tunnel wouldn't be found and they could return to it later. On the other hand, the tunnel could be like a hornet's nest with a couple hundred NVA hiding down there, just waiting to pounce all over one of our units.

The first order of business was to locate the trapdoors leading to the tunnel. Z and Cap'n Buck headed west, scouring every square inch of ground in search of the tunnel entrance. I headed east doing the same thing. By nightfall we had moved about thirty meters out from the first air vent. Z and Cap'n Buck had found one more air vent, and that was it. Instead of coming back together we spent the night apart in two listening posts.

On Z's second watch of the night the activity began. About seven meters behind Z and Cap'n Buck a little square piece of the jungle swung open, and two gray shadows climbed out. The shadows carefully plugged the opening back up and tiptoed out toward the north trail. They were carrying satchels, possibly containing documents of some sort. One of them was in an NVA uniform and the other was dressed like a Vietnamese civilian bureaucrat—white shirt and khaki slacks. I was oblivious to all this and didn't get involved in this action. Obviously, Z needed to somehow seize the two satchels and get them back to Military Intelligence for analysis. If would be a real plus if he could also capture the NVA soldier and the VC civilian.

How Z was going to manage this was the problem. He'd need to follow them a ways from the tunnel so any ruckus he created wouldn't be linked back to our discovery of their hideout. To capture them Z would need help, and Cap'n Buck wasn't skilled enough yet to track these men at night without being detected. The two subjects were already moving away, so Z didn't have time to summon me to help him. Plus, I had our only radio with me. If Z captured them he'd need to call for an extraction. Worse still, we were within a thousand meters of Cambodian, and the two VC more than likely would head across the border and be out of bounds before Z could catch them.

Z had to move quickly to stay up with them in the dark. He signaled for Cap'n Buck to stay put, and he started out after them on his own. Z would have to figure out the rest as he went along.

Once the NVA soldier and the VC civilian reached a trail, they started moving at a pretty good clip. Z tried to move only when they moved so they couldn't hear him following them.

After a while, it appeared to Z that the two VC had picked up an escort. He could hear somebody moving behind him, with Z sandwiched in the middle. Z decided to get off the trail and try to keep up with them by working parallel through the jungle. Soon Z lost contact with the soldier, but the man with the white shirt kept moving on down the trail. Z couldn't tell if they had split company or if the soldier was doubling back to ambush him. All Z could do was stay on the tail of the man with the white shirt while guarding against an ambush from the rear or flanks. Not long afterwards Z heard a scuffle on the trail behind him, and the civilian official doubled back. Z carefully worked his way back through the jungle to the edge of the trail. To Z's surprise, he observed that the NVA soldier had taken an American prisoner—Cap'n Buck!

With foolish intentions of being helpful, Cap'n Buck had lumbered clumsily down the trail behind Z and had been detected by the two subjects. The soldier had then concealed himself to set an ambush while the man with the white shirt continued down the trail as a decoy. Z could tell the NVA soldier was an officer who was ecstatic about capturing an American officer. On the other hand, the NVA officer would have been quite a prize for Z to capture and send back to American Intelligence for interrogation. But Z had no time to entertain that possibility now. While tying Cap'n Buck's hands behind him, the NVA officer rotated his back toward Z for a moment. Z took that opportunity to leap out of the brush and slash the NVA soldier's throat with his K-bar.

For an instant the civilian man drew back in shock. Then he grabbed both satchels and took off down the trail at a full gallop. Z dropped the NVA soldier in a heap and took out after him. Z was never the swiftest afoot, and this little guy wasn't so easy for him to catch. Z chased him up and down and around the curves in the trail for a couple of minutes.

When Z finally closed the gap and was just about ready to make his final lunge and wrestle him to the ground, the VC civilian suddenly flipped up in the air with a loud BOOM! He had stepped on one of their own land mines buried in the trail and was killed instantly. Z quickly searched the dead man's pockets and stuffed whatever papers he could find into one of the satchels. Z went back and also searched the NVA officer before Z and Cap'n Buck headed back to the tunnel system. Z could tell Cap'n Buck was feeling sheepish about messing up Z's plan, and rightfully so. Cap'n Buck's stupidity had placed both of their lives in jeopardy and had foiled an opportunity to capture some key prisoners. This was exactly the kind of bumbling that made me wary of placing an inexperienced officer in charge of a unit which depended on precision and skill for its survival.

By the time Z and Cap'n Buck reached the tunnel system it was almost dawn. We needed to get the two captured satchels to Intelligence quickly. Running out of time, we had no choice but to search the tunnel system, come what may. Being better rested than the other two, I volunteered to be the one to go below. I cautiously pulled the hatch open. With my K-bar strapped to one leg and Z's .32 pistol in hand, I crept down the ladder into the dark rabbit hole.

The floor of the first level was about twelve feet below ground level. The light from the entrance above cast gray hues for several feet in both directions. I was in a bare anteroom just below the entrance. The earthwork was buttressed by timbers lashed together by leather thongs. I wondered how secure the shoring was down there. Hopefully, it had been safety tested by the VC.

Everything was still and quiet. There were a couple of lanterns on a ledge by the ladder. I lit one and started into the tunnel. Unfortunately, the VC only dug the tunnels tall enough for Vietnamese people to pass through, so I had to bend over quite a bit at the waist to move through it. I couldn't hear any signs of activity, so I kept moving ahead slowly but surely.

The tunnel opened up into a room. Catty-corner across this room I suddenly saw two figures in the shadows, staring at me. Instinctively, I dropped the lantern and wheeled to fire. Before pulling the trigger, I realized the figures were only statues of Ho Chi Minh and Vo Nguyen Giap. This room appeared to be an office, with papers and photos strewn about over several tables. Towards the rear there was a trap door going down to a lower level. I dangled the lantern down through the hole and noticed boxes of files and photographs stacked up below me.

Moving along, I came out into a room outfitted into a photo lab. Down below this room was a storage room filled with hundreds of cans of film on racks. Next in the tunnel was a room used for living quarters. There were several bunks with personal gear set beside them. At the other end of the tunnel was a room stockpiled with rice and other food staples. There were also rifles, rocket launchers, mortars, and ammo. There was another ladder leading up to the tunnel's second entrance at ground level. After breathing that stale dirt odor, I gladly climbed back to the surface and enjoyed inhaling fresh air again.

Now that we knew the tunnel was empty, Cap'n Buck called in the troops. An infantry company quickly swooped in and cordoned off the area. They had a field day searching and re-searching the tunnel, which turned out to be the headquarters of the Viet Cong Central Information Office. The two satchels contained maps showing the location of American units and offices in and around Saigon, and lists of the Viet Cong infrastructure in the Saigon region.

In my mind, Cap'n Buck received mixed grades for his first campaign. He made the jump with us at Junction City, and he got his first kill. But then he pulled that blunder at the end of the mission. I still doubted he had the intestinal fortitude for our kind of work.

I withheld final judgment on Cap'n Buck until he passed the acid test of having to plan and carry out a mission from scratch, all by himself. That time came when we were dropped off in the coastal rice fields north of Hinh Hoa to monitor enemy activity in the area. If possible, we were to bring back a prisoner for interrogation. Traffic on Highway One had been interdicted several times by Viet Cong patrols, and Headquarters wanted to determine if there was a sizable enemy unit in the area or if this was the work of the local VC cadre.

The part I hated about operating near rice paddies was the heat and humidity blistering off the water in the fields. And the leeches. I wasn't too keen on sharing my blood with those suckers. We spent two boring days watching three-wheeled Lambrettas chugging up and down the highway without any interference from Charlie.

Around midnight on the second night, using a Starlight Scope, we spotted dark silhouettes crossing the highway. There weren't any friendlies in the area, so this had to be a VC patrol. They were heading east toward Ben Goi Bay, which opened out onto the South China Sea. There had been reports from up near Quang Ngai of VC cadre rendezvousing with North Korean submarines. Could this VC patrol be heading to the bay to meet a boat or submarine? It was an interesting possibility.

By the time we got after them the VC squad was quite a ways ahead of us. Occasionally we glimpsed shadows bobbing at the other end of the rice field. We stayed one dike over from them, keeping on the side of the dike away from them and crouching as low as possible, but moving smartly to try to catch up. That kind of movement was tough, with your left foot constantly sliding down the mud into the water while you scrambled along. When we reached the other end of the field, my legs were like rubber.

Z couldn't pick up a trail from where we last spotted them, so we had to move forward very cautiously. The terrain closer to the bay consisted of a series of rolling sand dunes with scrubby underbrush on them. In the distance you could hear the slow, rhythmic pounding of the surf, and the exhilarating aroma of salt air wafted toward us.

When we came up over the last dune we spotted two of the VC right in front of us on the beach. There weren't any signs of the other three we had been following. We assumed they had moved on down the beach to set up another observation post farther south.

The two Charlies we were watching proceeded to build a little fire out on the beach. This was most likely a signal fire, which reinforced the possibility they were rendezvousing with a boat coming in from the South China Sea. We chuckled that if Z was as good in the water as he was in the jungle, we'd soon be claiming a North Korean submarine as a war trophy!

When the first hint of pink began to emerge on the seabound horizon, we heard the faint sound of a motor, and soon a boat appeared out on the bay. There were three figures on board. With the light behind it, I couldn't make out exactly what kind of boat it was, but it was bigger than a sampan.

The boat shut down its engine about one hundred feet from shore, and the two VC soldiers who had been at the bonfire waded out through the surf to meet it. That was our cue to go into action. Cap'n Buck and the Moon Dog spread out to cover us while Z and I jumped up and trotted right out on the beach, straight for the boat. We were hoping in the dark we'd look like a couple of their comrades and we'd be able to get up close to the boat before they realized who we really were. After that it would be a matter of zapping them before they zapped us.

However, luck wasn't with us that morning. Z and I had barely hit the water when shots rang out from back at the shore, and I took a round through the shoulder. Evidently the other three VC, the ones we had lost track of earlier in the evening, had closed in behind us and opened fire. Z immediately dropped the two VC who had waded out from shore and were standing in the water by the boat. A shot came from my left rear as the Moon Dog took out one of the silhouettes in the boat. The other two figures in the boat ducked down out of view.

There we were, standing ankle deep in water, with Z trying to hold me up, with no cover—vulnerable to return fire from either the boat or shore. I was wondering if Cap'n Buck was going to come through for us before we were gunned down in the water. At last there was a WHAM WHAM WHAM behind me. It was Cap'n Buck nailing the three VC on the shore. Z fired short bursts into the boat to keep the heads of the other two silhouettes down while he pulled me back toward the dunes. The leader on the boat motioned, and the other survivor started the engine. They began pulling away.

By the time Z and I limped back to the base of the dunes the boat was out of any meaningful rifle range. That was when we witnessed something I'll never forget. The leader on the boat stood up in plain sight and gazed back at us. In turn, Cap'n Buck climbed up on the top of the dune, staring back at him. For a long moment, although it was still too dark to distinguish any facial features, they stood there in mutual recognition of each other as if to say, "Yes, we are now arch enemies. May the best man win."

I was sent to Japan for a few weeks to let my shoulder heal up. Meanwhile, Z was able to recover one of the VC bodies floating in the surf. He had several thousand dollars in MPC and American greenbacks on him. There was also a slip of paper with that day's date written on it, and the words *Mot Tuoi*, which means "The One."

Cap'n Buck only reported recovering about one-fourth of the money which was actually there. Nobody but us would know the difference, and the Captain held the rest in a kitty to buy extra equipment and supplies we would need. He never let us use it for personal things. It had to be something that would help us accomplish our mission. Looking back, you could question his ethics on that. However, at the time we all thought it was quite clever. It helped us down the line to do our jobs better.

When we returned to Headquarters, Cap'n Buck was reprimanded for engaging the enemy when we were supposed to only observe and report. They claimed that we had spoiled a secret ARVN operation of some kind. All Cap'n Buck would say was, "We were attempting to take a prisoner as ordered, Sir." They couldn't fault him for that, so they begrudgingly let it drop. We thought it was very suspicious that we would be criticized for doing a good job, breaking up some kind of enemy rendezvous, and recovering a sum of money. Whoever *Mot Tuoi* was, he was highly connected with either the Vietnamese Province Chief or the ARVN's, and it was quite possible he was using his influence to make Cap'n Buck back off.

When people thought about it months later, the VC interdictions along that stretch of the highway ceased after this encounter. More importantly, Cap'n Buck had passed his test with me. The longer Cap'n Buck worked at it, the better he got. He never did anything to get us killed, and he even stuck up for us with the higher-ups. Those are the two things that an enlisted man looks for in an officer.

There was really nothing romantic about being a LRRP. Awaking before dawn, you ate a bite of cold LRRP rations and quickly got on the move. You crept very quietly and carefully with your senses honed, watching for trip wires and booby traps and listening for a twig snap or the click of a selector switch. No smoking or joking was allowed. The tension of doing this all day was exhausting. You battled your body and mind to stay focused. You forced your aching legs and back to trudge forward while enduring the elements: malaria-laden mosquitoes, bamboo vipers, blistering heat, monsoonal downpours, and leech-infested pools. You moved like that for a few kilometers, which took all day. By then it was late afternoon, and your Team Leader selected a bivouac site in the dense undergrowth. You ate another cold meal and then took your turn listening during the night while the others slept. There was no thought of changing clothes, shaving, or personal hygiene—Charlie could smell shaving lotion a mile away in the jungle. The next morning you got up and did it all over again. In that manner you put one day in front of the last, counting the days until your DEROS date, the day you could go home.

Collecting Purple Hearts was an occupational hazard in our line of work. All of us seemed to get nicked up every time we were involved in a major battle. While Z didn't get really ripped open until the second campaign at Dak To, the Moon Dog and Cap'n Buck got the worst of it during our first trip to Dak To. The Team's participation in that bloody battle evolved out of deadly encounters with *Mot Tuoi*. First a minor triumph, then a bitter defeat.

Chapter III

WE WERE OUT IN THE Plei Trap Valley searching for the remnants of a downed Bird Dog, a small single-engine plane used for directing artillery fire. The Plei Trap Valley consisted of steep hills and dense, triple-canopy jungle. This time our search was unsuccessful. We never found any trace of the plane crash. After four days of working the ridges, Cap'n Buck moved us down off the top to bivouac for the night on a ledge overlooking the valley below.

During the night we were awakened by the engine sounds of vehicles, possibly a whole convoy. Each of us heard it distinctly. We edged our way over where we could see down the steep hill. The sighting was definite. We saw the headlights of trucks driving along the dirt road in the valley below us. Confirmed.

That far into South Vietnam we had never seen portions of the Ho Chi Minh Trail wide enough to carry anything larger than carts and bicycles. Yet, those trucks rumbled right on past us for the better part of the night. This would definitely call for American countermeasures—air strikes, blocking actions by ground forces, etc.

At daybreak, we quickly made our way to our pickup point to warn headquarters about what we had seen. Major Balker, the Brigade S-2, at least listened to us. However, the G-2 down in Nha Trang at II Corps didn't believe a word of it. It was impossible to him. He downgraded the reliability of the information to questionable, even though we swore we had seen it with our own eyes.

When Cap'n Buck heard that they doubted our word he really got a case. He stomped out of the Operations Center mumbling, "If they want proof, I'll get them proof!" He was determined to get hard evidence of the trucks. A couple of weeks later when the S-2 didn't have a specific target that needed to be reconned, Cap'n Buck told him we'd be out to the west checking for enemy activity. The S-2 assumed Cap'n Buck meant an area just west of our fire bases, but we "lost our bearings" and ended up out by the Cambodian border again.

The Ho Chi Minh Trail was, of course, not one trail but a nickname for the many supply routes through which the NVA channeled a steady stream of supplies to their comrades-in-arms in South Vietnam. We moved down the same trail we had seen the trucks on, heading south out the lower end of the Plei Trap Valley, along the Nam Sathay and Se San Rivers. The trail forded or employed low bridges at most of the smaller streams it crossed. Where the trail intersected the Se San River the VC had found a narrow point, which was concealed from the air by overhanging trees tied together, and had built a substantial bridge across the river.

Cap'n Buck selected this site to set up an ambush. We planted plastic explosives under the substructure of the bridge and left the Moon Dog behind to detonate it at the proper time.

Cap'n Buck, Z and I moved down the trail about a thousand meters and sawed most of the way through a big tree that hung out over the trail. We tied a rope around the tree to keep it from falling until the right time. Z and Cap'n Buck took up positions within the ambush zone, and I was stationed at the tree to cut the rope, which would allow the tree to fall across the trail and prevent vehicles from continuing down the trail. This would keep the targeted vehicles from escaping our trap. It was the same ploy you see in old Robin Hood movies.

We waited through two nights with only bicycles and foot traffic passing along the trail. In the middle of the third night things started to happen. I heard a series of loud explosions from up the road. The Moon Dog was blowing up the bridge, which meant some vehicles had just crossed over it. Now it was up to me to make the tree fall across the road in time to block their forward progress. Using my knife, I set to work sawing away at the rope supporting the tree. Then the first problem occurred. After I cut through the rope, the tree didn't budge. According to the plan, the Moon Dog had been instructed to let the first three vehicles through and then blow up the bridge. The destroyed bridge would stop any pursuit from the north end of the trail, but it was critical that the falling tree stop all three vehicles from escaping to the south. If any of them got through, they would bring back reinforcements to hunt us down.

I reached for the bow saw and began sawing deeper into our original cut in the tree. I could tell by the sound of the engine of the first vehicle that it was approaching and would soon be right under me. I wasn't sure I could finish in time, but I kept my head down and kept sawing feverishly. The trunk shifted, and the bow saw got wedged in the bind so I couldn't move it. I stood up and ran out on the trunk and started jumping up and down while the first vehicle passed beneath me. There was a snap, and the tree gave way under my feet. I began falling along with the tree. I reached out in the shadows, my hands flailing. I managed to grasp the limb of a neighboring tree and swinging myself hand-over-hand above the road until I reached the bank. Immediately I grabbed my rifle.

The vehicle which had passed under the tree was a jeep. It had almost cleared the falling main branch, but a limb had caught the back end, causing the vehicle to swerve sharply to the right and bounce off the side of the uphill bank. The abrupt stop caused the shadowy passenger riding on the right side to lurch forward and bang his head into the front window frame. The driver started to get out, but the passenger shouted "*DI DI! DI DI!*" Obediently, the driver backed up and started peeling off down the trail.

Behind me I could hear brakes squealing. The other two vehicles had been stopped in the trap. I knew that any gunfire from me might mess up Z and Cap'n Buck's chances of surprising the drivers of the two trucks, but the Captain's orders came ringing through to me, "We positively cannot let anyone get through the ambush zone." I sat down and steadied my rifle. Just before the jeep careened out of sight around a curve, I squeezed off one round aimed at the back of the driver. Immediately, I slid down the bank to the trail and started running after the jeep. I heard gunfire and shouting behind me. I rounded the bend and saw an explosion flare up from below the trail. With the driver hit, the jeep had gone over the edge of the bank and caught fire. It was hung up on a tree about sixty feet down the steep incline. The driver lay motionless against the steering wheel in the burning jeep. The passenger's side was empty. I dropped to one knee and scanned the surrounding terrain. When a flash of light came from the burning jeep, I spotted a figure stumbling away. For an instant he wheeled and looked up at me fiercely. I got off one shot at him before he disappeared into the undergrowth.

In his condition, and especially since he was on foot, I knew if the passenger survived he wouldn't be able to get ahead of us and warn anyone. I left him and ran back up the trail to help Cap'n Buck and Z.

When I reached them, I noticed two dead Viet Cong soldiers in black pajamas hanging out of the back of the truck. Z was guarding two other soldiers wearing O.D. military fatigues who were laid out spread eagle along the trail.

Cap'n Buck was in a hurry to get out of there. He told Z to take one of the trucks back to pick up the Moon Dog. I started tying up the two soldiers Z had been guarding. As I turned one of them over, I was shocked by what I saw. "Sir, this guy's an ARVN soldier!"

Cap'n Buck came to my side. "Yes. ARVN soldiers riding alongside VC soldiers in ARVN trucks, carrying enemy contraband, and possibly weapons. We've stepped in the middle of a very messy situation."

By the time Z returned with the Moon Dog, Cap'n Buck and I had loaded the ARVN soldiers on the truck, and we were ready to move out. We began bumping and winding our way down the trail, with Z and the Moon Dog following in the second truck. Driving down a narrow, unfamiliar dirt trail at night in hostile territory was pretty hairy. We were also getting low on gas. Cap'n Buck urged me to go faster. He wanted to reach the Special Forces Camp at Duc Co by dawn.

Along the way I had to tell Cap'n Buck what I had been piecing together in my mind. "Sir, that boat launch at the beach last spring. I could swear that was an ARVN boat. And that man back there at the wrecked jeep that made off into the jungle was wearing an ARVN uniform. He could have been *Mot Tuoi.*"

We bounced our way down the trail for twenty miles before reaching the Special Forces Camp at Duc Co. Cap'n Buck went over to the guard bunker and asked to speak to the A Team Commander.

In a few minutes the commander came out, and Cap'n Buck explained what had happened.

The commander became quite perturbed about the situation. "What in the hell were you doing out here?" he asked.

"We were on a routine patrol, and we must have been confused about our location." Cap'n Buck answered.

"Confused, my ass! You knew enough about where you were to drive straight into my camp. The 173rd has no business being in my area of operation without my knowledge. I'm calling Nha Trang about this."

"If I was in your AO without your permission, I take full responsibility. That aside, we have a serious problem here. We have what appears to be ARVN involvement in the movement of Communist supplies down the Ho Chi Minh Trail."

"Things aren't always as they seem, Captain. What you think you see in the dark from your limited perspective may not be the actual case. You don't know who these men are or what their mission is. It could be a simple matter of a couple of trucks getting lost. We'll take charge of the detainees and the trucks now, Captain."

"As you wish."

At the direction of the Green Berets a group of Montagnard mercenaries unloaded the trucks. They pulled out cases of jewelry, ivory carvings, whiskey, and drug derivatives. There was also equipment for warfare: Russian-made canteens, web gear, bandoliers, helmets, gas masks, and Ho Chi Minh sandals.

When we returned to Brigade Headquarters, our Commanding General really tore Cap'n Buck a new one over this incident. Afterwards, Cap'n Buck was summoned to Nha Trang to talk to Major Jack Daniels about it. He was the personal aide to the I Field Force Commander.

I Field Force Headquarters in Nha Trang was located in a downtown building two kilometers down the boulevard from the Vietnamese Hall of Justice building. Cap'n Buck passed through the MP gate and crossed the small court-yard to the main door. He was directed up the main stair-case and down the hall where he was greeted by Major Daniels.

"Captain Rogers, you had quite an adventure out there west of Pleiku."

"Yes, Sir."

"I know you must be a little nervous being called to Nha Trang like this. Granted it's a little unusual. But, trust me, I'm on your side on this. I know what it's like being a com-mander out there in the field. You're caught in the middle. You've got to have the latitude to do your job—within limits, of course. Now, the reason you're here is the General asked me to talk to you, *mano a mano*, to cut through all the bull-shit and find out what really went on out there. He's got to get unfiltered information so he knows how to accomplish the mission. You understand that, don't you?"

"Yes, Sir."

"Very good. I've read your report where you say you ambushed two ARVN trucks and drove them to Duc Co. Were those the only two vehicles you ambushed?"

"There was a lead jeep that went over the precipice and crashed and burned."

"Ah, I see. And why wasn't that in any of your previous reports?"

"I stated that there was a convoy. Identifying the various vehicles in the convoy, other than the captured trucks, did-n't seem important to me."

"No, that's fine. I'm not here to criticize your report. I'm just trying to piece as many facts together as I can. You never know what might end up being relevant."

"Yes, Sir. I can appreciate that. I'm relieved that someone's finally interested in listening to me. I want to cooperate with you any way I can."

"Outstanding. Now, about that jeep. Was there just the driver, or were there any passengers, or did you notice anything unusual about it?"

"I really couldn't tell anything about it in the dark. A limb must have hooked the back of the jeep as it drove through, and the driver lost control and went over the side of the hill. We were busy with the two trucks, and we didn't have time to go down and check out the jeep."

"I see. You know, this thing has really developed into a problem for us. And, I know how these things happen. You're out there bucking for major, and you let things get a little carried away. When I was a company commander one of my platoons found a large rice and arms cache, and I can certainly attest that something big like that gives your career a nice boost. The General and I don't want to stand in the way of that. Do you know what I mean?"

"Yes, Sir."

"On the other hand, this thing could have terrible repercussions for you, without a little help in the right places."

"I'm not sure what you mean, Sir."

"Come on, Rogers. Let's stop screwing around and get down to brass tacks on this thing. You blew it out there. You were outside of your AO without permission, fumbling around out there in the dark, way over your head, and you ambushed a friendly convoy. In the confusion, you kill an ARVN soldier, the very people we were sent over here to defend. And since then, the General has been in the next room working night and day to keep this from becoming an international incident. My God, What do you think Cronkite would do with something like this?"

"ARVN's out driving at night along the Ho Chi Minh Trail? I guess they just lost their way, Sir?"

"Those guys are entitled to take some risks on their own. It's their country. You and I, or even General

Westmoreland, don't know everything they're doing out there. Maybe somebody was a little greedy and was trying to make a few bucks on the side. We don't get involved in their business like that."

"What about the Soviet military equipment?"

"You and your men were just mistaken about those items. You were exhausted and those things happen. Believe me, I know. I have the complete inventory right here of everything that was in those trucks. There were civilian supplies and clothes, but no military equipment. I've got photographs of the seized items that substantiate the official report. Witnesses have conflicts all the time in their testimony. I'm sorry, Captain. I respect your ability. But, in this case, I have no choice after examining all the other information but to conclude that you and your men were pushing the whole thing a bit too hard and simply didn't see what you thought you saw."

"I guess we dreamed up the two dead VC, too?"

"That's where you really lost it. The ARVN drivers swear up and down there were no VC riding with them. Like I said, I'm trying to work with you on this. And, I think it will be better for all concerned if this whole matter is forgotten right now."

"Naturally, you'll want me to write a formal apology to Ho Chi Minh for blowing up his bridge by mistake. I was wondering why there had been no B-52 strikes along that section of the trail, and now I know."

"Captain, your cynicism is uncalled for. After all, I'm not the one who screwed up here. If we understand each other, I see no reason to continue this meeting."

"I've got one question for you, Major. Have you ever heard of a Vietnamese official known as *Mot Tuoi*?"

A flicker of surprise crossed Daniels' face before he regained his composure.

Cap'n Buck saluted and started to leave. "You don't have to answer that, Major. I think we understand each other completely."

Cap'n Buck closed the door and paused briefly out in the hallway, taking a few deep breaths to collect himself. Just then the door to the General's office opened, and a WAC came out carrying a steno pad. As the door closed slowly behind her, Cap'n Buck caught a glimpse of a Vietnamese man in the General's office wearing the uniform of a field grade ARVN officer. The Vietnamese officer was sitting up proudly and expectantly on the edge of his seat, his jaw held high and both hands resting out in front of him on the arms of the chair. When he sensed Cap'n Buck's presence in the hall, he turned his head suddenly to see who was there. He scanned upwards quickly and then directed his fierce gaze right into Cap'n Buck's eyes as if to say, YOU! Before the door completely closed, Cap'n Buck noticed that the man was wearing a bandage over part of the left side of his face.

When Cap'n Buck signed out at the guard desk downstairs, he posed a casual comment to the MP on duty.

"Wow, that ARVN field grade who's in with the General looks like he really got clobbered in the face by Charlie!"

"Colonel Xi? Yes, Sir. That is pretty wicked. Only it wasn't from enemy action. I hear his stove at home blew up in his face when he was lighting it the other day."

"Is that right? One of those home accidents, huh? What is Colonel Xi's position?"

"He's the G-2 for ARVN II Corps, Sir."

Were Colonel Xi and *Mot Tuoi* one and the same? It was certainly beginning to look that way, even if we lacked that one piece of clear and convincing evidence. Who was this Colonel Xi? Was he merely a part-time rum runner—something almost every South Vietnamese citizen was guilty of to a degree—or was he something much more egregious?

Cap'n Buck dispatched the Moon Dog to Nha Trang to take some candid photos of Colonel Xi entering and leaving II Corps Headquarters. We thumbtacked these photographs to the timbers in the abandoned VC tunnel we used as our jungle hideaway. Cap'n Buck would stay down in the tunnel for hours staring at those pictures and pondering the connection between Colonel Xi and *Mot Tuoi*. The rest of us didn't take it very seriously back then. But all that changed at Dak To One.

It was early June, 1967. We had spent a couple of days goofing off at our tunnel in the mountains. On one of Z's nature walks he was intercepted by his friend Bo, the Montagnard woodcutter. I had thought that no one except the four of us on the Team knew the location of our tunnel, but I guess those Montagnards knew exactly where it was and when we were in it.

Bo was small and rugged, with brown, leathery skin, clad only in a loin cloth, and wearing brass earrings and a large necklace of carved bone pieces around his neck. Amid his wild outward appearance, his yearning eyes hinted that a part of him was trapped, longing to be set free. He was armed with a crossbow, and a quiver of arrows was slung across his back. Atop his bushy shock of wiry, black hair was a tiger-striped boonie hat which Z had given him. I never saw him without it. In return Bo had given Z a brass bracelet which Z never took off.

Z, who had learned a fair amount of the Vietnamese language on the streets, wasn't very conversant in the Mon-Khmer tribal language, but he and Bo got along pretty well using charades, with a few familiar Vietnamese words thrown in. The message was that Bo's chief wanted us to come to dinner. Very important.

We followed Bo up and down and around jungle trails for an hour before coming out into the clearing of the Montagnard hamlet. The thatch huts were built up on stilts to protect them from monsoonal flooding and to keep rats and wild animals out of the dwellings. The oblong huts were framed with logs which were notched and lashed together. Four or five families lived in each hut. The rats scurrying on the ground were huge, and the entire community reeked of human waste and decaying food. The bare-breasted women stayed in the background and eyed us shyly. They were taking turns pounding grain with a giant-sized mortar and pestle hewn of wood. Though the women appeared to take a back seat role in the life of the hamlet, Z explained that behind the scenes the women were very influential. Montagnard tribal rights were handed down through the maternal side of the family.

The children stepped out to look at us more closely. We were probably the first Americans they had seen. In the middle of all these tiny, dark brown bodies, we were struck by the appearance of one snow white little child standing behind and apart from the other children. Below his white fuzz of hair he was shading his eyes from the painful glare of the bright afternoon sun. I glimpsed the hint of two pink eyes peeking out from the shadow provided by his little hand. Then I knew. He was an albino.

We were invited to sit in a circle with the men of the tribe around a big vat of fermented rice swill. There was a long, hollow bamboo reed which they passed from man to man. We took turns sucking a swig of home-brewed spirits through the reed. The wine tasted terrible, and dinner was even worse. It's no wonder they liked to get a little buzz on before eating, because chow consisted of an unwashed gourd filled with rice speckled with some kind of meat particles. I didn't dare ask what the meat *du jour* was. It tasted putrid, but I just kept smiling and trying to eat enough of it without gagging so we could get out of there without offending anyone.

"Don't leave none of that rice," Z warned us. "Water and rice are protected by the tribal spirits. They won't take too kindly to us offending their spirits."

After that admonition, Cap'n Buck and the Moon Dog and I choked down the rest of our servings. Fortunately, Z licked his gourd clean and asked for seconds. He was the hit of the party. I expected at any time for them to go ahead and give him his blood initiation and admit him into the tribe.

After dinner there was plenty more rice swill to go around for everyone. The men of the tribe displayed their hunting prowess by picking off unsuspecting rats with their crossbows. They rarely missed. When it was our turn with the crossbow Cap'n Buck, the Moon Dog, and I missed our marks by wide margins, causing the Montagnards to roar with laughter. Then came Z's turn. He took careful aim with the crossbow and pinned a large rodent, wriggling and squealing, to a wooden pier, much to the approval of his new-found brethren.

Later, the chief called Z and Cap'n Buck and Bo up to his hut for a conference. Meanwhile, the Moon Dog and I continued to entertain the remaining hunters by missing a few more rats. Of course, the crossbow was not the Moon Dog's weapon of choice. If this had been a knife throwing contest, I'm sure the Moon Dog could have held his own with the tribesmen.

When Cap'n Buck returned from the meeting he had a serious look on his face. The Montagnard chief had received word from the tribes in the western mountains of large NVA battle units heading this way. We radioed for Cowboy, the helicopter pilot who was a good friend of Cap'n Buck's, to come and pick us up.

I waved good-bye to the little albino child. It hurt me to see how painful it was for him to see out of those little pink eyes. The tribe, no doubt, had no understanding of why he was born white skinned. His weak eyesight would make him a poor hunter, and he would probably be ostracized his whole life.

The Moon Dog stopped and knelt down beside the boy.

"Hey, Little Dude," he said softly, offering a finger for him to touch.

The boy, his little hand still shading his eyes, looked questioningly into the Moon Dog's dark face. Then he reached out and touched the Moon Dog's rifle and said, "POW!"

The Moon Dog reached up and took off his own aviator-style sunglasses and gently placed them on the little boy's face. They wobbled precariously on his nose from being so big. Through the years, I've often thought of the Moon Dog's generosity at that moment, and of the boy growing up with those shades helping him to live normally.

We learned from Cowboy that the Brigade was receiving other reports of enemy troop movements. The Special Forces Camp at Dak To had received mortar attacks, and a patrol had been ambushed. The Brigade's Commanding General was moving two battalions from Tuy Hoa to Dak To as soon as the airlift could be scheduled.

Cap'n Buck asked Cowboy to fly us straight out to the western border so we could check out the new enemy activity.

The monsoon season was upon us. In addition to dealing with daily deluges, the low-lying clouds and thick fog made transportation by chopper very dangerous. However, with Cowboy flying I never worried. He may have been somewhat of a character, but as a chopper pilot Warrant Officer John Mac Smith had no equal. To have a pilot who would fly anywhere, anytime, and could make a helicopter do the things he could make it do, was truly rare. There wasn't a month when Cowboy didn't have his Huey in the air over two hundred hours, and during crunch time you could count on him flying thirteen hours a day. More important to the Team, there was a special bond between Cap'n Buck and Cowboy. They'd do anything for each other. Cowboy always gave us special attention when we got in a jam.

Cowboy couldn't find a suitable landing place on the Vietnamese side of the mountains, so he dropped us off on the Cambodian side of the border, which was a no-no. This was in the steep valleys and merciless jungles where the backbone of the Chaine Annamitique mountains forms the border with Cambodia.

It seemed like you were always going straight up or straight down the jagged ridges. The entire area was a vast tropical rain forest. The trees loomed as high as a football field stood on end, with trunks six feet in diameter. There were smaller trees pushing up 40 or 50 feet in the space underneath the canopy of the giants. Finally came the part that we became intimately familiar with: dense undergrowth sprouting up from the floor of the jungle. So called "clearings" were choked with dense brakes of 10-foot high bamboo. Bullets just bounced off of that stuff. And, of course, the flat valleys were few and far between. The NVA anticipated the good landing sites and frequently had some sort of ambush or mines waiting for American troops when we landed. "Chollie's got a 'suhplize' waitin' for us every time we set down," Cowboy used to say.

We worked our way down to the low country in a northeasterly direction. We came across a series of waterfalls and followed them down into the valley. The river they fed into was swift and filled with big boulders. We rounded a bend and saw up ahead a big bridge spanning the river. This was not your usual makeshift, Viet Cong variety bridge. This was a real, fully-trussed road bridge. Since this was in

Cambodia, both vehicular and foot traffic were crossing it freely during daylight hours.

We maneuvered closer to get a better look. For all practical purposes, it appeared to be a peacetime operation. Many of the pedestrians weren't even armed. Unconcerned by the noise they made, the truck drivers didn't hesitate to honk when someone got in their way. The trucks came in from the north fully loaded, and the ones returning from the south were empty.

Staying well out of sight, we paralleled the road, heading south. It was slow going in that rugged terrain, and by nightfall we had only traveled a couple of kilometers.

As darkness fell, Cap'n Buck decided we'd hitch a ride back into Vietnam. We waited for the next convoy to come along. When the front of the column came to a curve, it slowed the back of the convoy down to almost a standstill. At that moment the four of us dashed out and jumped into the back of the last cargo truck. We were wedged between the wooden crates and sides of the truck, which made for a pretty uncomfortable ride. However, it was a treat to ride instead of walk for a change.

We bumped around back there for about 45 minutes while the truck wound its way along the dirt trail. Then the column came to a halt. I could hear some voices shouting orders up in front.

"They know we're here, run for it!" Z shouted. He slit open the canvas top with his K-bar, poked himself halfway up through the slit, and started blazing away with his Swedish K to keep the NVA soldiers pinned down while the rest of us clambered out of the back and scurried up the steep embankment into the jungle. The NVA returned fire with a heavy outburst of firepower. There must have been a hundred of them firing every which of way. We nuzzled in behind some trees and hoped no ricochets got us. But, Z wasn't able to get away from the truck, and they started closing in on him.

"WE'VE GOT TO GET Z," ordered Cap'n Buck.

We started firing on the soldiers closest to the truck to force them to take cover. This gave away our location, and the barrage they focused on us was almost like a wall of lead. Luckily it was pitch black, and they were only firing blindly in our direction. Slowly, we inched our way back down towards the road. Suddenly the truck backed up crazily, and the back end banged into the bank below us. Z had overpowered the driver and taken the wheel. Many of the NVA stopped firing momentarily to see what the truck was doing, and we took that opportunity to dive back into the back of the truck. Z jammed the gear into first and spun it away from the column, heading down the trail in the opposite direction as fast as he could drive in the dark. The three of us in the bed of the truck squeezed down behind the crates of cargo to shield ourselves from incoming hostile fire. Immediately the NVA turned two of their trucks around and started chasing us.

We tossed all of our hand grenades out on the road, hoping the trucks chasing us would drive over them as they went off. Though we didn't have any direct hits, one exploded right in front of a truck, causing it to run off the road.

The second truck peeled out from behind the first one and continued its pursuit of us. Another burst of automatic weapons fire opened up on us, and our remaining rear tires that had not already been hit were blown out. We were starting to cross a bridge over a river, and the truck careened out of control. We tore through the wooden guard rail, floating through the air momentarily before smashing down against the bed of the truck and splashing into the water. My head slammed against the side panel, and I sat stunned for a long moment.

Through my hazy consciousness I heard Cap'n Buck shouting for us to swim to shore. I felt like I was moving someone else's body, but somehow I rolled myself out into the water. The cold water shocked me halfway back into my senses. Bullets were flying all around us. Z ripped the seat cushion out, and we all clung to that and drifted downstream away from the truck. They couldn't see us in the dark, so we were soon out of their kill zone. Eventually the seat cushion became waterlogged and sank, and we swam the rest of the way to the shore. To save ourselves in the water we had to let go of our radio, and Claymore mines.

We moved up a short distance into a jungle thicket and drew in back-to-back to mend our aches and pains and wait for daylight. We were nervous about being without a radio, our lifeline to call for help. We had two star-cluster signal flares that were our last hope of communicating with the outside world. We could count on Cowboy to give us a fly-over the next morning at the usual time, but the truck ride had moved us much farther than he would expect. We'd need the flares to get his attention.

Sometimes you wonder how a situation can get any worse, but this one did.

At first light I opened my eyes and noticed Z half-raised up on one elbow, looking all around. I listened carefully. In the distance I could distinguish faint rustling noises. It took me a while to realize what was happening. This wasn't your usual twig snaps and limb whips caused by a few people sneaking around. This was a whole herd of people. I cocked my ear back. It sounded like it was coming from up the hill above us, too. I looked across the river and strained to focus on the few gaps in the leaves that revealed the far shore. I spied waves of cream-colored uniforms wearing pith helmets. An entire NVA battalion was closing in on us from all sides. Apparently they had not spotted us yet, since they had not opened fire. However, their sweep was so concentrated that they literally would be stepping on us very soon.

By now Cap'n Buck and the Moon Dog were awake. We all glanced at each other to see if anyone had any ideas. I was usually able to stay calm and keep my wits about me, but this time our plight had me so rattled I couldn't think clearly. This would have been a great time to have a radio. Even a hand grenade or two would have come in handy. Did they have a weak flank that we could attack to make a breakout? Or, could one of us sacrifice himself and draw their fire while the rest of the Team fled? There were so many NVA, and they had us so well surrounded, that those options seemed pointless. A scenario of being captured, tortured, and left to waste away in a death camp passed through my mind. This was unthinkable for a LRRP. I concluded that all of us going down together in an attempted breakout was the noblest course of action.

As usual, Z was way ahead of us. He recognized that we did have one natural ally: the river. The river created a gap in their encirclement, and gave us a chance, albeit slim, of eluding them. With Z leading the way, we low-crawled like slithering snakes back to the water's edge. We got up under the branches and roots of a low-lying tree whose branches reached out and touched the water. This gave us some cover from the NVA on the other side. Then Z, to my amazement, unloaded his Swedish K and collapsed the stock. He stuck branches in the breach so it would look like a floating piece of debris, put his mouth over the end of the barrel, and got down below the waterline. Submerged and using the barrel as an air tube, he began drifting downstream, with nothing but the clump of brush showing above the water. It looked pretty fakey to me, with that clump of brush floating out in the middle of the stream, but the NVA didn't notice it.

Cap'n Buck motioned for the Moon Dog and me to go next. We unloaded and removed the wooden stocks from our AK-47's, camouflaged them, and followed Z into the water. The river was cold, and it was only about five feet deep. I kept both hands up by the surface to hold the camouflage on and to gauge how much of the barrel I needed to keep below water. That left only my legs free to try to steady myself in the current and keep myself submerged. In addition to the muzzle knocking against my teeth, I was gagging from the gunpowder-laden air I was breathing through the barrel. I tried to relax and resist the urge to go to the surface for a big gulp of air.

I wondered how long we needed to keep this up. I had no idea how far down stream they were looking for us, or how much progress I was making. That question became moot, however, when we hit a series of rapids which pushed us down and over the chutes. I landed in a pool of deep water. When I came to the surface, I spotted Z over at the edge pulling the Moon Dog out. We quickly reassembled our rifles and tried to shake ourselves off and get our equipment squared away. All the while, we were wondering where

Cap'n Buck was. There was a collective sigh of relief when he came squirting through the chutes and tumbling over the cascade.

Moving to high ground we managed to signal Cowboy with the flares to pick us up. On the flight back we learned from Cowboy's crew that the Second Battalion had men trapped on a mountainside, and enemy fire was so intense that the Brigade couldn't get any choppers in to reinforce them. A major battle had begun.

Chapter IV

COWBOY FLEW US TO the village of Dak To, which was hastily being prepared as the new Brigade Headquarters. Cap'n Buck reported to the S-2 on the location of the NVA battalion that had been chasing us a few hours earlier. The Commanding General inserted part of the Fourth Battalion into that area as a blocking force. Although our Team was exhausted and due for a rest, that was out of the question under the circumstances. Cap'n Buck suggested we go back out west of Ben Het to monitor any large NVA units which might be moving against our flank from Laos.

"Negative," said Major Balker. "I've got orders from on high about where they want you. This hill right here to the south of us, Hill 1338. It's the highest, most rugged mountain around here. We need you to recon it for the feasibility of putting a fire base on it."

We got resupplied as rapidly as possible and headed to the chopper pad. Cowboy had to run three other missions before he could get to us. We waited nervously at the pad. Everything was so noisy and hectic back at Base, and it seemed like everywhere we tried to squat we were in someone's way. When Cowboy finally lifted us off, we felt at ease again. Out over the jungle where it was just us, we were in our element again. This was what we did and who we were, and we could predict what our environment might throw up against us, and we knew what steps were necessary to handle it. We could control our own destiny. Above all else, we knew each other. We knew our strengths and weaknesses and how to compensate and cover for each other to make a strong whole. We knew what each team member was thinking and what each one would be doing in a given situation. We trusted the other three every day with our lives, and, though we each had to deal with our own fears, we would willingly risk everything to save any of the other three.

By the time Cowboy dropped us off it was mid-afternoon. Once again we were facing a steep climb up the mountain through dense, triple canopy jungle. In the distance we could hear the constant BOOM, BOOM, BOOM of our artillery and the occasional brrrrrrp of the gatling guns on Ragged Scooper. Overhead F-100 Phantom jets were queuing up for bombing runs.

Cap'n Buck was anxious to get to the top by nightfall so we could radio Headquarters to start setting up the fire base the next morning. But Z, sensing that something was wrong, was moving more cautiously than usual. I couldn't detect any signs of enemy activity in the vicinity, and I didn't understand what Z's problem was. Cap'n Buck was getting impatient, too.

About halfway up the mountain Cap'n Buck signaled for us to form on line. We spread out about twenty meters apart and all moved up the hill together. This way we could get a wider perspective on the hill and pull Z along at the same time. Z was on the right flank, with me to his left, then the Moon Dog, and finally Cap'n Buck out on our left flank. We crept slowly up the hill, with each man keeping abreast of the man on either side, all of us edging forward for about one hundred meters in this manner. The afternoon monsoonal downpour burst upon us, and visibility was only a few meters. Time and again we slipped on the wet leaves and logs while pulling ourselves upward.

Without warning, there was a short burst from a machine gun to my left. Instinctively I dropped to the ground. The automatic weapons fire sounded like it was coming from point blank in front of where the Moon Dog had been standing. Simultaneously hostile fire erupted from several locations to our front. It seemed like the hill itself was spitting bullets at us. At first glance no enemy soldiers could be seen. Only after a close second look could I detect gun barrels protruding from small gunports in the side of the steep hill.

We were hopelessly pinned down. I had never seen this much enemy firepower sustained from dug-in positions. With no helmets or heavy weapons, we were ill-equipped to challenge this kind of entrenched force. Ordinarily we would break contact and call for reinforcements, but there was no way to get out of the kill zone, and our reinforcements were already fully engaged somewhere else on a hill of their own. Right on cue the mortars started exploding around us to finish us off. Despite burrowing down as deep as we could into the slash, all of us took superficial hits from the mortar shrapnel. Z realized that our only chance was straight ahead, because they would not rain mortars down on their own position. The trick was getting higher without being riddled by fire from the machine gun nests. Our infantry training came into play: take on one target at a time and neutralize it, starting with the one that is the greatest threat to yourself. I laid down suppressing fire while Z inched his way closer to the nearest gunport. He tried to pitch a hand grenade inside, but it hit the muzzle of the enemy machine gun and bounced back. Z batted the live grenade away with his rifle butt. It rolled away from us into a little rill, and we braced ourselves for more shrapnel, this time self-inflicted. I was shocked by the force the grenade had. The shrapnel wasn't so bad, but the wave of energy emanating from it was like running into a brick wall. Z was closer to it, and afterwards he was a bit cross-eyed when he looked over at me. His ears must have really been ringing.

It got Z's dander up that Charlie had made him do something dumb like that to himself. He pulled his bandanna off and used it to tie a grenade to the end of his rifle. While I covered him, he pulled the pin on the frag, reached up, and rammed the grenade into the gunport, snapping and jerking his rifle back out. There was a BOOM from inside the hill, and smoke blew out of the hole. Z grinned with satisfaction. We slithered up to that smoking gun port and methodically neutralized the emplacement nearest to me in similar fashion.

By the time Z and I looked over to our left to try to link up with the other two, Cap'n Buck had crawled over and tried to rouse the Moon Dog, who was lying limp, right at the spot where he had been standing when the first burst of fire opened up on us. Enemy fire prevented Cap'n Buck from getting up close to his head. The Moon Dog didn't budge when Cap'n Buck shook him. The Captain took out his K-bar and slit the Moon Dog's pants leg open with it. He reached up to the Moon Dog's inner thigh above the knee to feel for a pulse. Face gone ashen, the Captain looked over at us and shook his head in the negative. PFC Horace Armstrong, God rest his soul, had taken the first burst point blank in the chest and was killed instantly. The Moon Dog didn't talk much, and I knew very little about where he came from, but I knew everything about what kind of a man he was, and I loved him like a brother.

We saw death around us constantly, but this was the first time we had seen it in our own group. For the time being, the three of us remaining had to put his death aside and focus on working together to survive the ordeal. We had already dodged a bullet, a lot of them, actually. If Cap'n Buck hadn't spread us out on line when he did, we probably all would have been killed by that initial burst.

The machine gun nest in front of the Moon Dog was a tough one because the terrain around it was concave-shaped, making it impossible to get within ten feet of the gun port without drawing intense fire. We had to have the PRC-25 radio, which was strapped to the Moon Dog's back, to call for help to get ourselves out of this mess. Cap'n Buck lobbed a grenade up near the firing port and then tried to low-crawl toward the radio, while Z and I provided covering fire. He edged forward, shielded by the Moon Dog's body. Red shards of human flesh were exploding backwards, yielding to the withering fire from the gun embedded in the mountain. I strained to see whether the eruptions of exploding flesh were coming from the Moon Dog or the Captain. I was relieved to see the Captain continue to writhe his way upward. Cap'n Buck got close enough to strip the radio off of the Moon Dog's shoulder, and I thought he was going to make it out of there, but suddenly another heavy volley of fire erupted from the bunker hole. Helplessly I watched Cap'n Buck's shoulder peel backwards. Immediately Z snaked his way over there to try to get to him while I fired at the hole continually to keep the NVA occupied inside the bunker. When Z tried to get up close enough to pull Cap'n Buck and the Moon Dog away, another vicious volley of fire drove him back. I lobbed a grenade high so it would land up above the hole and roll down toward it. I didn't actually get a hole-in-one, but it went off close enough to the mouth to stun the NVA inside momentarily. Z seized that opportunity to make a lunge for Cap'n Buck's leg and drag him back down out of the line of direct fire. Z started back up for the Moon Dog's body, but the fire was too intense. At least he was able to reach out using Cap'n Buck's AK-47, hook onto the PRC-25 radio, and pull the radio down to him and the Captain. Meanwhile I slithered over to join them.

We worked our way a few feet down to get behind a tree stump, where I quickly applied direct pressure to the Captain's wound to try to slow down the bleeding. The wound was on the top of the shoulder and slightly toward the back. I couldn't tell if it hit any bones or not. There didn't appear to be any vital organs involved. Bleeding was the immediate problem.

Z told me to set up our Claymore mines on either side of us while he called for help over the radio.

"Scout Two to Eagle One. Over."

"This is Eagle One. Over."

"We've got one dead and three wounded, one seriously. We need a Dust Off. Over."

"All of our Med-Evacs are flying other missions, Scout Four. We'll get to you as soon as we can. Over."

Then Cowboy's voice interrupted. "Base, this is Bronco Seven. I'll take that Dust Off mission. Over."

"Roger, Bronco Seven."

"Scout Two, can you identify that KIA?" Cowboy asked from his chopper.

"Shoot the Moon." answered Z.

"How about that serious IRHA?"

"That's the one you're afraid it is."

"Okay, keep your motor runnin'. I'll be there in Zero Five. Over."

When Cowboy tried to land the NVA opened up on him from everywhere above us and to our flanks. Cowboy pulled off and tried coming in from the other side, but he ran into the same withering fire. Determined to make it in, he kept pushing down toward us, with bullets ripping into his underbelly.

"Get out of there, you crazy toad hopper!" Z barked at him over the radio. "I've got enough problems without having to scrape up your guts too!"

"Whooee!" exclaimed Cowboy. He banked his chopper back toward the open sky. "I've never seen anything like this before. Z, you'd better call in the jet jocks to loosen things up for me. I'll have a couple of Cobras come in on their smoke to lay down fire suppression. Buckie Boy, if you're listenin', hang on there. I'll be in directly. Z, there's a spot about two hundred mikes down the hill where I believe I could set 'er down, if you can get to it. Over."

"Roger. We'll be there. Bird Dog One, this is Scout Two. Fire Mission. Over."

"This is Bird Dog One, send your mission. Over."

"Request air strike against machine gun position on the east slope of Hill 1338. Over."

"What kind of ordnance on that strike, Scout Two? Over."

"Give me all the Captain Carpenter you've got. Over."

With that, Cap'n Buck tried to raise up, but he winced and slumped back down. "Negative," the Captain said. "We've got to get Armstrong out of there first."

"Captain, this is the only way," Z said. I could tell he was afraid we'd lose the Captain, too, if we didn't do something decisive right then. "We've got to get you dusted off *mau mau*, and this is the only way we can neutralize their position. It's okay. The Moon Dog would want it this way."

With us so close to the target bunker, Z calling for napalm was practically a suicidal move. But our chances were slim and none of getting off the mountain alive, anyway, so I went along with it. The machine gun had us pinned down where we couldn't move, and ground troops were closing in on us from the sides. Our only hope was a decisive strike of some kind to break ourselves loose and make a run for it.

The Forward Observer kept up a steady dialogue with Z in preparation for the strike. "This is Bird Dog One. Where do you want the goods? Over."

"I'm popping smoke," Z replied. "Please identify. Over."

Z nodded to me, and I pulled the pin on a can of yellow smoke and heaved it up close to the Moon Dog's body.

"I see yellow smoke. Over," the spotter plane responded.

"That's confirm. When the smoke drifts away, you'll see a body on the ground right there. A friendly. Drop your load two mikes in front of that body. Over."

"Scout Two, that's going to fry that body. Over."

"Roger. That's what we've got to do. Over."

Suddenly, my heart sank. I heard the war whoops of scores of NVA coming out of the wood line to our left, charging right at us. In addition to the machine gun fire from the bunker, now they were throwing a human wave attack against us. I quickly detonated our Claymore mines which slowed down the attack momentarily. Z grabbed the radio again.

"Bird Dog, we need that ordnance PDQ. We've got company on the ground, now. Over."

"Roger. Here comes the hot stuff. Keep your heads down. This'll singe the hair on the back of your necks. Over."

We each emptied a magazine and heaved our last grenades at the oncoming NVA soldiers and quickly dragged the Captain a little farther down the hill and dug in to try and protect ourselves from the napalm.

Z was sobbing. He pulled a poncho and liner over the three of us. Tears were welling up in my eyes, too. I closed them briefly and tried to remember a prayer. "Please, God" was as far as I got. I didn't know if I was asking for guidance to somehow get us off of that mountain, or forgiveness for what we were about to do, or mercy for the Moon Dog's soul. I kept repeating "Please, God. Please, God. Please, God." Nothing else would come.

The Phantom thundered right toward the gun position. At the last second it pulled up, and two black canisters plunged from the undercarriage of the aircraft toward the gunport in the mountain. There were two big pops and a WHOOOSH, and the whole side of the mountain was engulfed in a billow of flames. The heat was like something out of hell, and the shock wave sucked the oxygen out of our lungs. We gasped for breath. I thought we were too close and would be roasted alive. The poncho completely melted, and the liner burst into flames. Z threw it off, and we did a check of our arms and legs to make sure they were still working.

After the inferno subsided a bit, I lifted up Cap'n Buck's head so he could see, and the three of us watched in silence, shielding our foreheads from the blast of heat with our arms. We were witnessing the funeral, ashes to ashes, dust to dust, of a fallen comrade. War had made the Moon Dog's conflagration a thousand times more intense than the noblest Indian funeral pyre. We watched in awe, fascinated and horrified at the same time. Was this really what the Moon Dog would have wanted? And what of our own frail existence? Would any of us be fortunate enough to have even three mourners at our gravesites? The Team was all we could count on in this world. Maybe the next of us to die would have two mourners, then one, then none.

When the fireball abated we couldn't tell if there was anything left of the Moon Dog's body. There was nothing but a sea of smoldering black soot to out front.

Z and I snapped back to the task of trying to save Cap'n Buck's life. The gunships came in, blazing away. There was still sporadic enemy fire around us, but the napalm had significantly reduced their hostilities. We slid down the slope, dragging Cap'n Buck with us to Cowboy's chopper.

"YOU STAY WITH CAP'N BUCK," Z shouted to me over the roar. "I'M GOING BACK FOR THE MOON DOG."

"IT'S ALMOST DARK!" I said.

"TELL COWBOY TO COME BACK FOR ME TOMORROW MORNING AT FIRST LIGHT."

Ducking the fury of the overhead propellers, we slid the Captain onto the floor of the chopper. Then Z boosted me up and waved for Cowboy to lift off. As we rose into the air, I pitched my canteen and ammo bandolier down to Z. He scooped up the extra supplies and retreated toward the jungle without looking back. I watched him zigzag toward the wood line and disappear, thinking that would be the last time I'd see him alive. Surrounded by hundreds of NVA, he was embarking on a hopeless mission.

Seeing how bad off Cap'n Buck was, panic grabbed hold of me. I cursed Z for leaving me by myself to watch the Captain die. With the Moon Dog dead and the Captain dying, my psyche desperately needed to keep together what was left of the Team. I knew full well I needed to stay with Cap'n Buck, and I understood why Z had to go back for the Moon Dog. Paratroopers don't leave a fallen comrade on the field of battle. Still, I felt totally alone and lost at that moment. Was this the end of the Team? Mechanically, I kept repeating in Cap'n Buck's ear encouragement for him to hang on, but I had nothing to hang on to myself.

The hospital at Pleiku was inundated with casualties, and Cowboy knew there'd be a long wait for treatment if he took Cap'n Buck there. So Cowboy took us up to five thousand feet and headed straight for the 8th Field Hospital at Nha Trang. I closed the side doors of the chopper and covered the Captain to keep him warm. One of Cowboy's door gunners had been an orderly in a hospital stateside and knew more than the rest of us about first aid. When we got some altitude he climbed out of his chair and reached over to me, taping a big gauze bandage on the back of my neck. That was the first time I realized that I, too, was burned and bleeding in several places.

The gunner leaned over and sliced the tape off of Cap'n Buck's dog tags. My heart sank as I expected the gunner to stick one of the tags in Cap'n Buck's mouth. Instead the gunner hopped around checking the dog tags of the rest of the crew. He was looking for a blood donor. He came back to me and sliced the tape off my tags. After a quick examination he indicated I'd have to be the donor. Propping me up against the bulkhead so I'd be higher than the Captain, the gunner connected a tube from the First Aid kit to I.V.'s he opened in my arm and the Captain's. He motioned for me to keep up the direct pressure on the Captain's shoulder wound.

The flight seemed like it took forever. Cap'n Buck kept seeping blood no matter how much pressure I applied, and he was getting weaker. I squeezed down on the wound as hard as I could, but the blood kept sooching between my fingers. I sobbed bitterly, stung by the injustice of it all. I didn't know how much blood he had lost or how much he could afford to lose and still make it. Hopefully, the I.V. had been started in time and there was enough pressure left to get some of my blood into him.

At last, Cowboy gave me a five sign, and I told the Captain we were coming into the hospital, and he'd be in good hands soon.

The field litter ambulance was waiting at the helicopter pad. When we landed the orderlies met us with a stretcher. While they were lifting Cap'n Buck onto the stretcher, I noticed an ARVN jeep parked on the tarmac. As they carried the Captain over to the ambulance Cap'n Buck's gaze fell on the passenger in the ARVN jeep. Cap'n Buck strained for focus and recognition, and then his eyes crystallized into total understanding. He tried to raise his head up and, at the same time, faintly said, "*Mot Tuoi.*"

I looked over at the jeep, finally realizing who Cap'n Buck was referring to. Seated in the passenger side of the jeep was a man whose picture I had seen many times in our cave. It was Colonel Xi. The man we believed to be *Mot Tuoi.* A shrewd smile glimmered in the Colonel's eyes. He exulted in seeing his nemesis stretched out before him in total defeat, and he seemed to take pride in being recognized by Cap'n Buck so that there could be no doubt who had done this. Obviously, the orders from on high that sent us into the ambush were the result of Colonel Xi's influence. His eyes never left the Captain's until Cap'n Buck was loaded into the ambulance. Then Colonel Xi gave a nod. His driver put the jeep into gear, and they drove off.

My wounds were superficial. They patched me up, and then I sat up all night in a dimly lit hospital corridor, waiting for word on the Captain. I also wondered if Z would make it off the mountain alive.

They wouldn't let me in to see Cap'n Buck after surgery, so early the next morning I went out to the helipad. Cowboy picked me up, and we flew out to Z's rendezvous point. Higher up on the mountain, the charred terrain looked like a moonscape. I scanned the jungle's edge, anxiously looking for any sign of Z. Just when we were about to give up, Z emerged carrying a crumpled poncho. Although I was relieved to see him, it was not a time for rejoicing. The only remains of the Moon Dog that Z had been able to recover were his rib cage and his belt buckle. Worse still, Z had lost something of himself on that mountainside, too. There was a worn look of resignation in his eyes. He glared out the chopper door into the morning mist.

"How's the Captain?" he finally shouted over the roar.

I slid over next to him so we could talk in each other's ear.

"He was in surgery last night for four hours. He's in post op now, still under the gas."

"Are they gonna send him to Japan?"

"It didn't sound like it. They were thinking he'd rehabilitate okay there in Nha Trang. But, they won't allow any visitors for several days. They advised us to return to our unit and come back for a visit in a week or so. Cowboy's taking us back to Base now. Z, there's one more thing. It was Colonel Xi that sent us into that ambush. He was waiting on us, gloating, when I brought the Captain in yesterday."

Z turned immediately and started to climb over to tell Cowboy to take him to Nha Trang. I reached out and grabbed his shoulder firmly.

"No, Z. Not now. Not this way."

"Let go of my arm, Stoney," he said deliberately.

I knew it was risky to press my luck, but I held him tightly for another moment, determined to get his attention and make my point.

"Z, you'll be playing right into Colonel Xi's hands if you go after him now. That's exactly what he wants, to sucker us into an uneven fight. That's his way. The reason you're the best is because you're so unpredictable. But, if you go after him now, he will have the edge, not you."

He jerked his shoulder out of my grasp.

"Z, just listen to me for one second. Do you want to do something dumb and end up being another trophy they nail to the wall? Or do you want to get them? I mean get them good? Let's wait for Cap'n Buck and put it all together and do this thing right. If you walk into a trap and get yourself killed, we won't be able to finish it without you."

He knelt on one knee and stared out at the distant mountains drifting by, his chest heaving.

"Okay. But, we're going back out there after 'em."

Besides Cap'n Buck getting seriously wounded, Z was troubled by the Moon Dog's death. Not because he had become personally attached to him—Z knew better than to get close to anyone in a combat zone. Even with Cap'n Buck and me, I believe he respected us a great deal, but it was strictly on a professional basis. He had seen enough death that he dare not let himself take us into his heart. He would do anything for us, including give up his life. But at the same time, Z kept us at arm's length emotionally. If that time ever came, he could dispassionately snap the chain on our dog tags, stick one tag in our mouth, put the other in his pocket to send to Graves Registration, take the code book out of our pocket, and move on down the trail without looking back. It wasn't so much that he had a deep attachment to the Moon Dog. It was that this Colonel Xi deal was so much bigger than he was. Z was in control when facing up to company-size units in the jungle, but if Colonel Xi was so powerful that he could have the Team assigned wherever he wanted, the implications of that were too mind-boggling for Z.

Chapter V

Z KNEW THAT CAP'N BUCK would be after Colonel Xi when the Captain was released from the hospital in a month or so. So, true to his word, Z had us out searching for leads as soon as the two of us could travel. The doctor had instructed Major Balker not to send us out to the field for a couple of weeks until our wounds healed up. That gave us the free time we needed to hobble out there on our own and see what we could uncover.

"Stoney," Z said—that's what he called me, I guess for Stonewall Jackson. While everyone else shortened my last name to "Jax," Z always called me, "Stoney." One time early on, I was covering our rear, and Charlie hit us pretty hard from that direction. I was determined not to let the Team down, so I arched my back and held my ground like a stone wall. After that, Z started calling me "Stoney." It made me feel good that I had earned a special nickname from the guy who was the best in the business—"Stoney," he said, "Let's go get Cowboy to drop us off out in the boons."

"Where to?" I asked.

"Out west of Duc Co. I want to see what *Mot Tuoi* is up to now that he's put the Captain out of commission."

"We've scouted that trail for a long way and proved they're moving trucks down it. What more is there to find?"

"There's bound to be a depot further along," Z said. He folded a map of the area into a neat rectangle. "Those trucks we hijacked were only half-full of gas. I judge there's got to be a refueling site farther south. We'll backtrack to this fork in the trail and follow the other leg of it south along the Se San."

We went back out in the jungle, still taped up from our last excursion. After following the trail for a couple of days we came upon an NVA refueling depot, just as Z had predicted. The compound was located in a tiny jut of Cambodia which made it off limits to U.S. ground operations and B-52 strikes.

This was the end of the road, so to speak. Only one of the trails branching out to the south and southeast from there was large enough for small vehicles to travel on. The majority of the trucks that made it to this station would have to refuel and head back north. The one exception was a trail heading east. We guessed that trucks with civilian markings could use this trail to connect up with Highway 19. With safe passage from the Viet Cong, smugglers could refuel here and drive their trucks past Pleiku and on through the Mang Yang Pass to Qui Nhon and Highway One. From there, they would have access to anywhere in South Vietnam.

The compound featured several fuel tanks, a warehouse, a maintenance shop, some thatch-roofed living quarters, and one office-type building in the center. Military equipment and supplies were unloaded off the trucks, which also carried a variety of black market goods suitable for sale to American GI's. The munitions were divided into small loads and placed on carts, bicycles, or suspended between two people on poles before departing into the jungle. There were also some of the small three-wheeled Lambretta vehicles loading up with black market goods, probably heading for the GI strips in Pleiku, Kontum, and An Khe.

The second phase of our investigation was to determine how these goods were distributed elsewhere in Vietnam. Z and I made note of some identifying features on Lambrettas which were probably being used in the smuggling operation. We then radioed Cowboy to pick us up and move us to the intersection of Highways 19 and 14, outside of Pleiku.

Z and I took up a position in a thicket between the two highways. By mid morning the next day, the Lambrettas we had seen loading the day before began passing our observation point. As expected, most of the little three-wheeled trucks continued heading east on Highway Nineteen toward An Khe and Qui Nhon. A few veered off toward Pleiku and Kontum.

We hiked into Pleiku to see how the goods were distributed there. With ARVN II Corps and the American Fourth Division headquartered there, Pleiku had become a boomtown of gyp joints. Every vice that a GI would spend money on was for sale there. The original marketplace, where vegetables and raw meats were sold, had been overshadowed by the shops lining the highways that catered to American soldiers.

Z and I must have looked otherworldly to the GI's from the Fourth Division. We stepped right out from the jungle in typical LRRP attire—boonie hats, tiger-striped camouflaged fatigues, a PRC-25 radio, a full load of water, food, equipment, and ammunition, and carrying an AK-47 and a Swedish K. We were in sharp contrast to the other GI's in town who were all scrubbed and pressed for shore leave, carrying standard-issue M-16's and wearing the regular OD jungle fatigues.

Some of the GI's wore brand new fatigues and were still white complected. They couldn't have been in country more than a week. I thought back to my first week in country down at Bien Hoa. My innocence and uncertainty back then were worlds away from what I had become. I remembered how apprehensive I was about my new duty assignment. These strange new surroundings demanded that I throw out all of my mores and cultural biases if I was to survive. I had wondered what it would be like when the moment of truth came. Could I kill a man, or would I hesitate for that instant that would result in my own undoing? Could I live with the consequences of letting my buddies down, or perhaps even getting them killed? Or, could I live with doing my job right? Whatever happened, was there any chance I'd ever again be the person I was before the War?

Z and I spent the afternoon dropping in on the shops where the Lambrettas we had noted were unloading. The drivers appeared to be independent middle men who bought merchandise wherever they could find it, no questions asked, and sold it at a profit to the mama sans who ran the shops along the strip. The merchandise for sale consisted of such things as wristwatches, jewelry, velvet paintings, and hand-carved trinkets. These goods could have been made anywhere in Indo-China and then smuggled down through North Vietnam and the Ho Chi Minh Trail into South Vietnam.

Late in the afternoon, with the Fourth Division's curfew hour approaching, the GI's began driving away in their jeeps and three-quarter ton trucks to return to the Fourth Division's base camp.

Z and I stopped in a little cafe to have a cold one. An iced-cold American beer was a luxury we seldom enjoyed. While sipping our brews, we were taken by the beauty and innocence of the young girl who waited on us. She was the daughter of the Mama San who owned the shop. The girl couldn't have been more than fifteen or sixteen years old. She smiled and tried diffidently to answer our questions in the pigeon English she had picked up from her American customers. We were struck by how delicate and demure she was, in contrast to the typical girls you encountered along these strips who would tease you and even sit in your lap to entice you to spend money in their shop. This girl had a purity and radiance about her that put her in a class by herself. She was also dressed more formally than the other coke girls. She wore a traditional *ao dai* instead of an American-style blouse and shorts.

When she brought out our beers, Z asked her name.

"Ten ye, Co?"

"Hai," she answered with a timid smile, almost in a whisper. She was a bit flustered that Z had spoken to her in her native tongue.

"Hi to you, too!" I said. She giggled nervously at my play on words.

It was almost dusk, and the last of the soldiers from the Fourth, who were pressing their luck by staying later than was allowed, sped off down the main drag.

The Mama San switched off the American radio station and started playing Vietnamese music. Z seemed to enjoy the change in music. He closed his eyes, cocked his head back, and began humming along to the tune.

"I love this song. It's about a lonely soldier in hostile territory. It goes:

Toi o mien xa, troi quen dat la.
[I am living in the remote region.]
Nhac tinh sao lam loi!
[How many words the love music has!]
Den voi toi, hay den voi toi;
[Come to me, now come to me;]
Dung yeu linh bang loi!
[Don't love a soldier with mere words!]"

We enjoyed mellowing out and listening to the music. After a while an overweight Vietnamese man drove up in a Lambretta. Z and I suspected he was one of the men we had seen at the refueling depot, but we weren't sure. He got out of his vehicle slowly, checking up and down the street before entering the shop. Behind his sunglasses his puffy cheeks made his head appear remarkably round. The fat paunch he was balancing in front made him waddle when he walked.

He was annoyed to see two Americans still in the shop. He asked Mama San something, probably what we were doing there so late. She shrugged her shoulders and mumbled something, busying herself in her work. Looking over at us he hesitated for a moment, deciding whether or not it was wise to conduct his business with us around.

He tested us with a question in Vietnamese: "*Hom nay ong lich-su hau-hanh duoc gap?*"

Z pretended not to comprehend. Satisfied, the chubby man motioned for Mama San to step in the back with him. As he passed by the girl, the man attempted to give her a familiar pat. Hai dodged his reach without looking up, pretending to wipe the tables she had previously cleaned. From the time the man arrived, Hai had obviously become very nervous.

Mama San and the man talked for about ten minutes, with the man getting loud and domineering and the woman whining and saying "no, no, no" a lot. Toward the end of the conversation, something was said that frightened the girl. She gasped and had to fight back tears. The man then waddled out of the shop, grunting and nodding to us as he passed by. He squeezed his large corpus back into the little cab of his Lambretta and drove off.

The girl ran into her mother's arms, sobbing. Z got up and asked them if we could help, but Mama San was beside herself. She shooed us out of the shop and closed and locked the outside doors behind us.

We ambled down the street a short distance. Z was troubled by the incident we had just witnessed. "That deal really stinks," he said finally.

"What were they saying?"

"Aw, I couldn't understand all of it, but apparently Mama San owes that fat guy a lot of money, and he's calling in his markers. She can't pay him, so he's demanding other considerations."

"What would that be?"

"He wants the girl. Something about making her a Numbah One bar girl in Saigon."

I knew right away from the way Z was talking that he was letting himself get emotionally involved in this situation. He wasn't going to be able to shrug this one off and move on. It didn't sit well with me, either. But it wasn't our duty to right every wrong we encountered.

"That's too bad," I said. "However, we don't know these people or the background to all this. We tried to talk to the Mama San about it, and she ran us off. Let's drop it and stick to accomplishing our job over here. It's not our place to get involved."

"If it's not our place to get involved, whose is it? We was sent over here to protect these people from oppression, wasn't we? I'm not going to let that butt gut take a nice girl like her and ruin her life by pimping her out. Aw, think of what she'll be like a couple of years from now if we don't do something."

"Z, let's be realistic. It'd be nice to help, but what can we really do? I'm sure we don't have enough dough to pay off Mama San's debt. What do you propose to do?"

"I don't know yet. But, I've got to at least monitor this situation for a while. Are you in or out?"

"In," I sighed.

"Okay. The sun's almost down. To figure our next move we need to set up somewhere for the night and keep an eye on that shop."

Z looked around and then asked some information from a Vietnamese passerby. The man pointed to an establishment a few doors down. The place was brightly colored and about twice the size of a typical shop. The big, hand-painted sign above the door proudly proclaimed "*LA VEGAS GIRLS.*" I took one look at it and knew we'd be spending the night in a brothel. It had already closed for the day, but Z kept knocking until one of the girls opened the door. She looked up and down the street, and then let us in.

The brothel's mama san wasn't so hospitable. She scurried down the corridor, jabbering all the way. She tried to block us from advancing any further. She told Z the MP's would close her down if they caught her harboring GI's after curfew. However, Z was not to be denied, and she finally relented.

The kitchen was built onto the back of the building and had an A-frame ceiling. A half-dozen girls were sitting around a table eating supper. They invited us to join them, scooting around to make room for us. A couple of the girls were feeding babies in their laps. Having seen very few Western visitors in their kitchen, the infants stared at us in wonderment.

"They American babies," one of the girls said.

One baby looked like it had a white father and the other one a black father. I pondered the grim future in store for them, especially when the American forces left, which had to happen sooner or later. It was a sobering thought, how a man's wild gasp of hormonal relief could cause misery and hardship years later to offspring he never knew he had.

Z asked the youngest girl how old she was. She answered that she was eighteen, but she couldn't have been much older than the girl, Hai, in the shop across the street. I knew that was what Z was thinking, too.

Dinner was typical Vietnamese fare—a bowl of rice with bits of meat and vegetables in it, and a tiny cup of hot tea. It was the type of victuals that Z loved, and I only tolerated. I tried my skills with a chopstick, to the amusement of the girls. I finally had to resort to holding the bowl up to my lips and pulling the food into my mouth with the sticks. I hammed it up while I was doing this, and they all had a good laugh.

Playfully, one of the girls picked up a strip of cooked meat out of the serving bowl with her chop sticks and tried to feed it to me.

"No thanks," I said, turning my head. I knew the Vietnamese eat dog meat, and those unidentified chunks of meat always made me suspicious that Rover was being served up. My uneasy expression made everyone howl all the more.

Our fun was interrupted by the sound of a jeep screeching to a halt in the street out front.

"MP's!" said the mama san. "Come with me, *mau mau!*"

The girls quickly placed a stool on top of a bureau next to the wall facing the bedrooms. One of the girls jumped up on the bureau and took down a wall hanging. Behind the drape was a hatch door leading to the crawl space above the bedrooms. Z and I grabbed our gear and leaped up into the black hole. The circle of light was quickly plugged up behind us.

For a while everything was dark around us. Our eyes gradually got used to the subdued light supplied by pinholes of light piercing through the frail ceiling below us. The attic was mostly unfinished. Nailed to the rafters were a few boards leading toward the front, where there was a makeshift bed. We both kept very still, listening to the goings on below us.

"MAMA SAN," announced one of the MP's loudly from below us. "You got some GI's here tonight?"

"No GI here," she answered.

"Come on, now. They were seen coming in here. Do you want us to close you down?"

"No, no. All GI leave."

The MP's began searching for us. We could hear their boots clomping from room to room.

"Okay, Mama San. But, we better not catch you hiding any GI's here."

"No, no. GI only come daytime."

We heard the MP's get back in their jeep and drive off. Z crawled up to the front to check it out. There was a louvered vent at the front wall facing out on the street below. The vent allowed a good view of the store where the young girl and her Mama San lived. It was an ideal location for us to monitor the comings and goings at the shop.

Z and I took turns sleeping on the bed and keeping watch through the night. Just before dawn Z shook me awake. I quietly slipped out of bed and joined him at the vent. Two shadows furtively left Mama San's shop, carrying a box and a suitcase. They hurried up the street in our direction, passing below us. Apparently the girl and her mother were sneaking away in the night.

Hastily we grabbed our gear and monkey-walked across the planks to the hatch door. Z tossed some money on the kitchen table, and we hustled out the back door, then up the narrow passage between the buildings, and out into the dim, gray street.

The two figures cut over to the main street and continued on to the bus depot at the edge of town. We stayed well behind them so they couldn't see us. The woman and her daughter stopped where a group of people were waiting for the bus. They melded into the middle of the group.

Z and I backtracked and circled around the depot through a tea plantation. Paralleling the highway, we moved through the tea fields for about a mile. We finally settled into a hedgerow thicket along the highway, sitting back to back, to protect ourselves from either direction.

"What are we doing?" I whispered.

"Looks like Mama San is putting Co Hai on the bus for Qui Nhon. By the time Cowboy gives us our morning flyover, it'll be too late to follow her. The only way we can stay up with her is to flag down the bus."

"Co Hai? So, it's Co Hai now? What is it with you and this girl? You've never even been formerly introduced to her, and you're acting as if you're her Godfather or something. All we have to do is make sure she gets on the bus. She'll be long gone before Butt Gut gets wind of it. Then she can go on about her business, and we can go on about ours."

"I judge this thing's not over yet. Butt Gut was pretty insistent about wanting her last night. We need to stay with her, at least until she makes connections in Qui Nhon. If you don't want to go along on the bus, you can wait here for Cowboy to pick you up."

"If we're going along to protect her, why didn't we get on the bus with her at the depot?"

"What would it look like for two GI's to buy bus tickets to Qui Nhon at the depot? Have you ever seen an American soldier ride on a Vietnamese bus?"

We had a bite of cold breakfast while we waited. Soon the minesweeper team from the Cav detachment passed by on their way out of town. After that, a trickle of civilian traffic began to pass by, and finally the bus.

Z stood in the middle of the highway and flagged the bus down while I covered him from the wood line. The driver didn't want to let us on because the bus was full, causing Z to negotiate vigorously. Finally Z motioned for me to join him. I was in for another surprise.

"We get the scenic seats," Z said. "Up top."

The old French bus was about half the size of a Trailways Bus, and it had a rack on the top for cargo. Walking around to the ladder in the back, I caught a glimpse of Co Hai seated inside. She was staring straight ahead. I gathered she recognized us and didn't know what to think about us reappearing in her life.

Z was only halfway up the ladder when the bus started rolling. I grabbed onto the side rail to give myself leverage to hoist Z up. We had to lie low amid the cargo to cut down on the wind drag. There was a wide variety of items up there, from live chickens to decent-looking luggage. With my usual luck, a goat with bad breath was tied down right in front of me. He tried to lick my nose, and I gave him a warning smack on the mouth with an ear of corn.

We wound our way across the high plateau, heading for the first stop at An Khe. Riding outside of a vehicle was a lot windier and colder than I had expected. The worst part was when it started to rain. The rain drops hitting your face at 40 mph felt like hundreds of sharp pin pricks. We dug down and buried our faces amid the cargo.

Just before we reached the Mang Yang Pass, the bus started squealing to a halt. Z looked up ahead and flicked the safety switch on his Swedish K to Auto.

"VC taxation squad," he whispered.

I couldn't tell how many there were or how they were deployed. I knew it wouldn't take them long before they climbed up to see what they could loot from the cargo on top. We were trapped in a kill-or-be-killed situation. Using hand grenades was out, because we couldn't risk injury to the people on the bus. I thought it would be better to open up on the VC squad immediately. This type of group was usually helter-skelter, and we might be able to pin them down long enough for the bus to drive through the ambush. But Z held back. He waited to determine the total number we were up against, where each was located, and how they were armed.

A couple of the highwaymen entered the bus and began shaking down the passengers by passing the hat for "donations." At the same time, a third soldier climbed halfway up the back ladder and started poking around at the fruit tied down at the back. He bumped Z's boot without realizing it. Then he spotted a big bag of rice along the back edge of the load. He pulled it down over the side and jumped down to pick it up.

We heard a commotion inside the bus. One of them said, "*Mau len*," and then dragged Co Hai off the bus. She was clutching her shoulder bag in terror.

A second tax collector began to climb up the outside ladder, but a vehicle appearing behind us in the distance altered his intentions. "*Di thi di!*" he warned the others. They dragged Co Hai with them off the road and disappeared into the jungle.

When the thieves left the road, the driver put the bus in gear and took off. We stayed low on the top until we rounded the first bend, then Z hung over the side and knocked on the window, signaling for the driver to stop. We grabbed Co Hai's box and suitcase off the roof and jumped to the ground.

Slipping into the jungle, it took us a moment to adjust to the subdued light. Cautiously we worked our way back toward where they had dragged Co Hai into the shadows. Blending ourselves into our surroundings, we crept close enough to assess the situation. There were six of them, and they obviously knew more about collecting taxes than flank security. One of them was keeping an eye on the road, but there was no one back on rear security, and they were all talking in normal tones. They were sorting through the loot commandeered from the bus. Co Hai was cowering down at the edge of the clearing, whimpering. Because the trees and undergrowth obstructed our view, we couldn't get a bead on them to zap them without endangering her. Again, we waited.

During the next hour the highwaymen stopped a couple of Lambrettas and exacted more taxes. Later a third Lambretta putt-putted toward us. The lookout yelled to them, and four of them headed back out to the road. Z motioned for me to stay back and watch Co Hai while he maneuvered over to the edge to see what was going on. The newly arrived Lambretta carried none other than Butt Gut himself! He was chummy with the VC. It didn't take long to figure out that Butt Gut had contacted the VC and requested them to stop the bus and take Co Hai off if she happened to be on it. It was an easy set up for Butt Gut. When Co Hai was missing and her mother tried to track her down, the other riders on the bus would say she was abducted by the VC. By the time any word got back to her mother about her whereabouts, Co Hai would be corrupted through drugs and enslavement into a hardened prostitute.

Butt Gut got out and opened the back of his Lambretta. The VC unloaded some boxes of supplies. Then they dragged Co Hai screaming and begging and struggling out of the bushes and gagged and lashed her next to Butt Gut on the little front bench seat of the Lambretta.

She went limp with fear and exhaustion after so much anxiety and manhandling. Seeing her so pitifully helpless was breaking Z's heart. He had his K aimed at the lead man, waiting until they separated themselves from the vehicle a few feet so he could get a clean shot without placing Co Hai in jeopardy. In his eagerness to save her, he made one of the few mistakes I ever saw him make. A pod popped under his foot, and the VC soldier down in the brushline spotted us and opened fire. We returned fire immediately. After emptying one magazine, I automatically rotated down and around to the left to try to flank them. We dropped three of them in the first few seconds, but the other three managed to hold the high ground and keep us at bay momentarily. They were behind trees, so we didn't have good targets.

Butt Gut started the engine of his Lambretta and lurched forward. Then Z did another dumb thing. He ran right out there on the road to try to stop the vehicle. The two VC who were engaging me wheeled to shoot at Z, and I was able to nail them. Z managed to get over far enough so the truck was between him and the last VC. Z aimed right at Butt Gut's head, but he couldn't bring himself to pull the trigger. I guess he was afraid Co Hai would be hurt in the crash if he killed the driver. The mini-truck was barreling right for Z. He stepped out of the way just in time, giving it a shove when it went by to try to tip it over. The Lambretta rocked a little but scooted by. After the three-wheeler passed him, Z whipped his rifle around in a blur and with one shot zapped the last VC, who was concealed at the edge of the jungle. Immediately Z dropped down on the road in a prone firing position and fired three aimed shots at the tires of the vehicle, but he couldn't hit them at that distance with a K.

"Search 'em for papers," said Z. He ran back and fetched our radio and gear.

It was mid-morning, past the time that Cowboy usually checked up on us. Z tried several times but couldn't raise Cowboy on the radio. This frustrated Z to no end. All tensed up, he prowled back and forth. We pitched the bodies of the VC into the undergrowth, and Z ran back and retrieved Co Hai's box and suitcase. A couple of Lambrettas passed by that were too small for us to ride in. Z kept pacing up and down along the road. I blended back into the underbrush and tried to keep my ears open for more trouble. Highway Nineteen was quasi-secure, but this squad we had just eliminated was bound to have friends who may have heard the firefight.

Finally Z flagged down an ARVN three-quarter ton truck which was headed east. Three ARVN soldiers were riding in the front seat with a few supplies stacked in the bed. Z opened the driver's door and ordered one of the soldiers to get out and ride in the back. Making the driver scoot over, Z jumped in and took the wheel. I tossed our equipment in the truck bed and hopped in the back with the displaced ARVN soldier.

Z roared off like a madman, swerving around the curves and bumping and banging all over the place. We started out about forty minutes behind Butt Gut and Co Hai. Unfortunately, although we probably closed the gap by thirty minutes, we weren't able to catch up to them before reaching An Khe. I could see through the back glass that Z was beside himself. As we sped through town I saw some Lambrettas that could have been Butt Gut's, but I couldn't tell for sure without stopping and checking each one.

Z halted at the far edge of town.

"He couldn't be more than ten minutes ahead of us," Z said. "He was bound to stop for gas before going on to Qui Nhon. He's already seen me, so I'll wait here and make sure he doesn't pass on through to Qui Nhon. You check out all the Lambrettas that look like his that are parked in town."

The ARVN's dropped me off at the edge of the business district. I needed to be on foot to make a careful vehicle-by-vehicle search. The shopping district catering to GI's—trinket shops, tailors, snack shops, marijuana dens, bars, massage parlors, brothels—was even gaudier than in Pleiku. The raunchiest section of bars and brothels was called "Sin City." The First Cav had been headquartered near An Khe at

Camp Radcliff for several months, and the strip was busy with GI's partaking of the pleasures of town life.

After working my way through a fourth of the strip, I spotted Butt Gut driving by in his Lambretta. Co Hai was not with him. I had no choice but to chase him on foot. I tried to zig in and out of shop entrances rather than run down the middle of the street, which he would be more likely to notice in his rearview mirror. Weighted down by all of my equipment, I watched him get farther and farther away until he almost disappeared in the sea of traffic ahead. Leaping up on a sidewalk table to keep him in view, I spied his Lambretta turning off to the left several blocks ahead. I jogged down to that side street and noticed Butt Gut's Lambretta parked outside a honky-tonk about halfway down the block. The place was called *Saigon Palace*. Rock and roll music drifted out from inside. It was a large, two-story storefront with a big, garish sign encircled in blinking lights.

I flagged down a teenager on a motor bike and paid him to go out and pick up Z. The kid returned in twenty minutes with Z's legs dangling off the sides of the scooter.

"What kind of a joint is that, Kid?" Z asked, eyeing the club from the corner.

"Everything happen in there. Even my mother afraid to work there. Drugs. Gambling. Girls. It beaucoup crazy in there."

Z whined as he listened to the boy's description. "Stoney, have this kid take you over to Camp Radcliff. Go to their chopper command center, and have them find Cowboy wherever he is and get him over here with his chopper. I'm going inside."

Z screwed the silencer onto his K and buried the rifle in his pack, covering the protruding butt with his poncho. He swung the doors open and stepped inside, pausing for a moment to let his senses grow accustomed to the sudden darkness, thick smoke, and blaring music. In the front, naked girls were dancing on the stage. Money was busily changing hands at card and crap games. Along the back and side walls girls were dancing on the round tables or sitting in GI's laps. Every so often a girl would take a GI by the hand and lead him up the stairs and down the hall into one of the rooms on the second floor. Twenty minutes later the girl would lead her trick back downstairs, give him a big good-bye kiss, and parade over to the lineup at the bar.

Through the smoke Z strained to examine the face of each girl, searching for Co Hai. She was nowhere to be found. Z cringed at the thought that she might already be upstairs. Soon the music faded into a dramatic drum roll. Butt Gut appeared from a room behind the stage, pulling Co Hai along with him. He forced her to stand up on the stage, holding her arms tightly in his grasp. Too frightened to look up, she appeared utterly humiliated and helpless.

The manager of the club stepped up to the microphone. "Gentlemen! Gentlemen! Give me full attention, please. We have very good delight and honor today. We have new girl here, just arrived. Guaranteed virgin. This is big chance for some lucky GI to give her first pleasure. We auction her to highest bidder. Bidding start at one hundred MPC."

"One hundred," came a drunken but enthusiastic shout from across the room. The crowd cheered.

"Two hundred."

"Two fifty."

"Three hundred."

"Four hundred."

"Four fifty."

"Five hundred," said a big, burly GI.

The crowd silenced. "We have five hundred," said the manager. "Does anyone say five fifty?"

He looked around the room, but the other bidders shook their heads.

"Five hundred once, five hundred twice "

"Six hundred," shouted Z, entering the bidding for the first time. Butt Gut peered out at him and then whispered something to the club's big Korean bouncer.

There was a tittering of voices before a hush fell over the patrons. "Six fifty," countered the burly GI

Z pulled all of his money out of his pocket and hastily counted it. "Seven hundred dollars," he announced.

"Seven ten," came the counter offer.

Z smoothed out a couple of wrinkled bills. "Seven twenty," he said, in desperation.

"Seven fifty."

Z looked around. The other GI's were looking at him with amusement. There wasn't a friendly face in the house. He stared blankly up at the stage.

"Seven fifty once, twice. Sold to this lucky man over here."

There was a roar of cheering, applause, hooting, and whistling as the burly GI triumphantly made his way to the stage. He ceremoniously counted out his money and presented it to the maitre d'. Then he rubbed his hands together hungrily and took Co Hai's arm, dragging her toward the stairs. She was crying and fighting to get away, to the entertainment of the crowd. The music started up again, and the patrons turned their attention to their own pursuits.

Everyone except Z. He made his way through the crowd toward the stairs, spurning several alluring propositions from girls along the way. When he reached the steps, the bouncer was already on the stairs in front of him, blocking his way. Z did not stop to argue with his adversary but immediately swung his ice axe, whopping the bouncer on the side of the head and knocking him down to the bottom of the stairs. While Z was still off-balance from his swing, Butt Gut rushed him, knocking him down and wrenching his pack away from him. Z connected to Butt Gut's chin with a right cross, sending him sailing backwards. Meanwhile the bouncer had recovered and drew out a pistol. Z was sprawled out spread eagle on the stairs, with his K out of reach. His only remaining defense was to lift his right leg, placing his boot between himself and his assailant. The Korean cackled and aimed his gun at Z. There was a gunshot. The look on the Korean's face changed to wonder, blood bubbled out of his mouth, and he collapsed to the floor. Z had reached down and fired, through his britches, the .32 he kept strapped to his leg. The bullet struck the Korean in the gut.

Z grabbed his gear and scrambled up the stairs, wheeling on the landing and firing a burst from his K into the mirror behind the bar to keep the bartender's shotgun out of the action. Girls were screaming, and GI's were diving for cover. Z bounded the rest of the way up the stairs and ran down the hallway, kicking down several doors before he found Co Hai. The burly GI had her pinned down on the bed.

"I have no beef with you," Z said. "Here's seven hundred and twenty dollars. I'll send you the rest when I get paid. Now, get on out of here."

The GI rushed him angrily. Z stepped aside and slammed his opponent into the wall, adding a karate chop to the back of his neck, and then slamming the chamber pot down on his head. Shoving his adversary out into the hallway, Z locked the door behind him. Immediately Z jumped up on the night stand and chopped a hole through the corrugated metal roof with his ice axe. Fetching a yellow smoke grenade from his pack, he pulled the pin and pitched it out onto the roof. Then he continued hacking away at the hole in the roof until he had enlarged it enough for a person to fit through. Without hesitating he boosted Co Hai up through the opening. Before Z could get out himself, the bartender burst into the room toting a shotgun. Z ducked the first blast, wrested the shotgun away from the bartender, and butt whipped him with it. Taking another smoke round from his pack, Z pulled the pin and threw it out into the hallway, firing the pump-action shotgun three times down the smoke-filled hallway to discourage any additional pursuers. Returning to the room, he shoved his equipment out the hole and, using his axe, pulled himself up onto the roof. Quickly he looked around in vain for a means of escape for Co Hai and himself. The distance to adjacent buildings was too long to risk jumping. At that moment he spotted Cowboy's chopper coming in. I was riding with Cowboy, watching Z's rooftop grow larger and larger below me. Because of surrounding antennas and trees Cowboy wouldn't be able to get low enough for Co Hai and Z to jump aboard. Co Hai screamed as gunfire started coming up at them through the roof. The bullet holes were opening up the tin roof like a soup can.

Z hugged Co Hai and tried to comfort her. "Come on. I've got you. *Khong co chi!*"

Cowboy flew over as low as he dared. He couldn't quite reach the rooftop. There would be no time for a second pass. As the chopper passed near the corner of the building, Z slung his pack over his shoulder and picked up Co Hai in one arm. He swung his ice axe over his head and flung it out towards the chopper. The axe head wrapped around the bottom runner and held fast. Z wound the rope around his arm as the slack tightened and he and Co Hai were jerked off the roof.

My heart was in my throat as I watched the two of them dangling below me, floating above the rooftops. Z strained desperately to maintain his grasp on the rope. It was a wild ride for Co Hai, swaying by that rope, totally reliant on Z's grip for her life. When Cowboy spotted a clearing at the edge of town, he gently landed the helicopter. I was relieved when I saw Z and Co Hai touch the ground. Cowboy set the chopper down in the clearing long enough for me to pull them on board. Z lay on his back on the metal floor of the chopper, his chest heaving from the strain. He slowly rubbed the deep red rope burns on his arm.

Chapter VI

THE DEBATE BEGAN ABOUT what to do with the girl. I should have insisted that we take her back to her Mama San right then. However, I stayed out of it, and Z finally persuaded Cowboy to hide her out at the airfield at Nha Trang for a few days until we could decide on the right course of action (which was their way of saying: let Cap'n Buck settle it). The airmen at Nha Trang had a nice two-story barracks with plenty of room to accommodate extra flight crews which might have to lay over at Nha Trang. Cowboy arranged for Z and me to stay there with his crew, and we sneaked Co Hai in with us. Z and I were assigned private rooms on different floors, but we doubled up in the ground floor room so Co Hai could have the room on the second floor to herself.

I had hoped for a peaceful night's sleep. Instead I worried about the problem we had gotten ourselves into. Upstairs we had a minor, of no more than sixteen years of age, who we had sneaked onto an American military installation during wartime without her parents' permission. What's more, she appeared to be a proper Vietnamese girl who is not allowed to be visited by a man without her mother being present, much less living in a hooch full of horny aviators. And our only rationale for doing all this was to save her from ruining her reputation, which, ironically, we had just ruined ourselves by saving her in this manner.

Looking back, it may have been Co Hai's introduction into our lives, rather than Cap'n Buck's getting wounded, that really marked the beginning of the end for the Team.

73

It's hard to say, since the two events happened so close together, and we wouldn't have found Co Hai if we hadn't been out trying to dig up evidence on Colonel Xi. At the very least, after Co Hai came into our lives her well-being figured into every decision we made. At the worst, her presence opened a gulf that never again let us work and live together effectively as a team.

The next morning, Z ran down to the chow line early to get some breakfast for Co Hai. He came back crestfallen. Cowboy had already beaten him to it, having delivered breakfast to her before he and his crew left to fly back to Kontum to support the 173rd's ground operations for the day. And, so it went. Z and Cowboy couldn't do enough for her. It was like they had adopted a child and were caught up in all the excitement of providing for her. I'll have to admit that she was a delight to be around. For someone who only spoke "Coke girl" English, Co Hai could communicate pretty well, and she managed to make each of us feel like we were her special friend. Her laugh simply made you melt. Occasionally she worried out loud about returning home to her mother, but Z and Cowboy quickly impressed upon her how dangerous and unwise that would be, what with Butt Gut still out there lurking about.

No one talked about it, but we all knew this situation would have to be resolved soon. In addition to her childlike beauty and innocence, her budding womanhood became apparent from time to time, reminding us that there was a whole other side to this situation that could have serious consequences. To complicate things even further, I sensed that Z was actually getting jealous of Cowboy's attentions.

All of this came to a head during our fourth night in the barracks. I awakened in the middle of the night and noticed that Z wasn't in the room with me. I tiptoed into the hallway to listen. After a while I heard some movement upstairs. I caught a faint "No!" from Co Hai's lips accompanied by an anguished cry of shock and disbelief. Then a hand must have muffled her mouth, and I could hear signs of an ensuing struggle.

"Z, No!" I gasped. I raced down the hall and up the stairs. I thought I knew Z pretty well and couldn't believe he had snapped and would actually resort to forcing himself on the girl.

When I reached her room, Co Hai was cowering in the corner, and Z was on the floor wrestling with a door gunner from one of the local chopper crews. Z drew his K-bar from his leg sheath, letting out a savage "AHHHHH." He lunged to slit the crewman's throat. I dove between them, my hand catching Z's wrist just in time and holding him fast. Distraught and disoriented in the semi-darkness, Z looked up into my face with blank surprise.

"No, my friend. Don't let it end this way," I whispered. For the first time since I had known Z, I was the one being the wise adviser. Z's obsession with protecting Co Hai had pushed him near the brink.

Everyone had heard Z's attack yell and had clambered out of their rooms. Cowboy pushed his way through the onlookers.

"What's goin' on?" he asked.

"This animal nearly killed me," said the door gunner, still pinned to the ground under Z. The man reeked of alcohol.

Z's eyes got round, and his nostrils heaved. "He did it! He hurt Co Hai!"

"How'd this girl get in here, anyway? And why are these LRRP's staying here, Smith?" asked the Detachment Commander.

"These are my buds, and I'll take responsibility for 'em," Cowboy said. "Whether the girl belongs here or not is neither here nor there right now. I've seen a lot of crazy things goin' on in this place. But, your gunner had no bizness messin' with her, Captain."

At that moment it became evident to all of us what was really happening here, and what we had become. I glanced at Co Hai, and I think she knew, too. I stepped over to her and offered her my hand. Helping her up, I gently escorted her over to her bed. She sat down on the edge. I looked back at Z and Cowboy.

"It's time we went to see Cap'n Buck," I said.

The next morning Cowboy borrowed a jeep, and we all piled in and headed for downtown Nha Trang. It was a gorgeous, sunny day. We decided to take Co Hai shopping in Nha Trang before going to the hospital. She had never visited Nha Trang before, and we couldn't wait to share it with her. In addition, the three of us were excited and nervous by the prospect of introducing her to Cap'n Buck. It was like bringing your first love home to meet your dad.

We headed for the downtown shopping area first, and Co Hai oohed and aahed over all the wonderful things in the open shops. The three of us chipped in and bought her a new turquoise-colored *ao dai*, consisting of the long trousers and traditional long-sleeved, slit tunic.

We stopped at the little PX to buy Cap'n Buck some books to read. While Co Hai waited in the jeep, each of us scurried about searching for our own special American gift for her. Z bought her a gold bracelet. Cowboy got her a little three-mirror vanity set and some make-up. I picked out a cassette player and some tapes: the Supremes, Elvis, and Loretta Lynn. I was covering all the bases since I didn't know what kind of American music she might take a fancy to.

When we gave her the gifts she shrieked with excitement, which made each of us feel ten feet tall.

Finally we couldn't put off the day of reckoning any longer, so we headed for the hospital. We left Co Hai down in the lobby and climbed the stairs to the ward where Cap'n Buck was recuperating. He was in the middle of a long double row of sick and wounded. It had been nearly two weeks since I had brought Cap'n Buck to the hospital. I was eager to see how he was doing. He was propped up in bed reading, with his shoulder and half of his torso bandaged up.

"Hey, now!" Cowboy said with a grin.

"Hey, Guys. Come on over here." said Cap'n Buck. "Z, Jax. How're you doing?"

"Fine, Sir," I answered. Z nodded.

"Well, Buckie Boy," said Cowboy. "You sure look better than when Jax and I brought you in here. When's the Doc gonna let you *Di Di Mau*?"

"They wanted to send me to Japan, but I talked them out of it. I'm supposed to start rehab on Monday. And then, maybe three more weeks."

"Monday! Will you guys listen to that Monday stuff? He's been out of the boonies so long he knows what day of the week it is! If you don't look out, Bud, they'll have to send you back to In-country Processin' to get you re-indoctrinated!"

Cap'n Buck laughed. "Man, it's sure good to see you guys. Lying here day after day, staring at that fan up there going around, it's enough to make a guy go crazy. Z, while I'm still laid up I need you and Jax to train our new man for me. I've received word from Major Balker that we're getting a replacement for Armstrong. His name is PFC Anthony Silvestri, and he's just arrived in country. He'll be finishing up his in-country Brigade training the day after tomorrow. I don't want him to join the Team in a Base Camp setting, I want a baptism of fire. Mac, why don't you drop him off out by the cave and let the boys train him out there. Z, I want him ready by the time I get back, so you'll have to give him a crash course."

Z nodded. "If he's got it in him to make the Team, we'll know by then."

"Hey, now. We brought you some reading material to help pass the time," said Cowboy. "These two squares brought you *The Green Berets* and *In Cold Blood*. But, your Bud knew what you really needed to get you back in shape." Cowboy held up the latest issue of *Playboy* and let the centerfold ripple down. "Joie Gibson!"

"Whoa! What have we here?" said the Captain. "Shame on you, tempting a married man like this! Oh, oh. Here's a pictorial on James Bond's Oriental Eyefuls. This looks like Jax' department! Thanks for your thoughtfulness, Mac. You're all heart!" Then he got serious. "Speaking of heart, I wrote to Armstrong's mother. It took me two days of staring at a blank sheet of paper. I keep going over it and over it in my mind, thinking about what I could have done differently."

"Captain, there wasn't anything you could have done," I said. "If you hadn't spread us out, we would have all been killed. It was a set up. Colonel Xi sent us out there into an ambush."

"Yes, Colonel Xi. I've thought a lot about him, too. When I get out of here I'll have to look into his business."

"We've already been out poking around some," Z said.

We explained to Cap'n Buck about our discovery of the refueling depot, and how Butt Gut later turned up in Pleiku. That got us around to explaining why we were now providing protective service for a sixteen year-old Vietnamese girl. The moment had come for which we were all waiting. I went down and brought her up on the ward to meet him.

She was radiant that afternoon. I couldn't see how she would fail to captivate his heart. She waited down at the foot of the bed and gave him a respectful bow.

"*Chao em,*" Cap'n Buck said.

"*Chao ong,*" she answered diffidently, bowing again.

"They've told me what you've been through," Cap'n Buck continued. "I know you've had a hard time, but now we must return you to your mother."

"Buck, she belongs in a nice school," Cowboy chimed in.

"Taking her back to her mother is the right thing to do," Cap'n Buck explained. "You want her to keep her honor, don't you? A Vietnamese girl has to be raised by her family. Mac, you're your own boss. I can't tell you what to do, but please consider this situation. This is the way it's got to be. We've got to get on with our jobs here."

Z translated this to Co Hai the best he could. She began shaking her head in distress and jabbering her response in an agitated manner.

"She says she wants to see her Mama San again more than anything in the world. But, she's afraid Mr. Nhat will find her and take her away again."

"She's right, Captain," I said. "Butt Gut's got connections everywhere. He'll find her anywhere she might be in the civilian populace."

"Well, what else are we going to do with her?" Cap'n Buck asked. "We can't continue to hide her out on an American base."

"I've been thinkin'," said Cowboy. "I've flown this attaché from the American Embassy, John Spencer, on a few hush-hush missions. I got to be pretty chummy with him, too. His family is over here living with him, a wife and two small kids. They live in an old French villa right around the corner from the Embassy. There's a whole colony of Embassy families livin' in that neighborhood, and they have an American school they send their kids to. Spenceer's one of those bleedin' heart types. I believe I could impose on him to take Co Hai in for a while, and maybe even let her study English at the school."

"Taking in a Vietnamese teenager is a lot to ask," I said. "Do you really think you could get him to do it?"

"It's worth a shot," nodded Cowboy. "He owes me big time."

"Then it's settled," said Cap'n Buck. "You can fly her down to Saigon this afternoon and get an answer from Spencer. If he says no, you can stay down there a couple of days and try to place her in a boarding school. That's all we can do."

Soon we were in the air on the way to Tan Son Nhut. Along the way Cowboy wowed Co Hai with his piloting skills. He laid it on thick with one story after another about his derring-do. Needless to say, this made Z quite jealous.

I don't know if Co Hai ever knew what she had in those two men. Both of them were the epitome of their profession. Cowboy was an extraordinary pilot. And Z—as a warrior his kind came along once in a lifetime. No matter how overrun or outgunned or outmaneuvered the situation might appear, you knew with Z on your side you had a chance. For me, he was the American version of Achilles in the Vietnam War. I eyed the developing storm clouds and hoped that Co Hai wouldn't turn out to be his Achilles' heel.

When we arrived at the Embassy, Cowboy called Spencer down to the guard gate and really gave him a sell job. Spencer called his wife and talked it over. It turned out the couple were looking for an *au pair* for their children. As a favor to Cowboy they agreed to try out Co Hai to see how she fit in with their family. Spencer walked us around to his villa, and his wife came out and welcomed Co Hai. They were a nice family, and I had a good feeling about how this would work out. Each of us had a lump in our throats when we said good-bye to Co Hai, but we knew it was for the best. We promised to visit her again soon.

That night Cowboy flew us back to Kontum, and we tried to concentrate once again on our combat assignments. Even though we all thought about Co Hai frequently, we rarely spoke of her. We regarded her too highly to bandy her name about in day-to-day conversation.

Our first order of business was to get the new guy, Silvestri, on board and up to speed quickly. Our effectiveness and our very lives depended on each team member functioning smoothly together. To this end, Z devised a baptism of fire for this new guy who we dubbed "Silver." We set it up with Cowboy to drop Silver off all alone in hostile territory, with Z and me keeping a watchful eye on the situation from nearby. By leaving Silver by himself in the jungle, we could find out a lot about his resourcefulness and presence of mind. Then we'd take him and force-feed him with everything he'd need to perform well as a scout. We could correct his mistakes right out there in the jungle where there was no room for error. Z also wanted him to get his first kill early on so we'd have the trauma of that experience behind us. Here again our plans hit a snag. Mother Nature had other ideas on how this training was to go down. It was Z who got his first kill of a different kind.

Cowboy dropped Silver off in a little glen at the edge of the jungle. Silver was right out of high school and six months of basic training, and the helicopter plopped him down all alone out there in the middle of Charlie land. With Z and me watching from a concealed location, Silver jumped off the helicopter with his gear. The door gunner pointed vaguely in our direction, and the chopper took off again. Silver dropped down low in the tall grass and lay there, frozen. He didn't move for about half an hour. I couldn't tell if he was hoping the chopper would come back for him, or what. Finally he began low-crawling in our general direction. He was armed to the teeth and lugging all kinds of equipment with him. With each push off with his legs, his gear banged around and jingled loudly. It was a good thing Z and I had made sure there was no enemy activity in the area before we gave Cowboy the go ahead to bring in.

Just before Silver reached the edge of the clearing, he suddenly froze in his tracks. At first Z and I were still laughing to ourselves about how spooked this rookie was. Then I heard a twig snap. I strained my ears and faintly picked up a strange purring-like noise. Z heard it, too. Silver raised his head and looked back over his shoulder. I scanned the terrain around him, at first not noticing anything unusual. Then I happened to catch something about twenty feet in back of Silver. It looked to be a pair of eyes, gazing at Silver through the tall savanna grass. There was something strange about those eyes. There were no whites around the pupils. Then it dawned on me that this was no human. This was an animal. Through the undergrowth I made out the coloring on part of the head and shoulder, and an electric shock of alarm bolted through me. I realized Silver was being stalked by a tiger. A bona fide, adult-size, man-eating tiger.

Silver's M-16 was in his right hand. He panicked and rolled over to try and get off a desperate shot, but he couldn't get his fingers to work right. Instantly, the tiger detected Silver's movement and sprang at its prey. Silver screamed in horror, awaiting his inevitable end. With the tiger in mid-air, I knew there'd only be one chance to get off a shot. But, I couldn't find the animal in my gun sights. A single BANG came from Z's K. At that instant the cat couldn't have been more than three feet from Silver. The tiger landed right on top of Silver. When the big cat didn't move and I saw Silver fidgeting underneath it, I breathed a sigh of relief. I scanned the area and detected no reaction to Z's rifle fire from the enemy. When Z saw Silver trying to roll the big beast off him, Z collected his cool and slipped over to Silver. After making sure Silver was okay, Z drew out his K-bar and began cutting the claws off of the tiger's front paws.

Without looking directly at Silver, Z whispered matter-of-factly as he worked, "All of that gear you're carrying is nothing but tiger bait. And Clyde bait. If you're going to run with us, Pack, you'll learn to run lean and quick and silent.

"Aw, as long as you're down on your belly, we might as well start your first lesson. Down there along the ground is where Clyde works. Look around you. That's Clyde's world. He don't fight up at shoulder level where Americans fight. He takes you on right there on the ground. That's where you look for Clyde. Always look down at you feet for signs of Clyde. Look for trip wires, for punji pits, for firing lanes. Clyde don't hack out big wide fields of fire like us Sammers. His firing lanes are no taller than your boot. He knocks your feet out from under you, then he's got your head and your heart in his field of fire. Clyde does it each and every day here in the Nam."

Z tossed a claw over to him. Dark purple blood dripped from one end of it. "There's a souvenir of your first day on the job."

Each of us received a souvenir from Silver's first day on the job. Z presented a tiger claw to Cap'n Buck, Cowboy, me, and his Montagnard friend, Bo. I still carry mine around my neck for good luck on special occasions.

When Cap'n Buck returned, the Team was fully operational again. It was a good feeling to be back together and doing our job again. This was a tense time for the Brigade, and while the line battalions were slugging it out in the grueling mountain jungles of western Kontum Province, the Team was out ahead of them, working along the border, trying to get a read on NVA troop and supply movements in and out of Vietnam.

Meanwhile, Cowboy was busy flying missions from sunrise until sunset. Once during July he flew a sortie down to Bien Hoa and was able to run over to Saigon to deliver a letter from Mama San to Co Hai, and bring her return letter back. Z sulked for days because Cowboy got to visit Co Hai and he didn't get to go along. He had to be content with knowing Co Hai was happy and everything was working out fine for her with the Spencers. Mrs. Spencer had arranged for Co Hai to attend some of the classes at the American school near the Embassy. The report that Co Hai was doing well made us all feel like proud papas.

In mid-August, the Brigade left the Fourth Battalion behind to anchor the Kontum area while the rest of us relocated to the coastal village of Tuy Hoa. Re-acquainting ourselves with this area of operation, it was almost like being on R&R after what the Brigade had just been through. We were matched against small VC units and could operate without the pressure of constant enemy contact.

During this time, whenever the Team had the chance, we continued to monitor the activities of Butt Gut and Colonel Xi. Although we couldn't get the type of hard evidence we'd need for a conviction, we were able to surmise a lot about their *modus operandi*. Butt Gut's operation was a piece of a much larger pie. Apparently he was one of the main regional distributors of black market goods in the Central Highlands. We speculated that there were other distributors for territories to the south and north of us.

There was more to it than what Butt Gut could carry around in his little Lambretta. Apparently they had bribed U.S. supply personnel at Cam Ranh Bay to assist them. Entire trucks filled with American beer, soda, cigarettes, candy, you name it, were rolling out of the supply yard at Cam Ranh Bay headed for the syndicate's black market warehouses. Some of the trucks used for transport were American, some were ARVN, and some were privately-owned. The syndicate was thriving by catering to the weaknesses of American servicemen. We wondered whether the bar and prostitution trade and drug trafficking were also controlled by them.

Meanwhile, American forces encountered more and more resistance from NVA regulars along the Laotian-Cambodian border. The 173rd Airborne Brigade was marching inexorably toward November and a date with destiny on Hill 875.

The Montagnard hamlet of Dak To is situated in a river valley surrounded by steep-sloped mountains of triple canopy jungle rising three-quarters of a mile high. The week before Thanksgiving a Special Forces Mike Force encountered a North Vietnamese regiment out west of Dak To on Hill 875. The enemy was dug into the mountain with bunkers and trenches. Most of the Brigade was already badly chewed up from vicious battles in recent days. The General had no choice but to send the Second Battalion up the mountain. The Second Batt was one of the toughest combat parachute battalions in the world, but the men were already battle weary from days of brutal fighting.

Deployment to Hill 875 began at dawn on Sunday, four days before Thanksgiving. We waited at the chopper pad for our turn to be lifted out. Huey after Huey rose and disappeared into the gray mist. Before we left, Chaplain Watters gathered some Sky Soldiers for a quick mass. He asked God to watch over us while we did His bidding so far from home. It was his last sermon.

Charlie and Delta Companies moved up the rugged north slope while Alpha Company stayed at the base of Hill 875 to clear a landing zone. Cap'n Buck, Z, Silver, and I were assigned to be perimeter lookouts for Alpha Company. The four of us were split up and sent out in front of the four sides of the perimeter to serve as one-man listening posts.

For a while everything was quiet down where we were, but our nerves were rubbed raw listening to the gunfire up above us. Struggling up the mountainside, Charlie and Delta Companies were up against constant sniper fire and attacks by small-sized units. Around noon the volleys became a steady downpour of gunfire. Charlie and Delta were getting hammered.

Without warning I heard automatic weapons fire out on the other side of our own makeshift perimeter, in the vicinity of where Z was positioned. I heard Silver and Cap'n Buck returning fire from their locations. I hurried back inside Alpha Company's line to help out. From out of nowhere a mass of NVA regulars, wearing cream-colored uniforms and pith helmets, assaulted our makeshift defensive line. They came storming through, their AK-47s blazing with volley after volley.

Alpha Company had a lot of heart, and they fought back with everything they had. There were so many NVA soldiers charging us that you could drop an enemy soldier with one shot almost anywhere you fired. No sooner had we pushed back the first wave then the second wave charged in right behind them. They overran the right side and poured into our perimeter. It was total chaos. We were firing in front of us and then wheeling around and shooting at someone behind us. This was no time to be wearing a boonie hat. I grabbed a helmet off a dead trooper, let the blood drain out of it, and put it on.

There was obviously no way to call in artillery or an air strike with the enemy that close. We were on our own, and it looked like the NVA were going to get the best of us. In the midst of the fighting, men were screaming for help, or quietly feeling their life ooze out of them, waiting for their moment of death.

The numbers of NVA were overwhelming. For every one we killed, three more popped up behind them. Half of our perimeter was getting slaughtered. The NVA were running through our position at will, bayoneting or shooting anyone who was still crawling. It was like one of those old frontier movies, where the Indians were swarming over the circled wagons, and the settlers, with no hope left, continued fighting on out of pride.

In a vicious hail of fire back and forth, the gutsy troopers on my side of the perimeter turned in desperation and pushed the NVA back enough to close ranks and form some semblance of a defensive line. Two Hueys tried to provide fire support and were shot down. A medic and a lieutenant tried to drag a wounded sergeant inside the lines, and all three of them were riddled with bullets.

Most of the officers and radio men in the Company were out of action. It was sheer bedlam. We were still fending off waves of NVA when our own artillery began exploding around our perimeter by mistake. Human limbs were flying up in the air from the exploding shells. Everyone was yelling to stop the artillery barrage, but no one knew how.

Then Cap'n Buck stepped in to fill the gap in the chain of command. "Don't panic. Hold your positions. We'll take care of the artillery. Who's got a radio that works? Soldier, does that radio work? How about that one there?"

He was speaking in a positive, level-headed way, and it helped to settle everyone down. I noticed that he was limping with pain at every step. He had been hit in the leg and left arm by shrapnel. At last he found a radio that worked.

"Check fire! Check fire! Left one hundred. Fire for effect."

Cap'n Buck dropped the radio's handset and began directing soldiers to shore up the defensive line, and to claw out a prone firing position for themselves anytime there was a moment's lull in the incoming fire. He moved an M-60 machine gun over so it had interlocking fire with guns on either side of it. He got the mortar squad better organized so their fire was more effective. He set up a better channel for getting the wounded back into the center of our small circle where Chaplain Watters was comforting the wounded and administering last rites to the dying.

Within a few minutes Cap'n Buck had us all fighting together again like a team. Our self-respect was restored. Hell, we were paratroopers, weren't we? "Living a life of guts and danger," as the ditty goes. We were going to let those boys from Hanoi know they were up against the best. They might outswarm us in numbers, but we'd never be beaten in spirit.

Cap'n Buck's morale boost didn't last long. I looked up and spotted an F-100 Phantom jet swooping our way. I was thinking, All right, Fly Boy, drop a little thunder right out there, and see how Charlie likes it! As it roared overhead a black dot left its undercarriage too soon. Helplessly, I watched a five hundred pound bomb plunge down right into the middle of our circle. I had just enough time to turn over and hug the ground before I felt the earth convulse, and I was slammed with a wave of hot energy and flying debris.

Immediately, Cap'n Buck was on the radio diverting the air strike. It was too late. The devastation had been done. The bomb landed in the middle of our wounded, and thirty-some soldiers were obliterated, including the Executive Officer, Chaplain, medical doctor, and most of the medics. Another two dozen troopers around the fringes were seriously wounded. People were shouting "AMMO!" and "MEDIC!" But, we were almost out of both.

The NVA seized that opportunity to launch another mass wave attack, driving right up to our defensive line again. Finally one of the jet jocks overhead got it right, and we were scorched from the heat of exploding napalm to our front. This caught the NVA inside our perimeter between us and a wall of flames. We managed to gain some momentum again, driving the enemy off to the flanks. Again Cap'n Buck steadied things, along with the few other officers who were still ambulatory. With our artillery and air power working effectively, we managed to keep the enemy in front of us.

I realized that I hadn't seen Z since that morning when we split up and went to our listening posts. Despite the ongoing confusion I headed downhill along the line, ducking enemy fire while checking the faces of bodies that resembled his. After working my way around about a third of the perimeter, I bumped into Cap'n Buck. He was out checking the defensive line.

"Cap'n, I can't find Z."

"He never came back inside the perimeter. How're you doing, Jax? You need a medic."

"Never mind me."

Pride welled up inside me that he was my commanding officer. Here was a man, wounded himself, one of the few captains or higher officer who was still functioning, directing the operations of a seriously outnumbered American force in the biggest battle of the War, and on top of all that, he was looking out for the men in his LRRP Team.

"Give me that napalm thirty mikes to the lima of that last batch, over," Cap'n Buck said into the handset of his radio. Then he turned to me. "Here, take the binocks. Z was on that ridge line over there. Go take a look."

"Yes, Sir."

"Keep your butt low!" he called after me.

I picked my way back over to the perimeter in the direction he had pointed out. The sun was getting low in the sky. The napalm strikes had taken the starch out of the NVA wave attacks, but we were still getting a steady diet of AK-47, mortar, and rocket fire from the jungle. I steadied the binoculars on top of the leg of a twisted NVA body and began scoping out the scene in front of me. For the first time that day my attention extended out beyond the focus of our own little piece of turf, which we had carved out with our bare hands and were sacrificing everything to defend. I was dumbfounded at what the world looked like around us. The wreckage of a dozen American helicopters were spread over the mountainside. The jungle to our flanks was in flames. The bombs and napalm had thinned out the triple canopy jungle around us. There were huge mounds of stumps and rubble where a mighty forest had stood only hours before. Most remarkable of all were the hundreds and hundreds of NVA bodies. They may have dealt a staggering blow to us, but we'd put a major hurt on them, too, to the tune of ten for every American killed.

I spotted something. In the middle of body after body clad in NVA uniforms, I noticed something twitching, reaching, and dragging, moving ever so slowly toward our perimeter. Eventually I made out the tiger camouflaged fatigues. I knew then it was Z. I could tell by the blood-soaked jersey and how he was moving that he was bad off. Somehow he was finding a way to push and pull himself along toward the general direction of our line. He was about fifty meters out, which was a long, long way under the circumstances. I quickly made my way back to Cap'n Buck, who was talking on the radio.

"We need plasma, morphine, ammo, and water, in that order." He turned to me. "Any luck, Jax?"

"Sir, Z's about 50 meters out. All shot up but still breathing. If you can get me five minutes of artillery cover behind him, we can try to drag him back inside."

"You've got it."

Returning to the east side of the perimeter, I yanked the chin strap tight on my helmet and prepared to go out. Taking off my gear and ammo bandoliers, I loaded a new magazine in my rifle and stuffed three full magazines behind me in my belt.

"I NEED A VOLUNTEER TO HELP BRING IN A WOUNDED!" I shouted.

"That would be me," answered a familiar voice.

I glanced around, and there was Silver. We looked at each other and nodded.

Moments later when the artillery barrage began landing behind Z, Silver and I slid up and over. Stateside, I would have set the record in the low crawl that day. Except, it's a lot harder in real life when you're keeping your rifle in front of you, being shot at constantly, and climbing over mounds of bodies and debris.

"You keeping up, Young Fella?" I shouted back to Silver.

"Right behind you, Big Guy."

When we reached Z, I couldn't believe he was still alive. He had been hit several times by small arms fire, plus he had an ugly shrapnel wound below his left shoulder. I ripped open his fatigue shirt and slapped makeshift bandages on his most gaping wounds. The artillery cover was working effectively until a machine gun got a bead on us and pinned us down behind a stump.

"I'll roll out and take out the machine gun," said Silver. "When I do, start dragging him back. I'll catch up later."

Silver slithered away. A minute later he opened fire on the machine gun. I started dragging Z with every ounce of strength I had in me. I dug in my heels, arched my back and tugged on him, and then again, and again. It was like rowing a boat, pull, pull, pull, forever and ever. I thought surely I had him almost to the perimeter, but I looked ahead and saw we had only gone about halfway. I pulled and pulled some more, up over dead NVA, and then down along the ground, then up over more dead. After our artillery support stopped, the sniper fire picked up, and bullets were pinging all around us. I looked ahead, and it still seemed like a long way to the perimeter. To their credit, the troopers back on the line were firing a barrage out over Z and me to give us cover.

"Let's go, Jax!" Silver said. He wiggled up and grabbed Z's other arm. "We're almost there. You better keep up with me!"

Together we dragged Z over the makeshift mound of dirt and into the perimeter, to the cheers of the troopers on that side of the line. We carried him back to the large group of seriously wounded. I laid down beside him and tried to help him the best I could. I still needed to get stitched up myself, but I told the medic to treat the serious ones first. The two medics that had survived had worked for seven hours straight under impossible field conditions. They were out of almost every medical supply needed, and there was no way to tend to everyone. Many had died during the day while waiting to be evacced out. Many more were still hanging on somehow. Every chopper that had braved the onslaught to get through to us had been shot down. After dark, using a circle of flashlights to signal with, we finally got a chopper to fly over and kick out medical supplies, ammo, and water to us. It was like manna from heaven.

While Alpha Company was staggering at the bottom of the mountain, Charlie and Delta were fighting for survival higher up on the mountainside, facing annihilation from the intense enemy barrage throughout the night. Meanwhile, it was a long night for us, too. All through the night the NVA continued to hit us with mortars and rockets. Our artillery fire base kept the perimeter lit up all night with illumination rounds, but the NVA probed our position numerous times through the night with squad-size assaults. The fresh ammo made us feel better, and our only option was to respond to each enemy action that came up. All you could do was hope you'd be one of the lucky ones still alive in the morning. Cap'n Buck stayed at the helm all night with no rest.

The next morning the Fourth Battalion came to our rescue. In a bold move, they left all their heavy gear behind and fought their way into our position. The plan was for them to link up with us in Alpha Company and then work their way up the mountain to break through to Charlie and Delta.

We cheered when the Fourth Batt joined our perimeter. We were able to expand the landing zone so that choppers could land to evacuate the wounded. We felt like we had a chance again. Z was still alive when we watched him being lifted off on the fifth Med-Evac chopper. Silver crossed himself, and I breathed a sigh of relief. I'm usually not very religious, but I felt if the Lord had let Z live through that terrible night, there'd be no reason to take him from us now.

The three of us left on the Team were pretty nicked up, too. They tried to make us go back to get patched up, but we wouldn't hear of it. We helped out at the point leading the Fourth Batt up the mountain to hook up with Charlie and Delta. That was a journey in itself with evidence of fierce fighting all along the way. We passed so many American bodies that we had to ask ourselves how many troopers were yet alive up there to save. It was nearly ten o'clock that night when we finally linked up with Charlie and Delta Companies. A lot of their guys sobbed uncontrollably when they saw us.

Then we turned our attention to taking the top of the mountain. That was two more days of fighting bunker by bunker, trenchline by trenchline, while our artillery kept pounding away and the Phantoms laid in one airstrike after the other on the hill above us.

When we reached the top they told us it was Thanksgiving Day, 1967. But the mood was somber. We were haunted by so many ghosts left behind us down the mountainside.

As 1967 drew to a close, the Team had not functioned at full strength for several weeks. Z had just returned to duty from his convalescence in Japan and was still not in shape to go out on patrol. Cowboy was just getting back from an R&R to Australia. And Cap'n Buck went to Hawaii on R&R to spend Christmas with his wife.

When Cap'n Buck returned from Hawaii, his priorities had changed. The goal of neutralizing Colonel Xi's operation became his driving force. His primary interest was finding ways to interdict the syndicate's supply lines and erode Colonel Xi's infrastructure. Cap'n Buck's time was running out, and he was determined to settle his score with Xi before it was over.

The GI's guarding the Green Line at Camp Radcliff celebrated the new year with a bang—machine guns blazed, and hundreds of star-cluster flares were launched skyward.

During January 1968, we continued to go after Colonel Xi at every opportunity. Although we were successful in intercepting some of the syndicate's supply trucks, we still had no indisputable evidence that would expose the syndicate's ringleaders and bust up the operation for good. Since Cap'n Buck's tour was scheduled to end soon, he grew impatient.

Cap'n Buck decided that we needed to force the issue by sneaking inside Colonel Xi's villa and gaining access to his secret records. This amounted to breaking and entering the home of an ARVN field grade officer. Silver was just returning from R&R, so it was left to the three of us to execute the plan.

Colonel Xi's villa was south of Nha Trang, about a mile down the beach beyond the airfield. It was near the five famous Bao Dai villas, one of which was used by President Thieu. The Colonel's villa overlooked the Bay and the glimmering turquoise waters of the South China Sea. The winding paths and lush tropical plants and trees behind and between the villas provided us with ample camouflage for our surveillance activities.

Z and I watched the house for several days, day and night, to determine the comings and goings of the Colonel, his wife, associates, and servants. The only apparent security at his mansion were ARVN soldiers, one of whom was on duty twenty-four hours a day at the guard shack by the front gate. The guard would get up two or three times during the night and check the doors and windows on the first floor around the house, and then return to the guard shack. We also noticed that the Colonel spent a lot of time by himself in a room in the corner of the cellar. Was he into woodworking? Or, was this where he recorded and stored his private transactions? We intended to find out.

We selected Sunday evening as the entry time because the housekeeper was off on Sundays, and Colonel Xi and his wife usually went to church after supper. Cap'n Buck would cover the front and keep an eye on the guard while Z and I actually entered the house.

We scaled the fence and made it across the lawn to the house. Z discovered the window over the kitchen sink was unlocked. He climbed in and let me in the kitchen door. The scent of Oriental teakwood permeated the home. Despite our efforts to be quiet, our boots clopped across the polished wooden floors, which surrounded the islands of Oriental throw rugs. For a wealthy man's home, I was surprised at how sparsely and austerely furnished it was. Their idea of luxury was so much simpler than ours.

We checked the ground and second floors and found nothing of interest. We made our way down into the cool and musty cellar. At the bottom of the stairs several doors led off of the main corridor. The door straight ahead opened into a large, well-fortified arms room, with reinforced concrete walls and firing ports. There were enough provisions and ammo stacked down there to hold a small army at bay.

Z paced off the length and width of the cellar and determined that the area where Xi spent so much time was not one of the apparent rooms in the cellar. We checked the walls on that side of the cellar inch by inch and finally discovered the concealed door to the old wine cellar behind a credenza. The steel door was locked with a fancy deadbolt system that we couldn't open. This was the room we needed to get into.

It was time to put Plan B into effect. I helped Z hide himself in a small room filled with firewood which had an angle view of the credenza with the wine cellar door concealed in it. Leaving Z hidden, I ransacked the arms room and the office upstairs, deliberately strewing his personal papers about the room, helter-skelter. Then I jimmied the outside lock to the kitchen door to make it look like a forced entry from the outside and slipped back over the wall without being detected by the guard at the front gate.

An hour or so later, Colonel Xi's car was admitted at the gate. He drove it around and parked in the garage, and he and his wife walked from there to the kitchen door. Right away, they noticed the door had been forced open. All the lights on the grounds suddenly came on, and the sentry was summoned from the guard house. The poor guy looked dumbfounded to see the back door had been jimmied. Xi reprimanded him severely, slapped him a couple of times, and sent him back to the guard house. Soon the local police arrived to search and investigate.

When all the inspectors had gone and his wife was asleep upstairs, Colonel Xi sneaked downstairs to make sure his wall safe was still intact and secure.

Opening the hidden room, Colonel Xi went straight over to the large wall safe. He hurriedly worked the combination and opened it. For a second he breathed a sigh of relief as he saw that the contents of the safe were untouched. Then Z pressed his pistol against Colonel Xi's temple.

"Ngung nghi!" said Z.

Z taped the Colonel's mouth and put a bag over the Colonel's head so Colonel Xi could not look around and identify his assailant. Then Z sat the Colonel down in a chair and tied him up.

With the Colonel well secured, Z shoveled the contents of the safe into a satchel. He took only the business papers—Cap'n Buck had given explicit orders that no money or valuables were to be removed from the house. Z then slipped out of the house and over the wall without being detected.

Once we were aboard Cowboy's helicopter we opened the satchel while his co-pilot began winding out the engine. We found a treasure trove of incriminating evidence against Colonel Xi. Although we couldn't read the Vietnamese writing we could make out the interspersed mentioning of Swiss banks and American names coupled with large sums of money. Hundreds of thousands of dollars had been deposited in Swiss bank accounts. In addition, we found payoffs to ARVN and American generals and field grade officers, with signed receipts from them which Xi kept as added insurance. There were names of what looked like co-conspirators and lists of every business venture connected with the syndicate. It went on and on. There seemed to be no end to the pies Xi had a finger in, or the high officials he had a finger on.

"Lookee here, Buck," said Cowboy. "This must be a list of his contacts in the United States."

Cap'n Buck took the ledger and thumbed through it. He centered on a page and scanned it quickly, then snapped the book shut. "This stuff's too hot for us to keep around. We've got to find a safe place to stash it for a while."

"Wait here," said Cowboy as he crammed everything back into the satchel. "KEEP HER REVVED UP. I'LL BE RIGHT BACK," he shouted to his co-pilot. Cowboy jumped down to the runway and jogged, in his double-time swagger, across the tarmac to the terminal. Soon he reappeared, and we lifted off. I never knew what Cowboy did with the documents inside the terminal.

Cap'n Buck was right. The information was too hot for us to keep around. The next day the MP's searched us and our quarters at An Khe, which the Brigade had recently occupied after the First Cav was relocated farther south. They also searched the helicopter platoon's barracks and Cowboy's chopper. Obviously, Colonel Xi had great influence over American commanders. The higher-ups were putting a lot of pressure on Cap'n Buck. He was called into the Operational Center a couple of times and came out looking very shaken. They grounded the Team from any further missions and barred us from leaving Camp Radcliff. Despite this, they couldn't turn up any trace of the documents, and all of us denied having any knowledge of them. But this time the trouble wouldn't pass. Our time was short.

Chapter VII

WITHIN A FEW DAYS we were summoned back to Nha
Trang for questioning. We were ordered to report to I Field
Force Headquarters at 0800 hours on January 30, 1968.

The day before the interviews were to begin, Cowboy
flew us down to Nha Trang. Cowboy and his crew stayed at
the transient flight crew quarters at the airfield. The Team,
no longer welcome at the airfield, went downtown and
checked into a civilian hotel a few blocks from the I Field
Force compound. Although Nha Trang didn't cater to GI's
like Pleiku and An Khe did, we decided to taste what there
was of the nightlife. Z started us out at a cafe which served
Vietnamese food and played native music. The *nuoc mam*
and rice got old pretty fast, so Cap'n Buck, Silver, and I split
from Z and ambled down the street, looking for a place that
was more Americanized. Happily, we found a bar where they
were playing all the sentimental favorites of American GI's:
wearing flowers in your hair in San Francisco; the green,
green grass of home; and best of all: "We've got to get out of
this place, if it's the last thing we ever do!"

One of the things I liked about Cap'n Buck was he
never pulled rank on us. We were a team, and in the field
we all had jobs that were just as important to our mutual
survival and success as the next person's. Although there
was no doubt about who was in charge, his not insisting
on rank made us respect him and follow his leadership
even more. Even Z, whose scouting skills were unparalleled and who did an excellent job of leading us anytime

the Captain wasn't with us, deferred to Cap'n Buck's judgment in the field. When we were in Base Camp or downtown Cap'n Buck could have stayed apart and gone off and done his thing with other officers, but he chose to sleep in the same tent with us at Base Camp and to hang out with us in town.

We were all getting to be short-timers over there. Even Silver was on the down side. Z and I had extended for an additional three months and had new DEROS dates set for March. Cap'n Buck only had two-and-a-half weeks to go. Usually when you got that short you lost your aggressiveness and started looking for the conservative way out of every situation. But Cap'n Buck wasn't thinking about home. Despite being grounded and facing a formal inquiry the next day, all Cap'n Buck could talk about was exposing Colonel Xi.

"If everybody's in on it except us, where are we going to go to get justice?" I asked.

"Things have a way of working themselves out," Cap'n Buck answered.

Z came in and joined us, looking worried.

"What happened, did the performer break his mandarin?" I joked.

"Naw, listen, now." I could tell by the deep lines around his eyes and the way he arched his eyebrow that he was nervous about something, which gave me a twinge of guilt. The rest of us were unwinding, but Z never stopped working. "Something's not right outside," he said.

"Tomorrow is the eve of the big Tet celebration," said Cap'n Buck. "The people are all bustling about in preparation for the holiday. That's probably what you feel."

"Naw, that's not it. I know their holiday spirit here. Something else is wrong out there. I can sense it. I think we better get back to our hotel. Please."

It was that last "please" that got us. Z never asked us to do anything, and how could we refuse a suggestion that was the right thing to do, anyway? After all, we had a long day of grilling under the hot lights coming up early the next morning. We finished our drinks and headed back.

In the hotel we circled up the marble staircase to our rooms on the third floor. Z and I were in one room, and Cap'n Buck was in the next room with Silver. All of us crashed forthwith, except Z. He got up and scanned the street from our window every 20 minutes. About one o'clock, Z left the room for a while. When he came back, he shook me awake.

"This city is crawling with Cong."

I stumbled over to the window, trying to shake off my grogginess. I could have kicked myself for consuming those two beers. The street was dark and empty. I watched for a few minutes until I saw a group of five black pajamas shuffling from shadow to shadow down the street, with a rifle slung over each man's shoulder.

"Jesus," I said, fumbling for my boots in the dark. "Go tell Cap'n Buck."

In a minute flat I grabbed all of our gear and joined the others next door. They were dressing hurriedly.

"You want to make a stand here, Cap'n?" I asked.

"Negative. Charlie's not after us. We've got to try to slip down to I Field Force Headquarters and warn them. No contact unless necessary. Z, get on the phone and try to raise someone at the Vietnamese side of the airfield and warn them."

Z picked up the phone and clicked several times, but couldn't get the desk clerk to answer.

"Let's go," Cap'n Buck said. "We'll try to call again from the switchboard when we get downstairs."

When we reached the lobby there was no sign of the desk clerk or the bellman. Z vaulted the front desk and worked on getting an outside line at the switchboard.

"This may take a while," Z said. "Go on ahead. I'll catch up."

I slipped out the front door first and slinked over to a shadow, motioning for the other two to follow. We managed to stay out of sight most of the way to the headquarters building. Then the dilemma. We needed to cross a major intersection and go another half block to the guard shack at the front entrance. The VC were bound to be in position all around the headquarters building to attack, and we didn't know the challenge and password to get past the gate guards. Cap'n Buck put an arm around me and the other around Silver, and we stumbled out into the moonlit center of the boulevard, pretending to be three sheets to the wind while singing the paratrooper's theme song:

There was blood upon his risers
and, his guts upon his chute,
AND, HE AIN'T GONNA JUMP NO MORE!
Gory, gory, what a hell of a way to die.
Gory, gory, what a hell of a way to die.
Gory, gory, what a hell of a way to die.
AND, HE AIN'T GONNA JUMP NO MORE!

With that, we made it to the front gate without being challenged.

We alerted the MP's guarding the compound and took up positions covering the front entrance. It didn't take long before Major Daniels heard of our intrusion and came storming downstairs.

"Captain, what in the hell do you think you're doing?"

"Major, we're about to come under a major attack. I recommend all ARVN and American installations in the city be alerted ASAP."

"That's ridiculous. There's been no indication of an attack in this region. Do you expect me to put the city on alert because you stagger in here after the bars have closed crying wolf?"

"With all due respect, Major, we are scouts. Warning higher-ups of enemy activity is what we do. Do you think I'm crouching behind this wall of sandbags just to be playing games with you?"

"You've played all the games you're ever going to play, Captain. Now get yourself and your men out of my compound, and report back here at 0800 as directed."

Just then automatic weapons fire erupted out in the street.

"GET DOWN!" Cap'n Buck shouted. He reached up and pulled the Major down.

Suddenly two rockets whistled into the entrance area, resulting in a tremendous jolt of energy. The wall of sandbags disintegrated, with the duty guard catching the force of it. He was blown back against the wall, his arm ripped open. Silver and I dragged him inside before hearing the familiar battle cry of a dozen VC soldiers. Their charge was accompanied by a heavy volley of small arms fire. Silver and I lobbed grenades out into the street and then opened up with our AK's. Despite our grenades and return fire, two VC from the first wave made it through the door. Cap'n Buck shot one point blank with his .45, and I smashed the face of the other with my rifle butt. The bodies tumbled down beside the crouching figure of Major Daniels.

"Attack confirmed, Sir," said Cap'n Buck.

It didn't look like we'd be successful in repelling the second wave. One rocket went straight through and exploded in the back of the lobby, followed by a half dozen VC storming the entrance. Bullets were bouncing around off all the walls. I didn't think we'd be able to hold them without reinforcements. Then there was the familiar firing of a different-sounding automatic weapon from out in the street behind the VC. Z's Swedish K was music to our ears. Now Charlie was being fired upon from two directions. Their attack soon dissolved.

"HOLD YOUR FIRE! FRIENDLY COMING IN," shouted Cap'n Buck. Through the smoke, Z hopped over the bodies and slid inside.

"I'll put the whole city on alert," said Major Daniels, running for the Communications Room.

Silver and I turned a desk over on its side and pushed it up to the door. We also tried to stack up any of the sandbags that were still intact.

"Aw, I judge that's the last of them," said Z. "We've cut down the squad assigned to attack this building. They're hitting different targets all over the city without no one objective. I doubt any reinforcements will show up tonight."

Z was right. It was a long night of waiting for the dawn to come, and you could hear heavy fighting going on all over the city, but that was the end of the attack on the I Field Force Headquarters.

A half-hour before dawn, Major Daniels came back downstairs carrying a map. "Captain, the provincial Hall of

Justice, right up the street a couple of clicks from here, is under siege. The VC are determined to take the building because there are political prisoners in the jail on the top floor. At this time it's being defended by a couple of janitors. They won't be able to hold it by themselves when daylight comes. We've got all our other combat units out securing bigger targets. We need your Team to go down and reinforce them."

"Does this mean our eight o'clock meeting is canceled?"

"Just postponed, Captain. We'll deal with that later."

"If we're going to get there before dawn, we'll need wheels."

"If you want to risk using a jeep, you're welcome to it."

"Did they take the airfield?"

"Victor Charlie has control of the fixed wing runway. We've sent an ARVN infantry company to clear them out."

"Is Nha Trang the only city under attack?"

"Ban Me Thuot, Kontum, Ninh Hoa, Qui Nhon, Pleiku, Tuy Hoa. It's an all-out blitz on the provincial capitals. That's why we need every fighting man out there trying to contain this thing."

"We're on our way, Sir," said Cap'n Buck.

The way Cap'n Buck drove, with no lights, I think he planned on a sixty-second trip. He was barreling straight ahead, no matter what. I was more afraid of bouncing off than I was of getting shot. When he'd hit pieces of debris in the street, I'd get jostled way up in the air. I prayed Charlie hadn't put out any mines.

There was gunfire here and there throughout the city, but we didn't take any direct hits until we got near the Hall of Justice. The Viet Cong had set up makeshift positions around the building, but we blazed our way through their line. Z, Silver, and I returned fire while Cap'n Buck bounced us right up the front steps. The jeep made it about halfway up before stalling out. Z and Silver rolled out on either side and laid down suppressing fire while Cap'n Buck and I scrambled up the steps to the door. Bullets were ricocheting all around us. Next, Cap'n Buck and I provided cover fire from behind the stone columns to allow Silver to sprint up to us. But our luck went sour again. A bullet ripped through Silver's right thigh. He flipped over in agony. Z dropped a grenade in the gas tank of the jeep and streaked up to help Silver. Emptying a magazine at the enemy's defensive line, I ran back down the steps to lend a hand. With Z and me on either shoulder, we lunged together with all our might to make it up and over the top step before the jeep exploded. The fire ball blew upward and then rained burning parts of the jeep down on us. We used that instant of mayhem to scurry inside the heavy, iron front doors of the massive building.

When I looked at Silver's leg there was no arterial bleeding. I hurriedly bandaged him.

"Z, find out who's in charge here and what their situation is," instructed Cap'n Buck. "Jax and I will check the rear of the building. Silver, cover the front the best you can."

We met the three gutsy irregulars who had kept the VC at bay for five hours. They consisted of an old night watchman and two young janitors. One janitor had his wife with him, and the other one had his whole family with him: his wife, a small boy, and an infant. With a meager arsenal of well-worn bolt-action rifles the trio had managed to hold off 20-odd Viet Cong sappers. The building would have fallen in the first five minutes had it not been for the architectural design. The VC were stymied by the way the imposing stone building locked up tighter than a drum at night. They couldn't figure out how to breach the seemingly impregnable exterior. Any overt attempts had been repulsed by the two janitors. The watchman devoted most of his time to guarding the prisoners upstairs.

Looking back, the Team would have been more effective had we not entered the building so quickly. If we had stayed behind the attackers we could have picked them off from the rear. However, Cap'n Buck had not known what kind of shape the defenders were in, and our orders were to relieve them. We only nailed a few of the VC soldiers on our way in, so there were still about 20 VC out there to deal with.

"Z, get this janitor to lead you up to the roof, and see how many VC you can pick off from up there. The best way to win this fight is to destroy them before they think to go for help. If some of their comrades have captured an ARVN tank, they could put us in a real hurt."

The light was improving outside, and there was movement among the VC as they tried to recon their objective better. Z took my AK-47, which had a better range than his K. He reported back in about 20 minutes.

"Any luck?" asked the Captain.

"Aw, I got a few of them, but after they saw me up there, they hunkered down out of sight. Captain, here's something else we can try. This janitor says he can get us down into the city sewer system from here. We might be able to come up behind them and give Clyde a surprise."

We decided to leave Silver inside with the janitors and watchman while the three of us tried to outflank Charlie. We followed a janitor through the main cellar and down a narrow, winding staircase to a sub-basement. The janitor pointed out a stone manhole cover with an iron ring in the center. The three of us climbed down and heaved together to lift and drag the stone out of the way.

Beneath the manhole cover was a black hole which dropped down into the building's sewer system. This was the hard part, because the pipe under the building wasn't very big, and we had to crawl through the water and sludge to reach the main line. We pried the bars open with our rifles and squeezed through into the main sewer channel, which was big enough to walk through.

We moved along under the street until we found the likely manhole cover. Z climbed up to have a look.

"We're in the street right behind them," said Z. "They've blown a hole in an air duct on the side of the building, and some sappers are forcing their way in. We've got to get back and help Silver."

"There's no time to go back," said Cap'n Buck. "The only way to save Silver is for us to knock them out from this side. Let's go."

Cap'n Buck scaled the ladder and slid the cover to one side. There were still eight or nine VC at the edge of the street, providing supporting fire for the assault team. They were so preoccupied with watching the sappers climb into the air vent that the Captain and Z were able to roll out onto the street before being noticed. I popped my head out of the hole, and the three of us opened fire simultaneously. It was over in a matter of seconds. The VC were so surprised and so vulnerable from the rear that none of them even had a chance to whirl and get off a decent shot at us. We moved up to their position and directed our fire at their assault team, most of whom were caught out in the open while waiting their turn to crawl into the air duct.

"We've got to push on through and get back to Silver," said Cap'n Buck. We dashed up the main entrance stairs again. Silver swung the front door open so we could dive back inside.

Once inside, Cap'n Buck and Z tracked down and neutralized the VC soldiers who had crawled into the ventilating ducts. Meanwhile, I borrowed a motor scooter from one of the janitors and carried Silver over to the Eighth Field Hospital for treatment. When I returned to the Hall, Cap'n Buck and Z had everything under control. By mid-afternoon, an ARVN squad relieved us, and we walked back to I Field Force Headquarters.

Cap'n Buck reported immediately to Major Daniels.

"Sir, you said Tuy Hoa was one of the places under attack. I request permission for my LRRP Team to return to Tuy Hoa to join the 173rd's Fourth Battalion in the battle there."

"Negative," replied Major Daniels. "They've got six hundred paratroopers to handle the situation there. We've got only three paratroopers to defend all of Nha Trang—YOU! Now, we've got a gun battle going on back and forth across the airfield. The Viet Cong have control of part of the runway. So far we've managed to keep them away from the chopper pad, but their ground fire's too heavy for us to get any choppers in or out. We've got Americans pinned down in the aviator's barracks and an ARVN unit holding on to the southwest edge of the runway. We need your Team to get over there and see what you can do to block or slow down the enemy advance on the chopper pad."

This time we didn't make the mistake of barging through the enemy lines and getting stuck inside. We spent the rest of the daylight hours skirting around the edges of the battle zone to determine Charlie's strengths and weaknesses. The VC were entrenched in a coffee plantation extending along the edge of the runway. Cap'n Buck sketched it out on a map and considered the enemy's possible courses of action before formulating a plan.

"A couple of hours after dark, the Viet Cong main force will likely assault the terminal and aviation control tower with rockets and small arms," said Cap'n Buck. "While that's going on, I expect a sapper squad to circle around the flank of the main attack force to destroy the helicopters parked on the helipad. As soon as it gets dark, we'll infiltrate their lines on the right side. When their evening attack begins, we'll be in a position to slide left and block the sappers. These are their crack commandos, and they will fight to the death, to the last man. They can't be repulsed, they must be destroyed. If even one sapper gets through, he'll inflict serious damage on our chopper fleet."

Z pointed to the map. "Cap'n," said Z, "Once we take their flank position here, I'd like to float out and intercept the sappers back here while they're moving into position. I might be able to zap some of them before they reach you and Stoney."

"Okay, but as soon as we open fire, you roll out to your left—our right—to avoid getting hit in our line of fire."

After nightfall the nervous ARVN's kept popping off illumination flares, forcing us to duck down low while the incendiaries silhouetted our location. As the three of us crawled along through the high-standing coffee plants, we bumped into small groups of VC moving up in preparation for their attack. We were so close that the VC thought we were stray parts of their own group and whispered to us to get back in formation.

The VC rocket attack on the terminal started about ten o'clock. Z looped back to intercept the sappers, and Cap'n Buck and I low-crawled across the friendly fire zone to the large dirt berm protecting the choppers from direct fire. We spread about twenty meters apart and set up fields of fire into low approach lanes. Meanwhile, there was a hellatious firefight going on behind us between the VC and ARVN regular forces. Both sides were going all out, with mortars, rockets, and fierce automatic weapons fire. Tracers and illumination rounds were lighting up the sky, as well as exposing our silhouettes on the berm.

Suddenly to our right front I heard Z's Swedish K firing off an entire magazine. That prompted a stiff return volley of enemy small arms fire. Apparently Z had run into trouble. It sounded like he was heavily outnumbered. Cap'n Buck motioned for me to see what was going on while the Captain held his position against what we still expected to be the direction of the main sapper attack.

I headed back along the inside of the berm until I was in front of the location of Z's firefight. It sounded like Z was caught in a crossfire. Constant firing from AK-47's was coming from several locations. I knew Z was still hanging in there because every so often Z's K could be heard, each time firing from a different location. Z was skillfully using fire and maneuver to maximize the enemy's confusion.

Before I could climb up on the berm to provide fire support, two sappers slipped over the top of the berm carrying satchel charges. They were heading toward two of the parked helicopters. They were too far away for me to chase them down, so I had to drop them with rifle fire.

Another sapper appeared, charging right at me. A flare lit up the sky, and I saw the determination and wildness in his cold, steel eyes. He sported a faint smile of exhilaration as he lunged to drive his knife in my chest. Instinctively I reached out and deflected the knife with my left arm. The knife slashed my hand open in the process. My assailant's momentum knocked me down, but I used this force to my advantage by flipping him over and then kipping up to apply a karate chop to his throat. He sprang up immediately with a "Hah" sound to let me know my move hadn't phased him. While the "Hah" was still coming out of his mouth I plunged my K-bar toward his heart. He caught my thrust, and I blocked his counter lunge. For a moment we were stalemated, both wrestling with one hand fending off the other's knife. We strained with all our might, face to face and chest to chest. I thought, so this is the way it is, the way it should be, the way it has to be—two men in the archetypal life or death struggle for survival. But I knew I had to finish it. I reversed his brute force by sitting down and flipping him over again, this time stabbing him through the neck with my K-bar. It was over.

I staggered up, gazing for an instant at his lifeless form. Lulled by this moment of triumph, I didn't hear the footsteps behind me until it was too late. I was jarred by the force of an assailant's forearm jammed against my shoulders. I knew the next sensation would be my last—the knife blade ripping through my heart. At that final moment I heard a rifle shot behind me, and the assailant slumped down at my feet. I looked back and saw Cap'n Buck take the rifle off his shoulder and continue running my way. Miraculously I had escaped certain death. Now anything I did for the rest of my life was a bonus, even if my life lasted only a few seconds more.

Cap'n Buck was almost at my side when two more sappers bounded up and over, charging us. We knelt down and fired into their chests at close range. After them, three more came up and over, running for the choppers. Cap'n Buck and I tackled and subdued two of the three. But the third ran right past us, heading straight for Cowboy's chopper. He started pulling the detonating fuse out of his satchel charge. I thought there was no way for us to stop him now and that all our efforts had been in vain. There was a jarring SHHUNK, and the sapper lurched forward and fell face down. I looked behind him, and there was Z, kneeling on one knee to catch his breath. He had appeared while we were engaged by the last two attackers and had run the last sapper down, hurling his ice axe with both hands, which hit his target square in the back. Z retrieved his axe, driving it into the earth and rocking it back and forth to clean the blood off. Z was superstitious about having his clothing or equipment sullied by enemy blood.

Cap'n Buck and I scrambled back up the berm to make sure there were no more attackers coming. Z got out the first aid kit, doused my hand in antiseptic, and bandaged it.

"That was the last of the sappers," Z whispered as he worked.

"What happened out there?"

"I hooked up with them and zapped a couple of their rear guard, but I realized they wasn't going to enter the berm over there where you was waiting for them. Instead of circling around, they was coming straight up off their flank. I knew there was no way you could stop them over where you was waiting, so I had to open fire without my silencer to give you warning of where they'd be coming in."

We had already accomplished a good night's worth of work, but Cap'n Buck wasn't finished yet.

"The ARVN's aren't making anything happen over there," said Cap'n Buck. "They're just laying back returning fire, and Charlie's gaining ground on the runway, inching ever closer to the terminal and barracks. We can't call in artillery or we'll destroy our own airfield, and our gunships are grounded. We're going to have to give this thing a kick in the rear before it slips away from us."

"What do you have in mind, Sir," I asked.

"They've moved forward out of their defensive positions and are now vulnerable from the flank and rear. We've got to double back and counterattack at their weakest point."

"Just the three of us?" I asked. I went along with risky maneuvers in the jungle where we could disappear into thin air. But, the three of us against a VC company in a conventional warfare setting, on a runway yet, seemed a bit much.

"Gather up the unused satchel charges the sappers were carrying. We'll blow their defensive trench line for starters. Then we can spread out, use the weapons off their dead as well as our own, and bring max pee. Maybe we can catch them out in the open from behind and put some fear and doubt into them."

Z and I picked up the unused satchel charges the sappers had been carrying, and the three of us slid back over the berm and maneuvered through the coffee fields to the rear of the VC's entrenchment line.

Our plans changed when a VC mortar battery unexpectedly sent up a volley of mortar fire. This meant the VC now had a mortar battery in place that could shell our choppers parked on the pad. The mortar emplacement was about two hundred meters behind us. Cap'n Buck signaled for us to go after the mortars. We carefully worked our way back to their deep rear, ducking both friendly and enemy fire along the way.

The mortar squad was hidden in a drainage gully. There were five VC manning two 82mm mortars. They had a good stockpile of rockets and mortar rounds.

On the count of three, we all lobbed grenades at the mortar emplacement. When the grenades exploded we charged through the area, shooting everything still moving We quickly established a defensive position in case of counterattack. Z collected the mortar tubes and munitions in one place, set the fuse on a satchel charge, and we raced for cover. When the satchel charge exploded we were pelted with burning debris.

With their mortars and munitions in flames behind them, the VC officers pushed their men into one more all-out attack in an effort to take control of the airfield before they lost their edge of fire superiority. After the second wave of VC soldiers had been hurled out across the runway, the three of us spread out into their vacated foxholes. I rounded up five additional enemy automatic weapons and laid them out in front of me all ready to go. At the signal from Cap'n Buck, I set the detonator on my explosive packet and tossed it two foxholes over. The charge stunned me momentarily when it went off, covering me with dirt and debris. Then I opened up with automatic weapons, two at once, until I had fired off my AK and the five other rifles in rapid succession. Z and Cap'n Buck did the same, creating an intimidating display of firepower.

Afterwards we crawled down to the foxhole on the far flank and opened fire on those VC who tried to retreat to their line. We picked off several more, causing panic in their ranks. They mounted a probing attack of our position which we succeeded in repulsing. Then we withdrew quickly before they attacked us in force.

Before dawn we returned to the berm of the heliport and held off enemy probes until an ARVN infantry company moved in to relieve us. At that point the three of us dragged ourselves back inside the aviator's barracks. We were exhausted. During the preceding thirty hours we had fought three significant, conventional warfare battles on two hours of sleep. I slumped down on the floor in the corner while the airmen fetched a medic to stitch up my hand. I was so tired I barely knew the medic was working on me. When he finished it looked like I was wearing a baseball glove on my hand because of the swelling and the bandage.

"Hey now, it's nice of you boys to drop in after all the excitement's over," Cowboy said. "I tell you what, I go out of my way to support you guys day in and day out, and where are you when I need a little help keepin' the gooks away from my chopper? We've been holed up here for two nights fightin' to keep our chopper fleet intact, and I Field Force won't even answer the phone when we call for help."

"Oh, they sent you help all right," said Cap'n Buck. "They sent us!'

Cowboy laughed heartily. This was the typical banter these two great friends engaged in when they really wanted to throw their arms around each other.

"Welcome to Tet 1968, Boys," Cowboy announced. "Happy Vietnamese New Year! We'll be passing out the noisemakers and paper hats shortly."

Our moment of levity vanished when we turned our attention to the radio which monitored transmissions from the control tower. A request was coming in from the Fourth Battalion of the 173rd Airborne Brigade in Tuy Hoa.

"Nha Trang, this is Parachute. We just had a Huey go down in the Song Ba Valley, north of Nui Vong Phu Mountain. We're receiving hostile fire here and can't get another chopper off the ground for search and rescue. Can you help us out? Over."

"Negative, Parachute. Charlie's on our runway right now. We can't get any traffic in or out, either. I guess An Khe's your best bet. Over."

"Roger, Nha Trang. We don't have time to get someone down from An Khe. We'll try to scramble a Phantom to take a look. Over."

Silence fell over the room. We all felt the helplessness of this situation. From out on the helipad we heard the faint whine of a Huey's jet engine beginning to stir into motion.

"Oh, Lordy!" Z exclaimed.

Z grabbed his rifle and ran outside toward the helipad. I realized what was happening and raced after him. While everyone had been listening to the radio transmission, Cap'n Buck and Cowboy had slipped outside by themselves and were cranking up Cowboy's chopper. Ignoring the danger of the hostile fire from across the runway, they were attempting to lift off to go after the downed chopper crew. Of course, Z and I weren't chasing them to try to stop them, but rather to get on board with them. We were hurt because they hadn't included us in their craziness.

Z, though running hard, couldn't quite reach them before they lifted off. He looked up at the ascending chopper and stretched out his arms to say: "After all my loyalty, why are you rejecting my service now?" Cap'n Buck shook his head and pumped his palms downward a couple of times and then saluted us.

Z and I stood there watching them rise into the air for a moment before the first sounds of small arms fire ricocheting off the fuselage of the chopper brought us back to our senses. We charged up to the top of a bunker, and kneeling there in full view, recklessly laid down suppressing fire to give the chopper a chance to get aloft. I cradled my AK-47 in my bandaged paw and blazed away. We furiously fired up all our magazines of ammo, and then continued to kneel there, stunned.

Enemy machine gun fire raked the top of the berm, skipping in our direction. Realizing the chopper had made it out, we raced back to the barracks to listen for Cowboy's radio transmissions.

There was a spooky silence while we awaited word from them. Finally, after Cowboy and Cap'n Buck reached the area where the helicopter went down, Cowboy's voice came through on the speaker.

"Eagle Seven, we're in the area now. We see some smoke over the next ridge. We'll check it out."

A couple of minutes later, Cowboy reported again. "Eagle Seven, we've got some burnin' debris. Looks like it could be part of a chopper. We're not drawin' any fire when we buzz over, so we're goin' in to have a look see."

We all nervously listened for Cowboy's next words.

"LOOK OUT! WE'RE HIT! I CAN'T HOLD 'ER! GOIN' DOWN. MAY DAY! MAY DAY!"

There was no further radio contact with Cowboy.

"Well, who's going to take me out there to find them?" asked Z.

An awkward pause ensued before the senior aviator answered. "We can't take off from here, and we've already lost two choppers out there. Maybe we can schedule a flight later today after things cool down."

"Later today!" Z was beside himself. "Have you ever heard Cowboy say 'Maybe later today' when there was a fellow pilot down? If they're alive, every second counts. WE'VE GOT TO GO NOW."

Z looked around at everyone in the room. Finally Cowboy's co-pilot said, "Will anybody lend me a chopper?"

There was a faint nod from the senior pilot. "Take mine," he sighed.

When we arrived at the crash site the co-pilot refused to land nearby. Z told him to drop us off on the other side of the ridge, and we hurriedly made our way back to the wreckage, carefully dodging enemy patrols along the way.

The crash scene was horrible. We were too late. There were no signs of life in the fiery wreckage. Cowboy's chopper, caught in the crossfire of the same VC ambush team, had essentially smashed down on top of the first chopper, and they had both gone up in flames in a tangled mass. We found Cap'n Buck's and Cowboy's charred boots with their dog tags attached, and a few bones, and that was it.

I tried to get Z out of there, but he was determined to personally recover what he could of Cowboy and Cap'n Buck's remains. The body recovery work was grisly, but Z religiously fulfilled his self-imposed duty.

Cap'n Buck and Cowboy weren't the only ones we lost that day. The old Z perished in that crash, too. Out of the embers a different Z emerged—one who was a stronger and mightier warrior, but one who had lost his humanity.

I tagged along as Z went off to fight his own personal war. I had the option of going back to the LRRP Platoon to finish out the short time I had remaining in country. But Z was all I had left of the Team, and I couldn't let him go off and do something crazy without going with him to cover his backside. When I asked him where we were going, all I could get out of him was, "Someplace where you can tell the good guys from the bad guys."

We headed west toward the border, into the jungle, the only place Z felt at home and where there were more bad guys than anywhere else for Z to take out his anger and frustration on.

This time we weren't out there as LRRP's to observe and report back. We were gunning for the enemy. We lived off of our victims, taking their food and ammo. We took on any platoon-size or smaller NVA forces we encountered. Time and again we surprised the enemy soldiers and decimated them. The risks were great, but we seemed untouchable. On more than one occasion the NVA sent out troops to hunt us down, but we managed to elude them and pick off the soldiers on their flanks. Z's crowning achievement was blowing up the fuel depot we had observed just over the border, from which Butt Gut got his supplies.

When we got to within a week of the date when we were scheduled to leave Vietnam and return to the States, Z still didn't have it out of his system. He was caught in a loop, doing the same thing over and over again because that's all he knew how to do. Each new incident fed off of the one before it. I didn't know how I could rein him in.

Finally I hit on a glimmer of light that Z could respond to: Co Hai. With Cowboy gone, Z must have felt responsible for her guardianship. He agreed to accompany me to Saigon to see her.

I waited across the Boulevard from the Spencer's villa and let him talk to her alone. I overheard her say she had something of his, and he told her he didn't need it anymore. I could tell Z broke the news to her about Cowboy and Cap'n

Buck because she melted into his arms, sobbing. He was a man of few words, and it must have been awkward for them to express their feelings. I don't know what was promised between them that day. Maybe he vowed to return to her some day. Or, maybe he intended to arrange for her to come to the United States. All I know is, when he came back across the street, there was a flicker of life in his eyes again.

Soon we were heading to Cam Ranh Bay and a homeward-bound Seven-O-Seven. One last obstacle was thrown at Z when the MP's at Cam Ranh refused to allow him to take home his K-bar knife. Z wheeled around angrily and strode rapidly over to the barracks where the incoming troops were housed. These were the green troops, right off the plane, who still had a whole year in Vietnam ahead of them. He stopped inside the door and gazed down through the Quonset hut, crowded with double-decked bunk beds.

"Anybody here headed to the 173rd?" Z asked.

"I am," answered a second looey, wearing a brand-new issue of jungle fatigues.

Z pitched his K-bar and sheath to the lieutenant. "Here, you'll be needing this."

"How many heavenly notches does it have on it?" came a wisecrack from another bunk.

Z glared at the soldier, his eyes piercing the shadows of the bottom bunk. "Nary a one," said Z. "They all went straight to hell!"

With that, Z surrendered his final weapon of the jungle. He could go home.

I was a bit surprised, more than thirty years later, to receive a collect call from Z. I had no idea after all those years how he even got my phone number. He asked me to meet him in a cemetery in his hometown of Philadelphia. And to bring a cassette tape player with me.

Chapter VIII

I STEPPED OVER THE low curb and walked down the remnants of a walk, the gravel path having long since been overtaken by leaves of grass. The morning sunlight dappled on the slabs of stone, beckoning me to learn their weathered histories. *Dearly Beloved of—* There was no end to them. Some of the plots were already two hundred years old. Pieces of section blocks and granite corner posts, no longer indicating any particular plot pattern, jutted haphazardly above the wavy rows of bent and twisted markers. On the side of a hill, under the futile vigil of a soot-sullied angel, a mounded mausoleum languished—a hollow tomb, rent open long ago by some ancient grave robber.

Faint sounds of the city creeping in from outside the walls were muffled by the stillness of the cold, moss-laden stone. Those resting below had been not unlike people of today—a few forging boldly out into life to build a homeland, leaving a trail of success in the wake of their industrious spirit, while the weak lingered to feed from the spilled spoils of their champions. For some grown men, there was no noteworthy accomplishment in life to distinguish them, other than *Son of Alfred and Rebecca Steele.* Now they all rested in the same earth together. As generations passed, even those obsessed to leave behind a lasting memorial to their good name and fortune languished with no admirers through acid-etched decades. Many of the plots stood half-empty, a lasting commentary on the patriarch's failed dreams of family grandeur and unity. Some simple markers

115

noting infants who only breathed life briefly outlasted the grander memorials of their parents and siblings, whose names had been rendered illegible by the inexorable rinsing of time.

A voice interrupted my reverie. "Is that you, Stoney?"

I looked back across the maze of grave markers. Slowly the form of a man emerged from the shadows. It was Z. A wild beard flowed out from under Z's faded boonie hat. There was a stale stench from his worn and soiled fatigues. He wheezed, causing his beard to quiver. His shrewd eyes searched me cautiously.

"Z," I said.

"Aw, you did come."

"It's good to see you, Z." I stepped forward and shook his hand.

"Did you bring a tape player?"

"My car has one built in that we can use. Z, what's this all about? Why did you need to see me?"

"Aw, I'll get to that. There's something I need you to look at that I can't get to just yet."

"No problem. I'm in no hurry. I'm relieved I was able to find you out here. This is a big cemetery. Didn't you mention you had a sister who lived in this area?"

"Aw, she throwed me out because I don't clean up nice like she wants. I prefer the open space anyhow. The cemetery is where I live now."

"How do you survive in the winter?"

"Aw, it's not that bad. I've hitched south a time or two. Sometimes I duck in that empty mausoleum over there to get out of the wind and rain. The Thorntons who live back along the south side let me sleep in their basement when it gets real cold. I do chill out quicker through the years."

We ambled aimlessly through the cemetery and then out into the streets of the surrounding neighborhoods. The cemetery was flanked on three sides by neighborhoods and by the Parkway on the fourth side. Each of the three neighborhoods had an entirely different character and culture. Z and I jumped from one idea and person to another as we reminisced about Vietnam.

"Z, after you went down on Hill 875 and were sent to Japan to convalesce, the Team floundered. By the time you returned just before Christmas, everything had changed. But I never knew why. Something happened that I wasn't clued in on."

"You do know Cap'n Buck's wife dumped him in Hawaii?"

"Yes, I gathered that."

"Aw, she didn't even stay the whole five days with him. On the second day she tells him there's someone else and leaves him there in Honolulu to spend Christmas by hisself."

"Wow! That was cruel. I guess that explains why he got so preoccupied with Colonel Xi at the end."

"The way that happened was Cowboy got a hot new lead on Colonel Xi while he was on R&R in Australia. He put us onto the final piece of the puzzle. And, he did it in typical Cowboy style—by dumb luck. Aw, Cowboy was in Australia on R&R, and he crossed paths with a guy named Clifton. It turned out Clifton was an embalmer who worked in Saigon preparing all the KIA's for the trip home.

"Cowboy was fascinated by that funeral stuff. He got Clifton to talking and found out all about how the Graves Registration procedure worked—embalming the bodies and shipping them in reusable transfer cases to Travis Air Force Base in California.

"The interesting part was when Clifton mentioned how the Vietnamese authorities had slowly taken over the shipping end of the business. Clifton and the other Americans still did the messy part, but the Vietnamese took charge of placing the bodies in the transfer cases, loading the transfer cases onto trucks, and delivering them back to Tan Son Nhut for the flight to the States. They even built a partition running down the middle of the warehouse to separate the shipping end from the identification and embalming end. Clifton was so busy doing the embalming that all this didn't bother him much. There was all kinds of people coming and going on the Vietnamese side. Usually Clifton paid them no mind. But, sometimes Clifton seen a senior Vietnamese ARVN officer pulling up in his jeep and going in to the shipping end of the warehouse. Well, this info got Cowboy's attention right quick. After quizzing Clifton some more, Cowboy became convinced that this heavyset Vietnamese field grade officer was none other than our Colonel Xi.

"When Cowboy told us about this, Cap'n Buck goes: 'It figures! They're up to their usual tricks—smuggling. They're using those caskets to smuggle black market goods into the United States—gold, jewels, dope. And, if they can get away with retrieving their merchandise at Travis, they must have a powerful organization Stateside, too.'

"Cap'n Buck wanted hard evidence of all this. He sent me down to Tan Son Nhut to observe the smuggling operation first hand and take pictures of it. The reason for my trip was a secret between Cap'n Buck, Cowboy, and me. Not even you was cut in on it. It gave me a chance to pay Co Hai a visit, too.

"I got down to Saigon about a month before Tet. At that time the mood of the people in Saigon was at its most confident level. The rich was getting richer off the War, and there was every reason to believe that the Americans would chase the Communists back up North for good.

"Co Hai had done grown up on me. She looked and acted like a young woman now. Still, she was glad to see me again. She understood what all we had done for her, and she made no bones about being thankful about it.

"I spent some time watching the Graves Registration routine from the outside. A work shift of Americans and a few Vietnamese arrived in the morning and left in the late afternoon. Then a night shift of Vietnamese came on and worked until the Americans returned in the morning. Body bags was trucked in from Tan Son Nhut, and a couple of truckloads of embalmed bodies in metal transfer cases was trucked back to the runway in the morning for the long flight back to the States.

"All of these guys was GI's who had landed in Vietnam thinking they was immortal—that maybe unthinkable things could happen to Careless Joe, but not to them. Eventually they all came through that warehouse on their final journey home, arriving at the warehouse piled up in a truckload of body bags, waiting to be methodically gutted and drained and pumped full of fluid by an embalmer who never bothered to look at their names or even glance at their faces.

"The next night I snuck inside the warehouse. There was a lot of work stations in there, and it was more crowded than I expected. A bunch of incoming bodies was stacked up waiting to be fingerprinted. Down the center was several embalming tables. Beyond them, against the adjacent wall from me, was offices, employee shower rooms, and the big walk-in refrigerator.

"At the far end of the embalming tables a big, double sliding door was locked shut. I judged the shipping area must be on the other side. I heard people moving about over there.

"Up above the double doors there was a louvered vent to allow air to circulate up in the rafters. I tied a rope to my ice axe and whipped it up over one of the rafters near the wall. Using the rope I walked up the wall to the rafters. From there I crawled over the cross beams to the vent in the center of the wall separating the two areas of the warehouse. Looking down through the vent, I could see a lot of what was going on in the other area.

"Most of it was on the up and up—placing the prepared bodies in the metal transfer cases, closing the cases, completing the paperwork, and loading them with a forklift into the back of a big box truck parked inside the warehouse. Except, every so often a Vietnamese man in civilian clothes would come out of the office carrying a cardboard box. After a body was placed in a transfer case, he'd place the box on top of the dead soldier's legs before the casket was closed. Then he'd place a green check mark on the outer shipping tag, and the forklift would load it into the truck. When the truck was loaded to the brim with cases they moved the truck just outside the back doors and parked it. Then they backed the next truck inside. I was snapping pictures of all this.

"The biggest surprise came when the second truck was almost loaded and the night's work was almost done. A bunch of people—mostly men, but also including some women and children—came out of the packaging room carrying food and water and personal belongings with them. Special transfer cases with hidden air vents in the sides was brought over, and these people stepped into the cases and laid down. The attendants got them situated with their food and water in reach, and then closed the lids on them. Colonel Xi wasn't only smuggling goods into the United States, he was smuggling people!

"Who was these people they was sneaking into the States? Wealthy Vietnamese seeking a better life in America? Political fugitives? Or even spies sent to infiltrate the Vietnamese communities sprouting up in America? I tried taking pictures of their faces when they climbed in the coffins, which is what got me in trouble. A woman looked up before they closed the lid on her and spotted my silhouette through the ceiling vent. She pointed at me and started jabbering.

"I ducked down, but it was too late. Everybody started shouting and running toward the big sliding doors just below me. I looked around to see what my courses of action was. Should I keep puttering up there and pretend to be a maintenance man? Should I let them take me into custody and hope for the best? No. I saw another way. There was a turbo-vent above me in the roof, and I went for it. They was shouting and gesturing below me. I popped the sheet metal screws apart with my K-bar, shoved the big vent off, and squeezed up through the hole.

"Bullets was bouncing off the roof from below. Outside a siren wailed, and dogs started barking. The roof was too high to jump to the ground and walk away from it. The sentries was moving back far enough to where they'd be able to shoot me from any place I might be at on the roof. Soon there'd be no place to hide.

"Then I remembered the box truck loaded with bodies that was parked at the far end of the warehouse. I made a dash for the end of the building, dodging bullets while I was running. With my ice axe I snagged the top of a tall light pole in the yard and swung down to the roof of the truck. I quickly squeezed through the open front window into the cab. I had my fingers crossed that the keys was in it, which they was, and it started right up. Bullets was ricocheting from everywhere. I ducked down to avoid the flying glass when they shot out the windshield. There was no time to look for a gate. Barreling ahead, I plowed into the fence at full speed. The truck stalled out and stopped abruptly. For a moment I was shocked by being thrown against the steering wheel. Then I seen that the force of the truck running into it had bent the fence outward at an angle. I pulled myself out through the broken windshield and desperately clawed my way up and over the fence. Only a few of them was shooting at this point because they had stopped to watch the crash and had not figured out that I was on the move. When I hit the ground, I wheeled and emptied a magazine from my K over their heads to make them hit the dirt. Then I sprinted for the military building next door, zigging and zagging to avoid their fire. Beyond the building I flagged down a Vietnamese truck out on the boulevard. After a high-speed chase with guns blazing, we managed to lose them.

"I left the film from Cap'n Buck's camera with Co Hai and told her to get it developed and hold onto the pictures for me. Then I sent word to Cowboy to fly down and pick me up.

"Back at Base Camp I went over with Cowboy and Cap'n Buck what I had seen on my trip. We now had evidence there was a big time Vietnamese smuggling ring shipping goods and people back to the States. Later when we hijacked Colonel Xi's satchel we got proof of all the rest. After that they never let up the heat on the Captain.

"I don't know how it would have turned out for Cap'n Buck if he hadn't went down in the chopper. It showed what kind of man he was that he could fight so tough during Tet with all that hanging over his head."

It was late. Z and I had been walking the neighborhood streets around the cemetery for hours. It seemed like Z kept circling around from different directions and walking us down the same street. He was watching the upstairs lights in a particular house.

Z was both stirred and troubled by the experiences we shared. "Some people are lucky enough to make the great sacrifice of their life while they're at their top," he said. "Others have to suffer through a long and bumpy down slide."

"What about Co Hai?" I asked. "Did you ever find out what happened to her?"

"Aw, she's the reason I got in touch with you. Out of the blue she up and sends me a cassette tape that we gotta listen to. But like I said, there's something I've got to show you first."

The hollow faces of the row houses looked pail and garish in the sodium glow of the street lights. Z led me into an alley which ran behind the houses.

"Follow me, real quiet like," he whispered.

Old clotheslines and rusty swing sets cast vacant shadows across broken furniture and well-worn gossip perches. Z carefully opened the back gate of one of the houses and ushered me into the tiny back yard. At first I wasn't sure where he was taking me, but then I realized this must be the rear of the house we had been walking past for the last few hours. It dawned on me that this was his sister's house.

Farther down the block a dog began barking. Z signaled me not to pay it any mind. He tiptoed up to the house and felt up underneath the back steps until his fingers located the key. Motioning me to stay put, he crept up the stairs to the kitchen door. Gently, he slipped the key into the lock and turned it. With a nudge on the knob, the door opened. He disappeared into the darkness, and the door snugged shut behind him.

In a few minutes I heard a faint click, and Z's head reappeared from the basement door below. He beckoned for me to come down, pointing downward with the beam from an old silver flashlight which dimly lit the concrete threshold at his feet. I descended the steps and entered the cellar.

The musty odor of damp cinder blocks permeated the air. I followed Z around several piles of dirty laundry, mounded in the aisle between stacks of abandoned hobbies and furniture. Venturing farther, we ducked under a low opening, following the dim beam of light into an adjoining cavern. The smaller room was lined with dusty cardboard boxes filled with old picture frames, flower pots, papers, and other knick-knacks. Z handed the flashlight to me and, bending to the task, carefully shuffled several boxes out of his way to expose an old trunk. Kneeling down in front of it, Z deliberately unsnapped the corroded, yawing hasps that kept its secrets sealed within. Fishing in his pocket for the key and successfully working the lock, he slowly lifted the lid on the mementos of his youth—baseball cards, old track trophies, a high school letter jacket, junior and senior yearbooks, old class pictures, clippings, a baseball glove carefully sponged in neat's-foot oil and wrapped in a towel for storage with a baseball still forming its pocket. Removing the top tier of high school memorabilia Z uncovered a Russian pistol resting on a neatly folded, almost new, North Vietnamese Army officer's uniform, complete with pith helmet, leather shoulder belt, and holster. Z's hand slid easily around the handle of the pistol. I recalled how proudly the Dai Uy had strutted in his new uniform around the jungle-hidden NVA camp, before Z gave him a final surprise. Now the officer lay buried in an unmarked grave in South Vietnam, while his uniform and sidearm rested, nearly forgotten, in a South Philly basement.

Scooping under and lifting up the uniform momentarily, Z groped below it and retrieved a large, bulky manila envelope, with "173rd" scribbled in pencil across the face of it. The envelope flopped perpetually open from the weight of the medals precariously shoved into the front—Silver and Bronze Stars and Purple Hearts, entombed in unopened blue cases. There was the familiar DD 214 and extensive medical records on various injuries.

Probing deeper, Z pricked his finger on his own crescent-shaped tiger claw. He sucked his finger for a moment as he thumbed through a few spare photographs which other GI's had taken and given to him. In the faltering yellow light, he searched until he found the only group snapshot he had of the Team: Cap'n Buck, Z, the Moon Dog, and me, lounging about the tent in Base Camp, all hamming it up for the picture taker. The youthful faces looked so real, as though we were still all there together. Even after what the Team had gone through to the point when the picture was taken, we all seemed so innocent. And only two of the four had made it home alive. Z let me keep the picture so I could study it later in better light.

At the very back of the big envelope Z retrieved a page ripped from a magazine. He now seemed satisfied that his search was completed. He placed the page in his pocket, returned all his treasures to their rightful place, and closed and locked the trunk.

Quietly Z and I began our retreat toward the outside door. Suddenly the bare ceiling bulb above our heads snapped on, blinding us momentarily. This was followed by floppy slippers plunking halfway down the wooden steps. Shielding my eyes, I made out the figure of a middle-aged woman glaring at us over the stair rail.

"Zeke! Is that you? What are you doing here?"

"We was just leaving," Z said.

"I've told you to stay out of here. How did you get in here, anyway?"

"I *said* we was leaving! You can board the damn place up for all I care. We're out of here."

Z scooted me out the door in front of him, with his sister nipping at our heels. She slammed and bolted the door behind us.

Drizzle was falling when we stepped back into the night. We paused in the shadows of the alley for a moment to get re-acclimated to the darkness. I could tell Z was embarrassed to have me see his sister chase him away like that.

Moving farther on we took refuge from the mist under the narrow overhang of a garage door next to an alley light. Z reached in his pocket and pulled out the folded page from the magazine.

"Here. You need to know this."

I unfolded the crooked creases and smoothed the slick paper out flat with my hand. I glanced at the bottom and noticed the page was from a *Newsweek* dated April 15, 1985. Upon checking the caption below the picture I discovered the scene it depicted occurred on April 29, 1975, when the collapse of Saigon was imminent. It was that famous picture of hordes of frenzied South Vietnamese trying desperately to scale the wall of the American Embassy in hopes of somehow making it out on one of the last choppers to freedom. There were hundreds of Vietnamese crushed up against the outside wall of the Embassy, looking upward with empty longing. An American soldier was on top of the wall, pushing back some boys who were trying to climb over the concertina wire.

"What's this for?" I asked.

"Look closer. Back behind the crowd."

Holding it so that the maximum light shone on it, I began carefully studying the photo. I focused on it at close range and let the picture immerse my vision, scrutinizing every detail.

Eventually, my eye was drawn to two of the figures, a man and a woman at the back of the crowd. The man was taller and fairer of skin than the others in the mob scene. A closer look indicated he was more than likely an American. The other oddity was that these two were not pressing up against the wall like the other frantic people. The angle of the picture showed a partial profile of their faces from the right rear. They actually appeared to be trying to move away from the Embassy through the crowd. Suddenly it became clear to me. My heart jumped.

"Co Hai and Cowboy?" I whispered.

"Maybe. Yes, I believe so."

"Seven years after the crash?" I murmured in shock. "How could this be?"

Z and I gazed at each other in wonderment, thinking back, using our own knowledge and perspective, to the fiery chopper crash. How could Cowboy have survived that horrible scene, and where had he been during all that time until 1975? Was he still alive today? Then, a whole new premise began to form in my thought. Z knew it was coming, and watched it build, waiting for me to mouth the words.

"If Cowboy somehow survived, maybe Cap'n Buck did, too."

Chapter IX

WE MADE OUR WAY back to my car parked at the gate to the cemetery. I shoved Co Hai's tape into the car's player, and we settled back to listen to a voice from the past.

"Hello, Z. I received your card many years ago, but I never could bring myself to answer you. Now I must. Now I must tell you everything before it is too late.

"You remember when you took me to live with the Spencers near the American Embassy? When I first arrived there I was a mere child of fifteen. I was very frightened. I spoke very little English. I was afraid I would make a mistake and they would throw me out on the street where Mr. Nhat could find me. I worked tirelessly taking care of their two children. Really, I felt more like the children's sister than their caretaker. In my free time I cleaned, cooked, ironed, and folded clothes constantly. I dare not let them ever find me idle. I was so homesick for my mother, but I knew it would be fatal to try and return to Pleiku under the circumstances. At night I wrote her letters. A few times John Mac came and gave me letters from my mother, and he took letters from me to deliver to her. I hid her letters under my mattress and read them over and over again. And wept.

"I guess the Spencers felt sorry for me and decided to let me stay on with them. Mr. Spencer spoke a fair amount of Vietnamese. One day they sat me down after the children were put to bed. Mrs. Spencer took both my hands in hers. Mr. Spencer explained to me that they had arranged for me to attend the American school and learn English. When I felt comfortable in the English language, I could take other courses as well. They assured me I did not have to work all the time. They wanted me to relax and have some fun, too. After that talk, I settled into my life with them more easily. I became more and more confident that I was pleasing them and my job with them was secure. Meanwhile, every chance I got I was furiously studying the English language.

"Little did I know there would be new worlds to conquer that I had not yet dreamed of.

"About six months after I came to the Spencers, you visited me and left some film to be developed. When the packet came back from Kodak, I opened the packet, expecting to see pictures of you and your Team. But, when I looked at the photographs, they were very strange. They showed Vietnamese workers loading things—packages and living people—into coffins. I sealed them up and hid them under my mattress.

"Sometime later a package arrived for me in the diplomatic pouch from Nha Trang. I was dumbfounded that someone would send me something by diplomatic pouch. I looked on the address label and saw it was from John Mac. His note said to hold it for him. I hid it under my bed, too.

"Sometimes I wondered if there was a connection between the your pictures and John Mac's package. Because I knew you two were watching Mr. Nhat's activities, I had the feeling this could have something to do with him also. I expected John Mac or you would come by and pick up the materials I was holding for you. When I did not hear from either of you for several weeks I began to worry something had happened to you. I was tempted to show the materials to Mr. Spencer, but I maintained my loyalty to you and kept them hidden.

"About that time, Mrs. Spencer asked me to take a file that Mr. Spencer had left at home over to his office in the Chancery Building. This was the first time I had been allowed to set foot on the grounds of the Embassy. It was nice and cool in the large building, and the air smelled so fresh. I thought only the Americans, who came from a cold country, could make their building cold in our hot climate!

"I stepped off the elevator onto the sixth floor. Everything seemed so quiet and clean. When I found the correct room number, Mr. Spencer opened the door and greeted me warmly. This put me at ease right away. Looking around, I wondered what kind of work Mr. Spencer did in this splendid place. It may have seemed like an ordinary office to you Americans, but to me it was wondrous.

"Mr. Spencer invited me over to the window where I became fascinated by the bustle of the city sprawling out in front of me. His office faced east, and I could look down and see people coming and going from the main gate. Beyond the fence there was a steady stream of small vehicles, motor scooters, and bicycles busily passing up and down Thong Nhut Boulevard. From this angle it took me a moment to recognize the Presidential Palace to my right. Also, the Cathedral straight in front of me looked so different from this vantage point. How massive and awe-inspiring it was! A few blocks farther on I recognized the Caravelle Hotel, and further still I caught a glimpse of the tops of sampans on the River.

"'It's quite a view,' Mr. Spencer said. I shook my head in agreement without taking my eyes off the magical sights before me.

"'Co Hai, Mrs. Spencer and I are very happy you are staying with us. Your rapid grasp of the English language shows you are eager to undertake difficult tasks.' They always spoke to me in English now, and I could understand most of what they were saying if I listened very hard. 'We want you to be happy, too, and we realize being cooped up with us all the time may get tiring for you.'

"Suddenly I realized he was leading up to some proposal, but I had no idea what it might be.

"'There is a part-time messenger position open here in the Administration Building, and we wondered if you would like to help out here while the kids are in school? You could still attend your language class, of course.'

"That's how it all started, me delivering mail and running messages at the Embassy.

"At first I would get mixed up and go the wrong way. Once I stumbled through a restricted door and alarms sounded from everywhere. I was so frightened and embarrassed! However, soon I knew the building backwards and forwards. Everyone would greet me in the morning with, 'Good morning, Co Hai.' And, I would answer back, 'Chao ong.' It became a very happy time of my life. I felt I was appreciated, and I was doing something important to help the Americans.

"After a while they started sending me down to the loading dock door when the guard at the rear gate signaled that a delivery was coming in. I opened up the overhead door and let them unload the goods in the receiving area. Then I would sign for the delivery. I was amazed at how many different types of wonderful things the Americans had coming into the building. Everything from desks and electronic equipment to chewing gum.

"Many of these goods came in large American military trucks from the air fields at Bien Hoa and Tan Son Nhut. However, there were also many deliveries from local Vietnamese businesses, and I came in contact with all types of delivery drivers. There were quiet, hard-working ones and big, ugly loudmouths who tried to put their hands all over me.

"The meat purveyor, a young man named Huanh, was neither of those, but rather a complainer. He complained about his boss, and the traffic, and too much inflation under the Thieu government, and everything else. One of his favorite gripes was with the Americans. They were the cause of everything going wrong in our country. Sometimes he would get so bitter and worked up he would pound the boxes of meat with his fist while unloading them, saying 'This is what I would like to do to the Americans. Why do you continue to work for them, anyway?'

"One day I had to move the boxes he had delivered over to the side to make way for another delivery. In so doing I noticed two boxes of chicken parts, both labeled to contain twenty pounds, did not feel like they were the same weight. I picked up each box again, side by side. There was a distinct difference in the weight. I thought the packing house must have made a mistake, and probably the heavier box weighed more than the stated twenty pounds. Out of curiosity I loaded the two boxes on a dolly and wheeled them down to Shipping to weigh them on the scales there. One box was right at twenty pounds, but the other one only weighed sixteen pounds. This really got me to thinking. Were any of the other food deliveries short? What should the Embassy be doing about this? I began to worry if the Embassy officials found out I could be fired for accepting short orders. Was this why I was the one being sent down to receive most of the food orders? The next day when I came to work, I brought Mrs. Spencer's bathroom scales with me. I decided I would weigh all the incoming deliveries and not sign for any that were short.

"When Huanh came again, both boxes of meat were below the stated weight. Huanh acted like it was not no deal. When I told him to go back and tell his company I would not sign for a short order any more, he smiled and drove off. He returned a half-hour later and said everything was okay now. I weighed the boxes again, and now one of them was three pounds over the stated weight. This made me suspicious—how could he have gone to the plant, had the boxes re-packed, and driven back to the Embassy in only thirty minutes? I opened the boxes and saw how the weight had increased so rapidly. The meat was now soaked in muddy water. Then it dawned on me that Huanh had been the one shorting the order every day, not the plant. I surmised he was taking a little meat from each box to make himself a nice 'take home' box, or possibly even to sell for extra money. Huanh smiled devilishly, seeing I had figured him out.

"'I believe we order meat from your company, not river water,' I observed coolly, speaking in Vietnamese.

"'The River of Life will do much to cleanse the souls of the American intruders.'

"'Your deception is reprehensible. Why do you not merely return the meat you have taken?'

"'Because it is no longer mine to give back. I have already dropped it off to our people.'

"'Enough of this. I will have my American boss call your company and report you.'

"'Your American boss! Where is your pride? The Vietnamese people should call no foreign imperialist their boss.'

"'No, he is a good boss.'

"'Good boss, ha.' He grasped my wrists tightly and looked deep into my eyes. At first I was mesmerized by him. 'Co Hai, listen to yourself. Can you not see there can be no happiness for our people while these outsiders are here dictating every move to their puppet government? Our people will never be truly happy until there is one unified government and country. I am going to leave you now to do the bidding of your conscience. If I am reported, then I will lose my job, and our people will go hungry. Deep inside, you know that would be wrong. If you do not report me, then you can be of great service to our people.'

"I watched him drive away. Then I mechanically busied myself with my work for the rest of the morning. What Huanh had said was very confusing and disconcerting to me. Who were the 'people' he was referring to? Did he mean his family or some bigger group? Was he a mere kook, or something more dangerous? He never used the word 'Cong,' but I wondered.

"By lunch time I had decided this man was very unpredictable and it was not wise to have him coming and going at the Embassy making deliveries every day. I went up to the sixth floor to Mr. Spencer's office and told him the whole story, word for word. I wondered if he would shrug it off and send me on my way. To the contrary, Mr. Spencer seemed very relieved and happy that I had told him, and he thanked me very much.

"A few days later I noticed Huanh's meat truck waiting outside the service gate, so I headed down to do my job. When I reached the dock level, the foreman from Shipping told me not to go out there, that the MP's would take care of it. This seemed very strange to me, so I slipped out onto the loading dock and ducked behind some boxes to see what was going on. Huanh had pulled up to the back gate in his usual manner, but this time the Marines drove a truck in behind him and did not raise the gate arm. A Marine walked around and asked him to get out of his delivery truck.

Huanh panicked and tried to back out of the driveway, ramming into the Marine's truck which was blocking him. Then he then put his truck into forward gear and barreled through the gate arm while the Marine on duty emptied the clip from his .45 into the back of the truck. I dropped to the floor, but I could not take my eyes off of the events unfolding in front of me. I do not know if Huanh was already wounded at this point or whether he decided to pull a kamikaze move, but the truck accelerated straight ahead until it crashed into the side of the Embassy building. By now the alert sirens were wailing, and Marines carrying rifles were pouring out from everywhere. Huanh was injured in the crash. He stumbled out of the truck and made a run for the loading dock. He was limping badly. Under his crafty smile I could tell he was in pain. He bolted right up on the dock past me. The door was locked. The Marines were shouting for him to halt. Huanh turned to face his adversaries, pulling out a machine pistol and opening fire on the Marines. Before he could get off more than two or three rounds, he was cut down by a barrage of gunfire. I saw his eyes clench closed and his hair fly in all directions as the bullets drove him back against the building, splattering blood on the double doors and wall. He slumped down so only his head and shoulders remained propped up against the door. His blood oozed down the door and soaked into his hair.

"I shuddered in horror. I was frightened for my own safety. Several of the bullets had bounced off the wall and almost hit me. The image of Huanh lying there motionless kept going through my mind. Here was a man I was acquainted with who now was dead. What had he done to deserve this? Later when the guilt set in I let myself believe all this had happened because I had turned him in. Mr. Spencer assured me it was not solely my report that did it. They would have found him out, anyway. Mr. Spencer counseled me not to get hung up on things like this—just step over the unpleasantness, put it behind me, and never look back. Despite his advice, this terrible experience worried me for months.

"To get my mind off of Huanh's tragedy, Mr. Spencer suggested I go out of the compound now and then to deliver envelopes or packages to other American offices around Saigon. It was good to finally get outside the walls and have some freedom. I felt very important delivering these envelopes around the city. When I announced I was from the Embassy, the guards would let me go right in. This made me feel very important.

"Eventually I progressed to the courier circuit. This was especially exciting because twice I got to see my mother. And, one of those times I actually held her in my arms. The courier business consisted of flying on Air America passenger planes to various provincial capitals and delivering or picking up parcels from American individuals who were assigned there. Many times I never saw the pickup person. I would leave the parcel I was carrying at a specified place for them. Sometimes I was instructed to wait in a secluded place for the contact person to make the exchange. I suspected some of these people were operating undercover, but I knew better than to ask questions. If Mr. Spencer sent me to do it, I was sure it was for the American cause and would eventually help my country. That's all I needed to know.

"Twice I had flown into Pleiku, but someone had met the plane and taken my packet there at the airfield, and I had flown on, so I had no chance to see my mother. It seemed strange to be so close to my mother and yet we were in different worlds, and a meeting was not to be. At those times, when the plane took off and pulled back up into the air, I really felt the heartache of missing my old, simple way of life.

"On my third trip to Pleiku I was instructed to switch packages with someone on a bench near the market. I was hoping the exchange would happen quickly so I would have time to visit my mother before my afternoon flight. However, I waited until past three o'clock, and my contact had not come yet.

"To while the time away I watched the crowd of people at the market. Among the shoppers buzzing around the vendors' stands a familiar-looking woman was picking out vegetables. It was my mother! Oh, how I longed to run to her, but I had to stay put until the exchange was made. She was moving in slow motion while others flickered by her like a silent movie. After all she had been through, losing everything, including me, she was still standing above it all. I watched her glide back down the street, not taking my eyes off of her until she disappeared at the end of the block. I was so moved by her display of dignity and character that I began to weep. Then I noticed a man sitting on the bench next to me, casually reading. He placed his newspaper-wrapped package next to mine. Leaving the package I had brought, I picked up his and walked back toward the airfield. I wanted so much to run after my mother, but there was not time. I did not dare look back.

"On my last courier visit to Pleiku my instructions were to leave the envelope, care of James Monroe at the hotel, and return by the next available flight. Now was my chance to visit my mother. Mr. Spencer knew my mother lived in Pleiku. Since he did not say one way or the other whether it was all right to visit her, I decided he was intentionally looking the other way. I dropped off the letter at the hotel and headed straight for Nguyen Van Troi Street. From the corner I looked down the long row of houses and stores, straining for my first glimpse of our shop. I was surprised to see it now had a bright red sign above the door, and there were lots of GI customers coming and going. I was afraid I would cause too much of a stir if I entered by the customer entrance. I ducked down the alley and made my way behind the row of shops, down the dirt path toward the back door. When I reached the rear of the shop, the back door opened and a familiar figure came out, tossed a bucket of dirty water onto the ground, and began wringing out a mop by hand. This person was not my mother but rather a man I knew. It was John Mac! His back was to me, and I watched him work for a few moments. He looked so cute doing domestic work. It had been several months since John Mac and Captain Rogers had appeared at the Embassy, returned from the dead. John Mac had written me a couple of letters since then, so I knew he had not yet returned to America, but I was not aware he was working with my mother. I stepped lightly up to him and touched him on the shoulder. Immediately his face lit up with delight.

"'Co Hai! Hey now. What are you doin' here?'

"'Embassy business,' I said.

"We embraced each other spontaneously. 'Wait 'til your Mama sees you. She'll have a hissy fit. Come to think of it, you'd better wait out here and let me send her out. She's liable to lose it if you walk in there.'

"Moments later my mother came running out, all wide-eyed and excited. She grabbed me tight, jabbering 'Toi tre con, toi tre con' through her tears. Hugging her, I realized for the first time that she was getting old. She was the little girl now, and I was the woman in this scene. I heard myself telling her over and over again that everything was okay, that I loved her, and she should not worry about me.

"Both my mother and John Mac seemed very proud of the restaurant and were eager to show it to me. It was so new and different from the last time I had seen it, on that horrible day when Mr. Nhat tried to take me away to pay for my mother's debt.

"Reluctantly I told them I had to go or I would miss my plane. I finally tore away from my mother, and John Mac walked me back to the airfield.

"'Mr. Smith, I have received two envelopes from the United States with American money in them. There was no name or address with them.'

"'That would be from Z. He's your Guardian Angel.'"

I looked at Z sitting next to me in the car. He stared straight ahead into the night, making no acknowledgement of whether or not the money had come from him. Co Hai's tape continued to play.

"John Mac asked me questions about what I was doing way up there by myself, away from the Embassy. He was very displeased to hear I was now a courier for Mr. Spencer.

"'Co Hai, do you realize what you're mixed up in? Remember, I am the one who arranged for you to live with the Spencers. I have flown some missions for him in the past. Now, I admit I don't know exactly who he's with or

what he does, but I know he's involved in some kind of intelligence work.'

"'It's okay. I am in no danger.'

"'Co Hai, for Christ sake! Spencer thinks he's pretty
crafty sendin' a teenage girl out to make his deliveries, but
I guarantee you, if Chollie gets on to you, Spencer's not goin'
to be around to bail you out.'

"'Mr. Smith, I am indebted to you for saving me from Mr.
Nhat, but I am old enough to make my own decisions. Look
around you. See how my mother and all my people are living because of the Communist insurgency. Some day you
will get tired of this country and will return to America. But
we Vietnamese must stay here and make something out of
our land. Children are dying here. Boys my age are carrying
rifles to defend their hamlets. Yet you say I am too young to
deliver letters? I am honored I can help my country in this
small way.'

"We continued along for some time without speaking. I
knew he was mulling over what I had just said. I felt surprised and pleased that I had spoken so well, and I hoped
he would accept this about me.

"When the plane taxied up to the little terminal building, John Mac spoke at last. 'Co Hai, I respect you for doin'
what you're doin'. I've invested a lot of effort in keepin' you
safe, and I don't want anything to happen to you now. So,
you be careful, you hear? Don't trust anybody, includin'
Spencer. Just remember, no matter how fond he is of you,
the mission will always come first with him. And one more
thing, you can tell him you saw me, and I'm available if he
needs a good chopper pilot. I'm listed KIA with the Army, so
startin' work for him tomorrow under an assumed name is
no problem. My talents are wastin' away here at the cafe. If
you're goin' to be involved with him, well maybe I'll be able
to keep an eye on you sometimes if we're workin' for the
same guy.'

"The next morning I went up to Mr. Spencer's office to
report on my trip. I told him about what John Mac had said,
and he seemed interested to know John Mac was still in country. But, there was something else on Mr. Spencer's mind.

"'Co Hai, you know Mrs. Spencer and I consider you like one of our own family. We do not want anything to happen to you. Your being a courier has been a big help to us and your country. I appreciate your willingness to help very much. But it seems our delivery locations are getting more and more dangerous.'

"I interrupted him, 'If you are suggesting that I stop being a courier, I beg you to give up your worries. Mr. Smith was talking the same way yesterday, and I know that both of you mean well. I want to be of service to my country, and I am grateful to you for giving me the opportunity to do this.'

"'Well, I am glad to hear you feel that way. The American government and your country thank you. There is a way I think you could help us even more, but I hesitate to place an added burden on you.'

"'Please give me the chance. I am eager to serve.'

"'Let me give you a little background first. That house next to the Italian Embassy on Cong-ly Street, the one with the guards inside the door where you have delivered some envelopes—do you know what that is all about?'

"'No. The man at the front desk always takes the envelopes. I do not know who works there.'

"'That's the headquarters for the Study and Observations Group, or SOG as we call it. I am the Embassy liaison for that group. SOG is involved in studying and working with some of the ethnic groups in Vietnam, like the Montagnards, the Nungs, the Chams, and the Khmers. A large group of Khmers live in the delta provinces of South Vietnam, but the majority of that group of people are inhabitants of Cambodia. In order for us to do our job, we need to stay in contact with some Khmer leaders who live in Cambodia. Since Cambodia is not friendly to the United States it is difficult for us to send documents back and forth to these leaders. However, I believe that you, a teenage girl, could do it.'

"'Yes. I will do it for you. Just tell me how you want me to go about it.'

"'We need deliveries made to the village of Svay Rieng. That's along Highway One, about forty-five kilometers over the border in Cambodia. You can take your bicycle along on the bus to the border hamlet of Go Dau Ha, then cross the border on your bicycle. When you reach Svay Rieng, your exchange will be similar to some you have already handled. You will wait on a bench in the town square until someone exchanges a fish wrapping with you.'

"I rode into the next phase of my new career on two wheels. On that first trip I made it across the border without a problem. Neither country had the means to maintain any kind of organized border control. The road passed through lowland jungles and rice paddies. I encountered a few other rural travelers walking along the way. I was afraid they would knock me down and take my bicycle, so I tried to stay clear of them. I also pedaled rapidly through the dark chasms of jungle which sometimes enveloped the road. I am not a superstitious person, but I was spooked by the stories of evil spirits lurking in the dark forests.

"When I had gone more than halfway I was beginning to breathe easier, thinking I could surely coast in from there. Then I rounded a bend in the road and ran into a small taxation roadblock, manned by four men. I did not know whose side they were on, but I knew they were up to no good. I could not get my speed up fast enough to zip past them. One of the men caught my bicycle and yanked me to an abrupt stop. They asked me something in a dialect I did not understand, and I shook my head no. They made some comments among themselves, and all of them laughed nervously. They eyed my bicycle, and especially me. I still was not very savvy to the ways of men, but they had the same look in their eyes that Mr. Nhat used to get when he ogled me in my mother's shop. I began trembling from fright. One of them began pawing at me and chuckling with a dumb-sounding 'yuk yuk yuk.' Another man pushed him away, and they tumbled to the ground fighting. The other two robbers reached down to pull them apart. I seized that opportunity to shove off and try to make my getaway. I focused on the crease of light at the far end of the road and never looked back. I heard running and shouting behind me, but I kept pedaling. I succeeded in getting away. When I had put a wide distance between me and them, I coasted over to the side of the road for a rest. I began trembling and sobbing uncontrollably. I was feeling too young and inexperienced for this task, and I did not see how I could possibly complete this mission successfully. However, I was more afraid of turning back than of going on to Svay Rieng, so I went ahead and completed my assignment.

"In that way, my courier missions now took on an international scope. I soon abandoned my bicycle and either walked or hitched a ride with other honest-looking travelers. I did not see John Mac at all during these months. I heard he was flying ethnic mercenaries in and out of Vietnam for SOG.

"After several months had passed, one day I was returning from Svay Rieng on foot, hurrying through that middle stretch of jungle which still gave me the creeps. Suddenly I heard the telltale whistles, and artillery shells began raining down around me. Big holes were exploding in the roadway ahead of me. I ran off the road into the jungle and crouched down behind a big tree.

"For a moment all was quiet again, and I thought the danger had passed. Then a new volley began hitting in the jungle near me. Dirt and debris splattered into my face. I started running blindly, deeper into the jungle. I slid down into a little ravine and started to scurry up the other side when two arms reached out and grabbed me, pulling me down under a huge fallen log.

"When the volley ended and I looked around, I saw I was in the middle of a squad of soldiers, all wearing black pajamas. Their dress could mean they were members of any one of several military irregular groups operating in that area, but my worst fears were soon realized when I determined they were Viet Cong soldiers. Although NVA supply columns sometimes crossed the highway through this stretch of jungle to supply their forces in the delta area below Saigon, VC units operating that far into Cambodia were very unusual. Perhaps they were guides or flank security for the NVA supply lines.

"Their leader studied me for a moment. 'What's a young girl like you doing out on the highway by yourself?' he asked in the Vietnamese language.

"I hastily made up a story to tell him. 'My father sent me to look after my uncle in Svay Rieng. He is very sick.'

"'Hmmm. You are Vietnamese?' I cringed inwardly at my blunder. If I had not answered him in Vietnamese and pretended only to know a Cambodian dialect, he might have left me alone. Now I was going to have to keep making up this cover story as I went along.

"'Yes. My father now farms some land near Cu Chio, but my uncle still farms the family homestead on the outskirts of Svay Rieng.'

"'I have seen her by herself on this road before, two or three times,' one of the soldiers reported.

"'Yes. My uncle has had a long illness. My father has sent me several times to take him medicine and to look after him.'

"The leader thought about that for a moment. 'On the road before, eh? A Vietnamese father would never send a young, unmarried girl like you out on the road alone several times. Maybe once in an extreme emergency, but never on a continuing basis. Search her.'

"One of the men searching my belongings brought the opened fish wrappings to the leader. 'We found this wrapped in a bundle of fish.'

"The leader examined the fish wrappings. 'Hmmm. Documents buried in a fish package? The writing does not make any sense, but it could be in some kind of code.'

"I had to really do some quick thinking to explain the documents.

"'Can you not see that I am really one of you, Comrade? Take me to your intelligence cadre. I insist on talking only to them.'

"They were a low-level group. After a while they decided it was too risky to ignore my request in case I was telling the truth. The leader assigned two of his men to escort me to headquarters.

"Near nightfall we arrived at an abandoned woodcutter's thatch-roofed hut. My escorts and I waited there through the night. Toward daybreak my interrogator appeared. He was a gaunt, nervous man named Mr. Li. He never smiled. Behind his wire-rim glasses he wore a white shirt and khaki pants. He mechanically satisfied his craving for nicotine by chain-smoking hand-rolled cigarettes, one after the other. In the pre-dawn darkness, the tip of his cigarettes barely illuminated the highest points of his facial craters, leaving the rest of his face a black void.

"'The information I have is only for the intelligence cadre,' I said.

"He took a couple of long puffs on his cigarette. 'You may rest assured that your story is being heard by the correct ears.'

"'I have been trying to establish contact with the Front for some time now. My father died before I was born, and my mother has had a very hard life. She finally sent me to be a nanny for an American family who work for the American Embassy in Saigon. While at the Embassy, I befriended a man named Huanh, who made meat deliveries to the Embassy. Huanh is the one who persuaded me that the ways of the American imperialists were wrong. I began providing him with information, however small it might be, which would help our people to liberate themselves from this aggression. One day I watched the Americans splatter his blood against the wall of the Embassy. I vowed then to ingratiate myself into the service of the imperialists and continue to gather the best information I could to help our people and to avenge Huanh's death. However, I have not been able to make contact with our comrades in the Saigon area without placing myself under suspicion. Now I have the perfect alibi to contact you. The Americans regularly send me to Svay Rieng to transmit messages back and forth with a Khmer Serei unit in Cambodia. I believe these messages, and other information I gather inside the Embassy, will be of assistance to our people.'

"Mr. Li was skeptical at first and questioned me extensively about every aspect of my story and my knowledge of the Embassy. He had difficulty believing a prime source had fallen into his lap so easily. On the other hand he did not dare dismiss me too lightly until he had tested the veracity of my statements. Mr. Li arranged a rendezvous point near the road at the date and time when I would be returning so we could meet again after he had time to evaluate my story more fully. I was then escorted to the border and released.

"I was elated. I had actually outwitted the Viet Cong and walked away with my life. I did not know if they would be able to break the code and decipher the Khmer Serei's message that they took from me. In case they did I would have to tell Mr. Spencer about this incident so any damage could be minimized.

"I fully expected that this episode had blown my cover and my courier duty to the Khmer Serei would be terminated. However, when I reported the incident to Mr. Spencer, he had an entirely different outlook on the whole business.

"Mr. Spencer said, 'Co Hai, you have been extremely helpful to us in the work you have been doing. I was very hesitant about asking someone so young to take on such a responsible assignment, but you have risen to the occasion. You are remarkably mature and reliable for someone your age.'

"'Yes. Thank you. I know what you are leading up to, and you do not have to mince words with me. After this last episode, I can no longer be used to take messages to Svay Rieng. I understand that.'

"'No. On the contrary, now you can be more useful than ever. A clandestine contact with the Viet Cong can be very valuable to our work here at the Embassy.'

"'But, how?'

"'You would continue delivering messages to Svay Rieng. But, at the same time, you could keep on making contact with the Viet Cong. Your activities will be tightly controlled by this office. However, Co Hai, you must understand this: It will be much more dangerous than what you have been doing so far. If you are found out by the National Liberation Front, it will almost certainly mean death. Taking this on will be totally voluntary on your part. If you do not want to do it, just say so.'

"'How would I go about making contact with the VC and still transport information to Svay Rieng?'

"'We will give you two sets of documents to carry with you—the real documents going to Svay Rieng and an altered set intended for the National Liberation Front. On the way to Svay Rieng you will stop off and give the altered information to the VC. We will provide you with carefully-prepared documents to give to them. These will contain enough factual information to be believable to them, but the documents you will give to them will mislead them and keep them off the focus of our main goals and policies. Besides the messages to Svay Rieng, from time to time we will give you other documents to take to the Viet Cong. These papers you can say you found in the trash or the copy room at the Embassy.

"'We will teach you to conceal the real set in your clothing where the VC will not find them. Meanwhile, you will continue to carry the altered documents, which you will share with the VC, in the old fish wrappings. Your handlers in the NLF will not trust you for quite some time. Meanwhile, you can give us information about who you contact and how they operate. The more committed they believe you are to their cause, the more they will accept you into their confidence and allow you to see more and more of their operations. As I said, this will be dangerous. Whether or not you want to perform these duties is up to you.'

"I thought of my father, executed by the Communists in the North before I was born, and how hard my mother had worked to support us. 'I will do it,' I said.

"'Good. But there is one thing I must caution you about from the start. You must trust no one. I will be your only contact person. No matter how trustworthy someone may seem, there are even leaks within this building. I will protect you here by not revealing you as my source to anyone, and you must protect yourself in the same way. No one else must know what you are doing. Not your mother, or my wife, or anyone else in the Embassy, and not your contacts in Svay Rieng.'

"And so, my life as a double agent began, although I had no idea at the time that this is what I had become. During my first meetings Mr. Li continued to interrogate me at the old hut where the VC had taken me the first time. I could tell they were still evaluating the quality of my information at arm's length before they got more closely involved with me. Mr. Li went over and over my cover story, trying to criss-cross and pick it apart from every direction. Those sessions left me drained, and I did not know whether or not I had succeeded in convincing him of my sincerity. Each time my escort took me back to the highway I expected to be shot and left for the wild animals. However, they always allowed me to go free.

"Besides Mr. Li, sometimes another man would talk to me who I assumed was Mr. Li's superior. He had a wiry frame, with concave cheeks, a long neck, and a protruding Adam's apple. He was called *Chuot Vang*. In English that is like a weasel. This man had such cruel eyes and his face was so strange that I could not look him in the eye when I talked to him.

"After some months they moved our meetings to an underground bunker. This was not where their main head-quarters was located, but I believed the command center to be nearby.

"My new role went on for several months. I was in the middle, a prized informant for both sides. I brought back real information for the Americans on what I observed, plus confusing the VC with the false information I was feeding them. The VC thought they were getting good intelligence from me, direct from the U.S. Embassy, so I was one of their star informants. One trick we used was for me to bring the Viet Cong information on new troop placements on the day U.S. or ARVN troops were deployed. This way my informa-tion was accurate, but they would soon confirm the news from their smaller units in the field, anyway. The VC would not be able to react quickly enough to make any use of the information that could place our troops in jeopardy.

"As different proposals were placed on the table at the Paris Peace Conference, my interrogators were always very interested in the slightest reaction from Embassy personnel which I might pick up around the water cooler. I would make things up, like: 'The Ambassador seemed very pleased with the progress of the talks.' And Mr. Li and his superiors readily accepted it.

"Although they tried to keep me isolated from their other contacts, from time to time I noticed other visitors entering or leaving the underground bunker. These could have been VC provincial cadre or NVA military officers, or even civilian smugglers who were involved in the VC supply process. Mr. Spencer was always very interested in a description of these other visitors.

"Z, I did not realize Side One of my tape ran out. Now that I have turned the tape over to Side Two, I will back track a bit to make sure you do not miss anything."

Chapter X

"IT WAS LATE SPRING of 1969, and the dry season was almost over. The black western clouds of the monsoon were beginning to soak us with their first brief, daily showers. One day I hitched a ride to Svay Rieng with a farmer and his son, who were leading two new oxen back to his farm near Kampong Trabek. I was relegated to riding in the back of the wagon with the hay. I watched the glazed eyes of the two animals tethered to the back and plodding along behind us. The farmer and his son seemed very nervous about encountering any trouble. If I had not been so young and innocent-looking, I am sure my request to ride with them would have been turned down. I got the impression their entire fortune was invested in those oxen, which they had to get back to the farm at all costs.

"The farmer and his son spoke very little during the trip, and I spent the morning rocking back and forth in the hay, either lying on my back and watching the clouds change shape in the blue sky, or staring at the two beasts clopping along behind.

"At noonday they stopped along a rice paddy and led their wagon team and their two new oxen down to a drainage ditch for watering. While the animals drank, the boy bailed water to cool the oxen's backs. He dipped a gourd in the ditch and let the muddy water trickle down their flanks. Then it was back on the road with more of the same bumpy boredom. The shadows of the jungle walls on either side of us looked very sinister and foreboding in contrast to the corridor of bright sunshine in which we rode. I buried myself in the hay to seek relief from the intense light and heat.

"The pace of the oxen picked up for a few strides. The boy anxiously asked something of his father in their dialect, but there was only a quick grunt for an answer. Then the wagon came to a stop. I started to sit up, but decided to stay hidden in the straw until I determined what was happening. I held my breath and strained to hear. From the road on the driver's side someone made a loud salutation to the driver— so overdone that its sincerity sounded dubious. At the same time there was a whistle from someone who I guessed was calming the harnessed ox in front. Then there came a 'yuk, yuk, yuk' from off to the side, which chilled my bones. I had heard that laugh before. Immediately I knew the worst: this was the group of bandits who had tried to jerk me off my bicycle on my first trip. I froze with fear. Hopefully they would not notice me in the hay.

"The leader knocked and thumped along the side of the wagon with a wooden club. He asked the farmer over and over again if there were any concealed valuables on board. The farmer repeatedly denied it in a very nervous manner. I wondered if the bandits would take the farmer's new oxen if he had nothing else to give them. But he did have something to offer them. In desperation the farmer gave his son an instruction. There was a brief pause. The farmer repeated his command forcefully. The boy climbed into the back of the wagon. I thought he would fish around somewhere in the hay and ante up a hidden box of valuables. Instead, to my dismay the boy raked the hay back from my face and pointed me out to the gang. There was another gap in the dialogue while the leader boosted himself up on the side. The wagon bed tilted slightly. When the leader leaned over, his ugly face interrupted my blue sky. He studied my face for a few moments before it registered on him who I was. He started cackling in a sinister tone. I feared this did not bode well for me. I expected them to jerk some of my things away or otherwise barter with the farmer. I never dreamed the bartering was already concluded. The leader and a confederate reached in and dragged me out the back until I crumpled down in the dust between the twin sets of oxen hooves. I lay there for a moment, startled and confused about what was happening. The farmer gave a cluck to his oxen, and the hooves clopped past my ears and proceeded on down the road. I bent my head backwards against the ground and watched, upside down, the wagon receding into the distance.

"'*NGUNG LAI! NGUNG LAI!*' I shrieked over and over again, in desperation. The only response was the nervous laughter and brutal hands of the gang. I continued to scream and scream, fighting against the determined animality of the men. The purple silhouettes of these monsters burned into the inside of my eyelids. Each took his turn pumping up and down, in and out of the sun's glare. They slammed my head against the ground repeatedly, stunning my brain into static pins and needles. I found release by compressing the pain and terror and helplessness into one lump and drifting above the grunting scene below.

"Something deep inside me was floating peacefully, carefully avoiding any cares or realities. Slowly I grew aware of the wetness and coldness around me. I sputtered. I could feel something wet running down my nose. Instinctively, I wanted to rub the tickle on my nose, but I had no power to do so until I willed my hovering being back to earth and attempted to make my body function again. When I tried to make my arms work it was like I was flopping someone else's arm to my face. I could only plop my fingers in the vicinity of my nose itch.

"The rain washed against my face relentlessly. A rivulet of water trickled into my ear. I struggled to open one eye. All was black. I let it shut again and tried to force the other one open. I could not make it function. Was I blind? I rolled my head to one side and shielded my eyes from the rain with my floppy hand. This time I got both of my eyes to open at the same time. I struggled to focus. Shadowy shapes began to form from the night. The blackness was not merely in me. The whole world was enveloped in darkness. A chill of horror gripped me when I recalled the image of the men brutalizing me. Panicking, I staggered up and tried to run away from that place before they caught me again. I ran blindly into the underbrush along the side of the road and crashed violently back into the ground. My heart was pounding, and I gasped for breath, afraid they would find me again. I slipped back into unconsciousness.

"When I awoke again, the rain had stopped. I pulled myself to my feet, trying to block out what had happened. My instinct told me I had to get up and find shelter in order to survive. There was some starlight now, and I faintly distinguished a gray road from the blackness on either side. I limped and staggered along through the haze, whimpering with the pain and horror of each step.

"Before the dawn, adrift in the cool grayness of first light, I found myself bumping up against a wooden barrier. I listened to a rhythmic pounding sound and traced the numbness and pain to my own hands, beating on the door to the woodcutter's old hut. The door swung open, and I sank down inside its shadows sobbing, curling up to fend off the shivering chill. I dreamed of running beside my father through a meadow filled with flowers.

"Everything felt warm, and comfortable, and safe. I strained to open my one functional eye and focus. There was the form of a man lurking about. I tried to sit up with a start, but the pain and soreness shackled by efforts. I was relieved when I recognized Mr. Li. Gently lifting up my head, Mr. Li spoon-fed me some rice broth. He tried to talk to me, but I let his words roll up and away without attempting to grasp them. I struggled to sip down a few spoonfuls through my swollen mouth, but it was too difficult, and I did not care anymore. I rolled gingerly over on my side, facing the wall, and let myself slip back into sleep.

"In a semi-conscious state, I drifted in and out of my feelings. My childhood was over. What would become of me now? Was I still tight enough to pass for a virgin, or had I been ruined? Would I be able to bear children? Was I pregnant already? When would the rawness and pain go away? Should I tell Mr. Li what had happened? Did I dare share my shame with anyone? Would any decent man have anything to do with me now? Or, would I be branded a whore?

Whatever happened from now on, my girlhood dreams were shattered.

"During the time it took me to heal physically, Mr. Li was very kind and gentle with me. I saw a tender side of him I had never seen before. After I recovered and resumed my duties as courier, Mr. Li again returned to his business-like tone. However, we had exposed our vulnerabilities to each other. We would never be the same again.

"I noticed that, beneath his poker-faced facade, Mr. Li seemed especially pleased to see me when I would come. Little by little I began to cultivate a more personal relationship with him. I was very fragile at this time, and my ego seemed to crave this kind of reinforcement.

"Eventually I became more and more forward with Mr. Li. I dared to see how far I could push him without crossing the line. Though he never let me touch him, one day I got close to him and whispered a teasing good-bye before prancing out. He showed no immediate reaction. When I stuck my head back in the room to say a formal good-bye, I saw he was clenching one fist very tightly and trying to drive it down through the table with all his might. I knew I was having a strong effect on him.

"'Mr. Li, do you care about me?' I asked him one day. 'You never pay any attention to me. Do you like me? Do you find me attractive?'

"He did not answer me. He continued to sit back in the shadows, puffing on his perpetual cigarette, staring at me with no external display of emotion.

"I surprised even myself with that bold approach. I asked myself later: What was I thinking of back there? My impulses disturbed me, both personally and professionally. One side was telling me I should be ashamed of myself for speaking to him in such a forward manner. I wondered if I was becoming the harlot those men on the highway had treated me like. Was that my true secret desire which they had only helped to bring to the surface? Was I doomed to a life of sinful and lascivious conduct? On the other hand, was not stringing Mr. Li along something that a good intelligence operative does—anything you have to do to get the information from your source? Was I really clever enough to handle this? Although I kept telling myself what a good agent I was, deep inside I knew I was nothing but a pawn in the great game of espionage played by the high rollers.

"I was not really attracted to Mr. Li physically, but I had a desire to establish a closer emotional relationship with him. At first my pride was bruised repeatedly by his seeming coldness. When I reflected on his reactions, I recognized a reverse pattern of response on his part. The more forward I tried to get the more turned off he seemed to be. Conversely, when I was doing something naive and low key I would glance over and notice I had his full attention. Finally, I made the connection. It was my unaffected, innocent, bloom-of-youth appearance he was interested in, not a woman-of-the-world image. After discovering this I started doing more subtle things to pique his interest. For example, when I came in from the rain, I would dry my hair with a towel and comb it out in an innocent way, with him watching me.

"To my surprise, he never pushed our encounters beyond that phase or allowed me to go any further with it. He never asked me for any favors. Instead he would sit there in the shadows, puffing on his cigarettes, and imbibe all my youthful movements. Surely he knew what I was doing to him—that all those bends and flips in rain-soaked clothes were not really accidental. Yet he allowed the game to continue to the point where I was in control. With the tidbits of information he let slip from time to time, and the fact he was allowing the peep shows to continue, we both knew I had enough on him to compromise his position with his superiors at any time.

"This went on for the next two years, during which time I managed to feed the VC phony information from the Embassy without being suspected of being a double. Most of my success was due to excellent document preparation by American intelligence specialists. They provided me with information which was believable and vaguely verifiable so that the Viet Cong thought I was on their side. Also, my control over Mr. Li helped me in this regard. He did not want to lose me. Without realizing it he had lost his objectivity. He would gloss over weaknesses in my stories and present me in his reports to his superiors as much more believable than I really was.

"In addition to helping our cause by providing misinformation, I was able to pick up a few nuggets of valuable intelligence along the way: the size of their intelligence and other support staffing; the debriefing techniques used by Mr. Li and others who talked to me; the way their bunkers were constructed; troop movements; new units moved down from the North; their anti-aircraft defenses; and, of course the locations of the fringe sites where Mr. Li met with me. These were all things of value to the Americans.

"My information about the location of NVA/VC headquarters elements was particularly valuable to the Americans during the spring of 1970 when they were planning the invasion of Cambodia. During the actual invasion Mr. Spencer held me back at the Embassy, since significant military action was waging along my usual route. I wondered if anyone would catch up to Mr. Li, and if they did, what would happen to him. I kept telling myself he was the enemy, and it did not matter what happened to him. But I did have a business and quasi-personal relationship with him, and I was concerned about his safety.

"When Mr. Spencer finally let me go back into Cambodia, I was very nervous about what I would find. When I arrived at the usual bunker sites, I was shocked to find there were no VC there and the area had been ransacked by American troops. The Central Office of South Vietnam Command Center had been forced to hastily relocate. Mr. Li left an escort soldier behind to guide me to a new meeting site. I was very glad to see that Mr. Li was safe. I ignored his reticence and flew into his arms.

"'I am so glad to see you are safe!' I said.

"'They came close this time,' he answered. 'But the imperialists bungled their chance once again.'

"'I was so worried about you, Mr. Li.' I continued to cling to him.

"'Were you really?' He grabbed my arms and pushed me back, clutching my wrists tightly and staring into my eyes. 'You knew about the attacks and did not try to warn me.'

"'No!'

"'Then why did you miss your last appointment the day before the offensive started? The Americans rolled right in here like they knew exactly where they were going! How do you suppose they did that?'

"'No! No! Please, Mr. Li, you are hurting me.' He continued to clench my wrists fiercely. 'I did not know they were going to attack you. If I had known, I would have tried to warn you. They do not tell me things like that. My contact person in the Embassy prevented me from coming to you. I did not know why. I do not know how they found the bunkers so easily. I did not tell them anything. Maybe they spotted the bunkers on the pictures they take from their airplanes.'

"I was frightened and whiny. He was still holding my wrists and gazing deep inside me. Abruptly, he let me go and walked briskly to his side of the table. Quickly taking his seat, he busied himself with examining the documents I had brought. His chest was heaving.

"'I was sick with worry about you,' I said. 'Was it difficult evading the Americans?'

"'We managed,' he said matter-of-factly, his head buried in the messages. He scanned each one and stuck them down on his paper spindle, as was his usual custom. I was relieved when he finally spoke. 'How do the Americans assess their offensive?'

"'They are calling it an impressive victory.'

"He laughed derisively. 'They miss our command infrastructure altogether, only manage rear guard skirmishes with our flanking units, and they still manage to claim victory. We do not have to defeat them on the battlefield, their own lies will strangle them!'

"'The Front—it is still strong?'

"'Their destruction of supply bases near Snoul and Sre Khtum has slowed down our timetable for the final offensive.

But, our battle units and command structure are still fully capable of waging war,' Mr. Li proclaimed proudly.

"'The Saigon newspapers are saying their offensive proved the capabilities of the ARVN units.'

"'This is true. It proved them to be weak and inferior. We now know if we wait patiently for the Americans to leave— which they will do eventually—then the ARVN's will collapse like a house of straw.'

"'Do you really think the Americans will withdraw?'

"'The Americans are no match for us. They are not dedicated to a cause like we are. They have no popular support at home. There is confusion at their highest ranks about what their policy should be. They are uncaring bureaucrats who think of nothing but leaving our country without personal injury and returning to their homeland.'

"When I relayed Mr. Li's prediction to Mr. Spencer, he assumed a stoic, noncommittal look. The look in his eye was one of resignation.

"Several months went by, and my exchanges of information with Mr. Li continued normally. Looking back on it, I should have noticed Mr. Li was growing progressively more nervous and detached. Still, he never stopped me from putting on my schoolgirl act for him.

"With the Occidental New Year approaching, Mr. Spencer asked me to do something he had never asked of me before. He wanted me to try to find out about NVA troop positions and supply depots along the Ho Chi Minh Trail up in Laos, in the area of Tchepone. Always before, any targeted information Mr. Spencer asked me to collect was attainable by observing the VC units in the local area. This time he requested maps and documents about a highly secure area in a different part of the theater of operations. This new assignment really seemed to be impossible to me. Tchepone is a Laotian village near the 17th Parallel, adjacent to the far northern border between North and South Vietnam. Any information the COSVN Command Center would have on that region would be well secured in the strategic command bunker complex. Of course, I had no access to such a place. I did not even know if Mr. Li was allowed in there, or whether he had access to such information.

"'How important is it that I get this information?' I asked Mr. Spencer.

"'Very important.'

"'Even at the risk of compromising my current operation and placing myself in danger?'

"'I do not want you to do something foolish and get yourself killed. But, yes. This information is critical, and we need it badly enough to take substantial risks to get it.'

"'I understand. All right. I will try. If I am successful in getting the information, I may need to get out quickly. I would like to arrange established return times and helicopter checkpoint flyovers, in case I am late getting back.'

"'Good idea. I will arrange it with Special Ops.'

"On the way to see Mr. Li, I planned out my method for acquiring the information. The Command Center was a denied area to me, and it was unrealistic for me to consider sneaking in there and stealing the maps myself. I would have to manipulate Mr. Li to risk getting the information for me. Furthermore, I did not have any time to gradually work up to this. I would have to force the issue right away. I had to look my best and be in top form on this trip.

"While he was reviewing the usual information I had brought, I sat down with one leg resting on the seat of a straight-backed chair, combing out my hair in front of him. 'Mr. Li, there is something I must talk to you about. I need your help.'

"'What is it?'

"'I received a letter from my mother in Pleiku the other day. She is getting older and is developing some maladies—nothing serious yet. The war and living alone is taking its toll on her. She has convinced herself she must make a pilgrimage to the graves of my father and her parents near Ha Tinh in the North.'

"'Impossible.'

"'My mother is very determined. She believes this to be her duty to her ancestors that she must accomplish before she dies. And I must accompany her. That is my duty.

"'No. I will not allow it. The area north of Hue is an intense battlefield with many troop formations on both sides. It is impossible to slip through the lines safely. Once Vietnam is unified again, these pilgrimages may resume. Your mother must put this nonsense out of her head for the time being.'

"'You are right. The road from Hue is too dangerous. But there is another way.'

"'What is that?'

"'The Trail.'

"'That's preposterous. The Trail is used only for military purposes, not for a silly woman's sightseeing trip.'

"'If I must have a military purpose, then give me one. If you need bearers to fetch mortar rounds to use here in the South, then I will carry back both my own and my mother's. I am a loyal member of the Front. Surely something useful could be arranged so my mother and I can make the trip.'

"'That's the point exactly. You are far too valuable to the Cause. You are needed here to continue providing information about the Embassy. Such a trip would take several months. We cannot afford to have you away from your duties for so long.'

""We" or "I"?'

"He squirmed a little.

"I got up and slowly approached the table. 'Mr. Li, you and I have worked very closely together for the Cause for a long time. I have grown very attached to you during that time. I depend on you for my inner strength, and I look forward to being with you. We've been through a lot together. You are my mentor and closest friend. I am indebted to you for this. You know I want to continue working with you to help the Cause. But, I cannot turn my back on my mother when she needs me. She raised me when we had nothing. She is the only family I have. I cannot deny her this last request. I must do this. She is anxious to leave before the monsoons come again, so I must choose a route soon and go to her.' I leaned forward on the table and touched his hand. He left it in mine for a moment, then withdrew it abruptly. I pouted and turned away. 'If you cannot help me, then I will go to my contact in the Embassy.'

"'That would be very foolish. You would lose the protection of the Front, and any attempt by the Americans to assist you would be quickly defeated by our comrades to the north.'

"'Then you must help me.'

"'You are dreaming if you think this would be easy. The Trail is not some straight and smooth highway. There are mountains and jungles and rivers to cross. Also, there are many forks in the road where American bombs have forced us to take detours.'

"'Surely there are maps showing the most recent routes, with way stations or friendly troop locations marked on them, where we might find safe havens during our journey.'

"'Impossible!'

"'Well, at least help me to find the nearest branch of the Trail from Pleiku. We will find our way from there.'

"Mr. Li sighed. 'Make an excuse with the Americans to come again next week. I will see what I can do.'

"When I returned the next week, Mr. Li seemed relieved to see me, but at the same time detesting the hold I had over him and the risk it was placing him under. He tried to act normally throughout the meeting. When I started to talk about my mother's pilgrimage, he shook his head and drowned me out. After I finished our business and prepared to climb out of the bunker, he slipped a folded map into my bag and whispered quickly, 'Here is some of it. Come again in a week, and I will try to have some travel documents for you.'

"Mr. Spencer was quite pleased when he examined the maps that Mr. Li had given to me. The maps indicated the locations of the branches of the Ho Chi Minh Trail and enemy troop positions in the area of Tchepone. Mr. Spencer said they confirmed the assessment made by SOG, and he would send the information forward immediately.

"'Mr. Li told me to return in a week for some travel documents.'

"'You have given us everything we were after here. It's probably best to let things cool off a bit before you go back.'

"'No, no. I must go back. Otherwise it will place my whole operation under suspicion. After this meeting, I can pretend I went to Ha Tinh and not return for a while.'

"'Hmmm. Are you sure you are not in jeopardy already?'

"'I am sure I am okay with Mr. Li. Why else would he give me these maps?'

"'Remember when I told you to trust no one? Do not forget Mr. Li is the enemy. All right. I will have these troop locations verified against our other intelligence sources. If they check out I will allow you to go in one more time. Just be sure to get in and out quickly. Some things are about to pop which could blow your cover. I will increase the helicopter flyovers to twice a day, just in case.'

"When I made my return journey a week later, I was not lucky in hitching a ride and ended up having to walk. I spent the night along the side of the highway and arrived at the bunker the next morning. Mr. Li was not there to greet me. *Chuot Vang* appeared in his place. I cringed when he spoke.

"'And so, Hai, is your mother feeling any better now?' His face was so narrow and drawn that there appeared to be dark pockets where his cheeks should have been.

"'Why, yes. She is better, thank you. I must visit her soon. Where is Mr. Li?'

"'She is better, is she? Well, I have good news for you, Hai. A cadreman from Pleiku is here meeting with us. He tells us your mother is running a restaurant which caters to American GI's. He also reports she is in fine health.'

"'Thank you for telling me. That's a relief to know. I must have misinterpreted something she said in her last letter. Where is Mr. Li? I really should be moving along before the Americans miss me. Perhaps I could give my information to you so I can be on my way.'

"'Are you, by chance, in a hurry to be on your way to Ha Tinh?'

"'Why, yes. Yes I am. But, how did you know about that?'

"'What's the matter? Are things becoming a little uneasy for you, Hai? Is this when you usually comb out your hair or bend over innocently to divert Mr. Li's attention away from the discrepancies in your information? Go ahead, do a little show for me now. I am sure I will enjoy it. But it will not make me neglect my duty, I assure you.'

"'What is going on here? I do not understand.'

"'It's very simple, Hai. Two weeks ago some maps were missing from the Command Center soon after Mr. Li paid an impromptu visit there. We had been suspecting you for some time because no information you ever gave us was timely enough to use. Consequently, we bugged your last meeting with Mr. Li. Does this sound familiar?'

"He turned on a tape recorder, and played, *'Here is some of it. Come again in a week.'*

"'Do you not think it strange he would get up from the table and pass something to you secretly when you were leaving?'

"'I asked him to give me directions for a pilgrimage to North Vietnam that I plan to take with my mother. I did not know he would have to obtain the maps from the Command Center. Mr. Li is a very dedicated Party member. I am sure he would use proper procedures for signing out any documents he might use.'

"'You are correct. Any *dedicated* Party member would do that. Does it not seem quite circumstantial that one of the maps he gave you was of our troop positions in the Tchepone area of Laos?'

"'I had planned to take my mother that way to Ha Tinh. Is there anything wrong with a loyal member of the Front using the Trail?'

"'Ah, a *loyal* member of the Front, are we? Well, I must apologize. You were on the road overnight and did not hear the news reports over the radio. If you had, you would know that ARVN tanks moved west on Highway Nine across the Laotian border this morning. Is it not rather coincidental that the maps you requested showed our troop positions in this exact area? It is enough to make one wonder just where your true loyalties really lie.'

"'My loyalties have always been with the Front. I have worked very hard for a long time, placing myself at great risk

at the Embassy to bring you all of the information I could
gather. If I were guilty, why would I have come back here? If
the Americans ever found out I was aiding the Cause, they
would place me in prison immediately. My dedication has
never been questioned and is not deserving of your snide
insinuations.'

"'Did your dedication to the Cause begin before or after
the death of your father?'

"'You are confusing and twisting everything to your
own conclusions. Where is Mr. Li? He will straighten everything out.'

"'Mr. Li has made a full confession of his betrayal of the
Front and is awaiting execution. So you see, you have no
collaborator to turn to. You are all alone. You can make it
easy on yourself by cooperating with us and perhaps be sent
to a re-indoctrination camp in the North, or you can make
it difficult on yourself by continuing this masquerade. I
assure you, either way you will eventually give us the information we are seeking. Should you choose the difficult
route, there will not be enough strength and health left in
your body for us to bother sending you north when we are
finished with you. It is your decision.'

"I started sobbing. 'Yes, of course I will help you. I will
always help the Front in whatever I do. You make me feel
very confused and ashamed. I am only a simple messenger
girl. I have never said or done anything to hurt the Front. If
my plans to travel to the North with my mother displease
you, I would want whatever form of correction the Front
thinks best.'

"'Very good. You are wise to cooperate. You will remain
in this bunker, and the interrogation will begin immediately.
I must warn you, if your repentance is found to be insincere,
you will be dealt with severely.'

"'Thank you for giving me the opportunity to prove my
dedication to the Front. I am certain the information which
I will give you will demonstrate my loyalty.'

"The interrogation lasted until late into the night. It was
very exhausting, both physically and mentally. I pretended
to be cooperating with them, telling them about my child-

hood in Pleiku, about how I came to live at the Embassy, the influence Huanh had over me, and how I started carrying messages from the Embassy to the Khmer Serei in Cambodia.

"Towards the end I was too exhausted to put two sentences together. Finally they left me in darkness with only a heel of bread and a cup of water for food. I hunkered down behind Mr. Li's table, too numb to fall asleep.

"It seemed like only moments later that the bare light dangling from the ceiling was switched back on. I scrambled incoherently to my feet, trying to prepare my muddled mind for further interrogation. Growing accustomed to the light, I was startled to see someone dressed in white shoes and white pants standing in the shadows at the other side of the bunker.

"'Surprised to see me?' asked a voice obscured by the darkness.

"His voice sounded dreadfully familiar, as if from a childhood nightmare.

"'Who are you?'

"There was a laugh. 'Why, you mean you do not know your Sugar Daddy's voice?'

"He stepped forward so that a swath of light draped across his face. My heart sank. It was Mr. Nhat. Instinctively I reached into the shadows of Mr. Li's desk for a means of defense.

"'What are you doing here?'

"He laughed again. 'The same thing you are doing— going along in order to get along. I have to admit you have done all right for yourself up until now. I was quite surprised when I saw you entering the bunker on my last trip down here. I recognized you right away. You have the type of face old men like me never forget. I have been doing some checking on you. Tsk, tsk, tsk. Living under U.S. Embassy protection all this time while I was turning Qui Nhon, Nha Trang, and Saigon upside down looking for you. Then you began making courier runs to the Khmer Serei, and now this.' He laughed again. 'You really had them fooled. They really thought you were their best informant. You see, they do not know you like I do. They had no idea your mother operated a cafe in Pleiku, a very lucrative capitalist enterprise. And they certainly did not know your father owned a farm in the North, until one day our comrades broke his door down, announced he had been convicted of crimes against the people, marched him out into his own rice paddy, and blew his brains out, while your mother watched with you in her womb.'

"'No. Stop it,' I sobbed.

"'No. Our comrades could not possibly have known those things. Because if they had, they would have realized you would rather die than to ever assist them in their cause. Lucky for them I came along to straighten them out. Oh, do not act so upset, My Dear. Those beautiful eyes of yours do not look nearly so appealing when they are all red and watery.'

"He laughed again. My shock and fear were now being replaced with the hatred and detestation I felt for him. I stared in disgust at his fat belly, which protruded out of the darkness into the light.

"'I do not have to endure your torment any longer,' I said. 'I will be dead by tomorrow, anyway. Get out, now! Or I will yell for the guard outside and have you thrown out.'

"'A noble idea. Except I do not think you will get a sympathetic ear from the guard. I paid him handsomely to look the other way for the next half hour until dawn. So you see, all we have for the time being is each other. And, you are right. It is a life or death matter: *My* life or *your* death.'

"'What do you want from me?'

"'Now, that's better. Let's get this back on a business-like basis. Ah, I will have to say your resourcefulness has far exceeded my humble expectations of you. I am the first to admit my mistakes. I was wrong to consider you a simple rural maiden who would learn to sell her soul for a thousand piasters a throw. You have proved your price to be much greater than that. I should have kept you all to myself back then, when you still came cheap.'

"'There were those who did not think I deserved to be sold so cheaply!'

"'Ah, yes. Those unfortunate Americans who became enamored with you. Look around. They are not here to save you now. They are either dead or back in America, leaving you all by yourself in a Viet Cong interrogation cell. After you have told the cadre all you dare to, they will torture the real truth out of you before the firing squad ends it. It's too bad you do not know someone with some influence around here. Or, do you?'

"Mr. Nhat cackled again, causing my skin to crawl. My nemesis had found me at last. He was right, I was doomed this time. Had they granted him one night of pleasure, or could he really have me released into his custody to become his slave? I was too tired to care anymore. Either way, he had me. I hated him for what he was going to force me to do, and what he had already done to so many others before me. I resigned myself to my fate.

"'Enough. Please. I am too tired to fight you. Even if I did, you would have the guard hold me down for you. And that would not be much fun for either of us, would it?'

"Slowly and seductively I circled the desk and approached him, with one hand on my hip and the other behind my back. 'You are such a man of the world, and I am merely a poor little coke girl. How do you know I will be able to make you happy?'

"Pausing in the pool of light, I slowly ran my fingers through my hair, letting the light dapple on my tresses. Then I continued my slow approach, first striding forward with one foot, then turning my hips and gliding out with the other. He laughed nervously without taking his eyes off me. Slowly I raised one leg until my thigh angled out in front of him. My free hand worked its way down my hip and out across my thigh. From there my fingers started working their way slowly up the inside of my thigh.

"He grunted and stepped out toward me, reaching out for me with his hands. In an instant of fury I swung my arm out from behind my back and plunged the paper spindle I had taken from Mr. Li's desk deep into the side of Butt Gut's neck. His eyes grew fierce. He grabbed me and pulled me down onto the floor under him. The stab wound was by no means fatal, and he struggled with me angrily, meaning to subdue me with his superior strength and weight. I never let go of the spindle, and I persisted in working and twisting it around in his neck. He rolled over on his back and clutched at the spindle to try to wrestle it from my grasp. Grabbing my hand which held the spindle, he forced it out and away from his body. We struggled for control of the spindle. His powerful grasp was wrenching my fingers back and slowly winning the battle. I shifted my weight up onto my elbow and mustered one good knee jerk into his groin. Wheezing with pain, he loosened his grasp on the spindle for one instant, and I seized that opportunity to stab it into the middle of his throat. Horror spread over him. He sputtered, with blood spewing everywhere. Both of his hands went to his throat, but it was too late to prevent me from one last deep thrust with the spindle which pierced his spinal cord.

"'That is for my mother. And all the girls you sold into whoredom,' I whispered in his ear. He wheezed a final 'uuhhh' and it was over.

"He is the only man I ever killed, and I have never regretted it for a moment.

"There was no time to savor my victory. I heard the latch slide open on the iron door. Jumping up, I grabbed a chair and stepped back into the shadows behind the door. Cracking the door, the guard saw Mr. Nhat's body on the floor and rushed in to assist him. I swung the chair down on his head with all my might. He reeled under the weight of the blow. I pushed past him and slammed and locked the door on my way out.

"Outside, there was no one else stirring in the pre-dawn stillness. I slipped out of the compound unchallenged and made my way up the hill through the jungle to my helicopter flyover checkpoint. I heard the faint noise of a chopper in the distance and prayed it was coming for me. In the grayness I reached the hilltop clearing, unearthed the two signal flares I had buried, and quickly launched one skyward. This signal roused the sentries in the area, and soon dozens of VC soldiers began closing in on my hilltop. Small arms fire from three sides opened up on the descending helicopter. The door gunners on the chopper returned fire with their machine guns, quelling the VC fire momentarily. One dark figure of a VC soldier broke through and charged toward me. I could see the look of determination on his face. I put a halt to him by firing my last flare into his chest.

"I knew it was no use against so many. No Allied chopper would attempt to land in the middle of a Viet Cong stronghold to pick up one expendable Vietnamese girl. I expected the chopper to cut its losses, wave me off, and head for home. To my surprise the chopper kept coming in, with bullets ricocheting off it from everywhere. Then I realized there was one pilot crazy enough to fly through hell to save me. It had to be my John Mac coming for me.

"The chopper set down, and I raced for the door. I found out later I was hit twice on the way, but I did not even feel the bullet wounds at the time. All I remember was seeing the chopper's big mouth getting closer and closer, feeling my cheek slide against the cold metal plate floor, and listening to the chopper roaring in liftoff. The chopper shook decidedly, straining to gain altitude. I fought to stay conscious long enough to see if we made it out of there, preparing myself for the fireball of death if that was to be. I waited, feeling the lift of the chopper pressing the steel floor against my prone body.

"'EEEEEEEAAAAHHHHH!!!' John Mac finally shouted.

"I let my eyes close.

"Now, dear Z, you know everything. And now that you do, I must ask you to come to me. I am under investigation by the authorities. My past may soon be revealed. I need your help. You can find me through Father Han at the Cathedral in Nha Trang. I look forward to that day."

Z studied the pole light down the street without saying a word. Then he glanced my way furtively. I knew that he could not refuse Co Hai's request. And, he knew that I knew.

"We better get you on the next flight," I said. "Don't worry about the money. I can loan you some. I've got savings I can dip into."

Z's decision to return to Vietnam was the only choice he could make. He was returning to the one place where he had really been alive. He had accomplished his crowning life's achievements in Vietnam and had never been able to find meaning in his life afterwards. To Z, going to Co Hai's aid wasn't merely a nice thing to do for a friend. She was the only person who had ever touched his heart, and her freedom was the be all, end all of his existence.

A month went by without word from Z. Then a cablegram came. It was from Father Han, sent on Z's behalf. Both Z and Co Hai had been arrested. The situation was very serious. They needed my help urgently.

Chapter XI

SURROUNDING US WAS AN endless expanse of azure-white haze. We soared onward, racing in vain to catch the dimming sunburst. Inevitably our guiding light faded into the blue distance, shrouding us in the gray hues of impending night.

For me, flying back to Vietnam was partially intellectual curiosity and partially a throwback to my youth. That the United States and Vietnam could find enough common ground to allow veterans to return as tourists was a marvel in itself. I didn't know what role I could play in gaining the release of Z and Co Hai from prison other than making sure they had good legal representation. Backing up Z when he asked me for help was reason enough for returning to Vietnam. And there was the added mystery of finding out what happened to Cowboy and Cap'n Buck.

The plane touched down at Ho Chi Minh City on the familiar runway that was formerly Tan Son Nhut Air Base. I took a cab to the train station, heading for Nha Trang where Co Hai lived. During the ride in the cab I was fascinated by the sights and sounds of old Saigon in peacetime. The city was renewing itself with enthusiastic energy. I was impressed with how the Vietnamese people, despite the tragedies of the past, could adapt to any form of government that might be imposed on them and still manage to go on with their lives. Among pockets of traditional French colonial building styles, decayed and obsolete structures were being replaced everywhere by new buildings. Yet, the signs of progress were interspersed with the waste products of social change—the poor.

So far as I knew, I could travel anywhere I liked in Vietnam and look at anything except military or government installations. No one was keeping track of my comings and goings.

The well-worn train bound for Nha Trang smelled of diesel fuel and smoke. Every two seats faced each other, and the people sitting on the wooden bench opposite me had their legs jammed up against mine. People from all walks of life were forced together as fellow travelers, from the most simple rural peasant to a dapper young man in his twenties, dressed in a white suit. Being a local train, it stopped at every crossing to let people and their boxes and animals on and off. Since there was only one main track between Ho Chi Minh City and Hanoi, our train had to pull off on a side track and wait until the northbound express train came through. While we were stopped local vendors climbed through the windows, wading through and over the passengers to hawk their tea, water, dried squid, and so on.

It was after five o'clock when the train arrived at Nha Trang. That late in the day there was no use trying to locate Father Han, the priest who worked with Co Hai and who had sent me the cablegram. I checked into the Royal Hotel, which was located near the train station and Cathedral.

Nha Trang, with a population of two hundred thousand, is an Asian sapphire waiting to be discovered. I was interested in seeing the changes in the city since my visits there during wartime. I decided to take a stroll through the city to stretch my legs. The streets glistened from the freshly fallen rain. As I headed into the heart of the city I noticed a woman giving her baby a bath at a public water trough. I ventured on until I came upon the large city market. The vendors' stalls were crowded with noisy shoppers. Fly-encrusted slabs of raw meat had been on display throughout the day awaiting a buyer. Next to a stall selling flowers a dentist proudly displayed his pile of pulled teeth. To whet my appetite a culinary merchant offered me *cha gio*. I politely declined. A novelty stall sold wood statuettes and objects made from tortoise shells. An open pet shop offered chickens, dogs, parrots, and monkeys. Towards the end of the day the man at the fish market used a piece of raffia to string up some fish through the gills for the trip home. There was as much social chattering going on as there was shopping. Nobody seemed to mind whether they sold anything or not.

I hailed a taxi and instructed the driver to cruise around the city and show me the sights. From the bustle of the business district we emerged at the Pasteur Institute and then turned south along the beach drive. The dark turquoise waters of the Bay looked spectacular in the waning light. It was hard to believe that something this serene and beautiful could exist in a country whose quasi-national pastime for the better part of two thousand years was fending off outside intruders.

Beyond the public beaches we approached a handsome row of French colonial-style villas overlooking the beach, the bay, and the glimmering South China Sea beyond. I recognized the mansion up ahead as Colonel Xi's old villa. I wondered who lived in it now and whether they were aware of its dubious history.

I directed the driver to head toward the airport. This brought back many memories which I soaked in against the backdrop of the setting sun. Cowboy had used that airport to fly the Team in and out of Nha Trang many times to spy on Colonel Xi. And on that runway the Team had interdicted the VC attack throughout that tenuous night when the friendlies inside the terminal held on by a wing and a prayer. I gazed in the direction where the old heliport had stood, where Cowboy and I had brought in Cap'n Buck, clinging to life, after being set up by Colonel Xi; and where Cowboy and Cap'n Buck impulsively had lifted off on their last flight together.

From there I told the driver to head for Tan Hung Dao Street. We proceeded slowly down to the building where the I Field Force Headquarters had been. The barbed wire and MP station and sandbags were gone now, leaving no trace of what once had been the city's American nerve center.

Farther down the street I got out of the cab at the Hall of Justice which the Team had fought to protect during the Tet Offensive. I gazed at the top floor windows, wondering if Co Hai and Z were being held prisoners there. In front of the building I found the manhole the Team had used to surprise the VC from the rear. I climbed the granite steps to the place where our jeep had been blown apart and Silver had been wounded. By looking closely I could see where the Vietnamese had patched the bullet holes in the steps and walls to efface any evidence of the battle. Memories of the past were painful, and the idea that Co Hai and Z were prisoners in the same building made me all the more reflective.

The next morning I went to the Cathedral to meet Father Han. I slowly mounted the ramped entranceway between the wall of plaques, each marking the remains of a deceased parishioner. The church's gray stone facade had a life and time all its own. The French gothic spires and medieval stained glass windows loomed high above the front plaza. The weathered tombstones surrounding the edifice only hinted at what this icon stood for. Here time was marked in centuries, not hours.

"Ah, this is very bad for Co Hai," said Father Han. "Very bad." His eyes were half-closed, and he was wringing his hands and shaking his head.

"Do you know her very well?" I asked.

"Ah, she do very good work for the Church and our people. She write letters and papers to help people go live with friends and relatives in other countries. The government say, 'No,' but she never stop trying. She help many, many people—men, women, children—leave this country. They so happy they call her, *Thien-Thanh*, that is like 'angel'."

"Is that why they arrested her, because her assistance to emigrants was embarrassing the government?"

"Ah, I do not know. Maybe some, yes. They say she help Americans many years ago when she was young girl. They say she steal secrets and commit crimes against the state. I cannot believe. She so wonderful here. Do many good things."

"What can we do to help her?"

"Ah, I do not know. This very bad. I get her good lawyer. He do everything he can. It look very, very bad. They have first hearing already."

"What happened at the hearing?"

"Ah, the judge, he not listen. No. He no believe what Hai's lawyer say. Judge in big hurry to end it. They show papers that Hai work at American Embassy many years ago. A lot of people work for Americans then, and they do not arrest them. They no prove she a spy. No. They no prove it."

"Where was Chandler during all this?"

"Ah, he no pay attention to me. I tell him not to go to hearing. I tell him it be very bad for Hai. He cannot stay away. He hear what they say and get very angry. He stand up shouting, 'Unfair, unfair, you lousy commies!' Then he try to run up to the front. The police grab him and drag him away. Very bad."

"What's the next step that's going to happen to Co Hai?"

"Judge say he set day for trial to begin soon. He look at calendar first."

"Where are Co Hai and Chandler now?"

"They in same jail. They upstairs in Hall of Justice. Hai, she in jail cell by herself. Chandler in with other prisoners."

"Is it possible that they will move Co Hai's trial to another location?"

"No, no. You not understand. Hai arrested by Nha Trang police. This is local matter. They have trial here."

"Well, I guess all I can do is wait."

"No. No. Hai say you must go *mau mau* to find her friend, Cowboy. She say Cowboy help save her."

"So, he's still alive, is he? Where can I find him?"

"He live in mountains alone. I do not know where. She say you know how to find friend named Bo. You find Bo, he take you to Cowboy. Hai say this very important. You must find Bo now and bring back Cowboy."

I was surprised that Co Hai was asking me to do this. My chances, alone and on foot, of finding Bo's tribe again deep in the mountainous jungles was probably a thousand to one. But if Co Hai said this was what must be done, who was I to say differently? I knew Z would definitely give it a try if our roles were reversed. So, I bought some hiking gear, hired a taxi to take me as far as the roads went, and headed out from there into the jungle.

There is something to the simile that the forest primeval is like a church. Moving through the jungle, the stillness, subdued light, and giant trees arching overhead gives you the feeling you are walking through a great cathedral. Dust-filled columns of light beamed down through the lush ceiling of vegetation to accent a lone blossom sprouting upward from the jungle floor. The chirping of distant birds was disturbed only by the groans I uttered while laboring under the burden of my heavy pack.

Eventually the trail I was following veered off in the wrong direction, so I left it and began beating my own trail through the brush and across the rocky crags, carefully avoiding slipping downhill under the weight of my top-heavy load. It was a thrill to be back in the jungle, but I had to face the reality that I wasn't twenty anymore.

I now had a greater appreciation for the spectacular vistas which appeared in the valley below. I spotted some elephants in a little glen along the water's edge. That indicated I was not in the hunting territory of any Montagnard tribe.

About an hour before dark, I found a little saddle in the ridge and made camp for the night. I was glad the food I ate for supper wouldn't be on my back the next day!

I rose at dawn, eating French bread with cheese and coffee before continuing my journey. I moved along the top of the ridge for most of the morning before zigzagging down the slope and through the valley to tackle the next peak. On I went for two more days.

When I finally reached the vicinity where I thought Bo's Montagnard village should be, I found nothing—no trails or other signs of human life. Using the cloverleaf method of exploration, I made a wide circle in each quadrant before returning to the starting point. I continued this throughout the afternoon, exploring three quadrants, with no positive results.

I knew I was close. I could feel the tribe watching me all afternoon. My equipment was the problem. Bo's tribe avoided contact with outsiders. I had to make myself equal to them before they would reveal themselves. I had to rid myself of the trappings of my world in order to join them in theirs.

I returned to an easily-recognizable rock formation and left all of my equipment behind. Then I headed into the final quadrant of the clover pattern I had started earlier. I eased slowly ahead, on and on, farther and farther. The jungle was growing darker and darker. I began to think it was time to camp for the night and try again in the morning.

Miraculously I stepped into a small glade, opening out of nowhere. I stood at one end of the clearing, marveling at the majesty of the jungle, which could part its thick crown and render up such a wondrous place so unexpectedly.

When my gaze returned to eye level, through the gathering grayness, there stood before me at some distance the form of a man. He was as natural as the trees and foliage from which he had mysteriously emerged. He appeared to be an elder statesman of a Montagnard tribe, typically small of stature, with the bushy hair of the hunters and clad only in a loin cloth. He carried no bow or spear and wore no war paint. Amid his worn and baked visage, there were longing eyes, caught in an evolutionary snare. I was impressed with his air of oneness with his environment.

On his head this Montagnard elder wore the tattered remnants of an old American boonie hat, which shaded his most distinguishing feature—his necklace. The necklace consisted of a series of smaller objects, perhaps animal teeth or small pieces of bone, leading down to a single sharp, crescent-shaped object. The pendant seemed familiar. Peering through the near darkness, I recognized the object. Slowly I unbuttoned my top buttons, reached inside my shirt, and drew out a similar ornament which dangled from a leather thong. It was the tiger claw Z had given me. I displayed it to the Montagnard man to signify our friendship.

Now I knew this ancient apparition standing before me was our old friend, Bo, another honored recipient of one of Z's tiger claws. I solemnly raised my right hand. Bo did the same. We stepped forward to approach one another ceremoniously.

Instantly there was a flash of light, and the ground jolted. Bo was shrouded in flying dirt and black smoke. A jarring BOOM rocked the jungle floor, tearing Bo's form apart. For a moment I tried to make some sense out of what was going on. Was this some sort of Montagnard hocus-pocus? Then I realized something was terribly wrong. I rushed forward shouting, "BO! NO! NO!" When I reached Bo's side I lifted Bo's head and the remaining part of his torso. Blood was still bubbling in spurts out of an empty socket where a leg used to be. Bo blinked and studied my face. A brief moment of recognition brightened his eyes before they glazed cold.

I looked around and saw I was surrounded by a dozen hunters, each with his crossbow aimed right at me. The Montagnards assumed I was responsible for Bo's accident, even though I was unarmed. Something totally beyond the ken of the Montagnard world had suddenly happened to their elder statesman at the same time a person from the outside world had arrived. It was logical for them to believe I was to blame. I felt completely defenseless, in the hands of a race lost in time with no concept of mercy in their society.

The hunters grunted and motioned at me. Their cross-bows were trained intently in my direction. I laid Bo's remains down and stepped back. The senior tribesman who was tending to Bo glanced over and uttered an order. Lowering their bows in unison, the hunters lashed my hands behind my back with vines and marched me away into the jungle.

In the growing darkness, I stumbled clumsily through the underbrush while my captors glided easily along beside me. By and by, we swung onto a rough trail, on which we continued in the dark for some time.

At last there were flickers of light ahead of us through the trees. We emerged into a clearing ringed with small huts built on stilts. They herded me toward a post protruding from the ground, about twenty yards from the central fire. There the hunters forced me to the ground and lashed my hands together behind me around the post. Two of the tribesmen stayed nearby as guards. The others returned to their huts.

Soon the rest of the hunters arrived carrying Bo's remains. A whimper of activity rippled through the dark hamlet. Bo's torso was laid out on the ground. Some Montagnard women came out to prepare it. Other women came back and forth to the fire bringing food to the men who had returned. My equipment, retrieved from the rock where I had left it, was stacked outside the central hut.

After a while all fell quiet. I was left alone to ponder my fate. I should have never attempted to find Bo. Not only had Bo died as a result, but I would probably be next. Or at the very least, without Bo's help there would be no way for me to find Cowboy and save Co Hai. The reality was, I was too old and out of shape to tackle this type of venture. In addition to being cold, hungry, and thirsty there was the pain from sitting up in an awkward position on the hard ground. I squirmed to try to shift my weight to keep my legs from going to sleep.

In analyzing the accident, I decided Bo must have stepped on an old, live artillery round. As a representative of the democracy which had fired the artillery shell, I was in part responsible for it. Tribesmen had no doubt walked through that glen many times, but this time Bo stepped in the wrong place, and BOOM.

The hunters could have killed me on the spot, so they apparently had not yet decided what to do with me. The death penalty was rarely imposed in the Montagnard culture. If one member of the tribe killed another tribesman, the murderer was not put to death. Montagnards were afraid the ghost of the murderer would stalk the hamlet. That was with members of their own tribe. With me, who knew?

During the night, even though I was exhausted and my legs were going numb, I struggled to keep myself awake. After the two men who were guarding me nodded off to sleep, I quietly began trying to fish my pocket knife out of my pocket. It must have taken fifty tries before I worked it up and out of my pocket. Then I spent the rest of the night sawing through the vines binding my wrists.

The grayness of the dawn was beginning to gather as I staggered to my feet, clutching the post to steady myself. I flexed my fingers and toes to make the pins and needles go away.

Unsteadily I lumbered toward my gear stacked outside the central hut. Though the bonfire had died down to red embers, I could make out shadowy objects with the help of the distant glimmer of morning's first light. I took my time, moving from shadow to shadow in a zigzag fashion. When I reached my pack I quietly hoisted it on my shoulder and headed toward the edge of the hamlet.

By that time the light of dawn was steadily illuminating the hamlet. There weren't many shadows left for me to duck into, leaving me in plain sight most of the time. One of the guards woke up with a start and spied my escape. He raised his crossbow and fired an arrow at me. Fearing the arrow had a poisonous tip, I shielded myself with my pack. The arrow pierced the canvas cover and lodged in it. Hastily the guard began reloading his crossbow. I charged straight at him, bulldozing him with my pack and knocking him to the ground. It was too late. The second guard awakened and thrust his loaded crossbow against my throat. I dropped my pack and slowly raised my hands in the air.

A hue and cry went up throughout the village. The hunters quickly surrounded me, with women and children peeking out from behind them. They began marching me back in the direction of the stake where I had been tied up overnight.

"COWBOY, COWBOY," I shouted in desperation. Everyone in the village stopped short, startled by hearing a stranger utter that name. Seizing the opportunity to communicate with them, I pantomimed the meaning of the words as I spoke. "I"—I pointed at my chest—"look"—I put my hand above my eyes and looked back and forth—"for Cowboy"—I held out my hand to show how tall Cowboy was and then began strutting around, mimicking Cowboy's swagger. They all laughed at my rendition of Cowboy's strut. My God, I thought, they must know Cowboy!

Now that I had their attention I forged ahead, trying the best I could to act out mental concepts. "Many moons ago, four men came to your village: Me, Z, Captain Buck, and the Moon Dog." I got out my wallet and pulled out the photo Z had lent me of the Team. Going around to each of the elders, I pointed at one of the figures in the picture, saying "me" and pointed to my chest. They seemed fascinated by the clear likenesses in the photograph. I made the circuit a second time pointing to the Moon Dog in the picture. To demonstrate, I took my sunglasses out of my pocket and put them on. "He"—pointing to the picture of the Moon Dog— "gave sunglasses to little boy *con trai mau trang*," I said. I knelt down and tried to act out the scene where the little albino boy is squinting and holding his hands over his eyes to shield them, and then the Moon Dog takes off his sunglasses and puts them on the boy.

After eyeing those histrionics, the entire village became very upset. They were highly offended by my depiction of that scene from the past. The warriors encircled me again and lifted their bows in readiness to fire.

Their actions were interrupted by movement from inside the central hut. A middle-aged female Montagnard came out of the hut and tied open the door flap. The woman held up a sun screen made out of woven bamboo palms. When all was in readiness, a Montagnard man who looked to be in his thirties stepped out of the shadows of the tent into the glow of dawn. He wore a ceremonial mantle made of brightly colored beads and fine stones. The tribesmen bowed their heads when he appeared. I also bowed. The chieftain gave one clap, and the tribesmen all stood erect again. This chieftain had all of the features of a Montagnard, but his skin was white as snow. I realized who it had to be—the albino the Team had seen when he was a little child. He was still wearing the same aviator's sunglasses the Moon Dog had given him on that day so long ago. The albino chieftain mumbled an order, and I was brought before him.

I bowed and pointed out the sunglasses on the Moon Dog in the picture and then pointed to the albino. The albino motioned, and one of the elders brought the picture up for his inspection.

I tried again to explain my mission. "Cowboy. I look for Cowboy." I did a bit of my impression of the swagger again.

"Cowboy!" said the albino, chuckling with recognition.

"Yes, Cowboy!" I said.

The chieftain summoned the elder who had been there the previous evening when Bo was killed. From the gestures, it was apparent they were discussing the circumstances of Bo's death. After completing his deliberations, the chieftain gave some directions and pointed west. I was handed my pack, and two hunters led me to a trail heading out of the village in a westerly direction.

One of my Montagnard escorts led the way, and the other trailed behind me. We stayed on the trail for some time and then moved off through the jungle, wading through a couple of streams and climbing some steep hills before connecting up with another trail. Since we had obviously passed out of the tribe's hunting territory, it became apparent the two hunters' assignment was not merely to banish me from the tribe. They were leading me somewhere beyond that, maybe all the way to Cowboy.

We spent the night in the foothills of the mountains. The next morning we began the ascent up the mountainside. Although we were no longer on a trail, the two guides showed me how to zig and zag my way up the crags and crevices of the mountain. The terrain was rugged, and I had to move carefully, but the guides led me to passable avenues where the going seemed impossible to the uninformed eye.

By noon of the second day we emerged onto the lip of the vast Plateau du Darlac. The terrain on top of the plateau is mostly a high savanna, broken up by large, jagged patches of jungle and rocky hills.

In the late afternoon my guides stopped at the edge of a clearing. They did not advance any further. Their job was done. They waited, allowing me to continue alone.

There at the opposite end of the field, sitting on the edge of the esplanade, facing out away from me toward the mountains and valleys beyond, looking like it had been plopped down there by mistake, was a house, a large, two-story, European-style lodge. It looked rather dilapidated now, but in its day it must have been a grand house.

There were several acres of cultivated tea and coffee plants around the house, but on this day there was no sign of human activity around it. Approaching the house warily, I turned the back door knob and nudged the door with my shoulder. It wouldn't budge. Working my way around to the front of the house I tried to peer through each window. The facade, though largely raw, weather-beaten wood, showed a hint of worn paint in the protected areas. When I stepped up onto the large front porch, it creaked under my steps. I knocked at the front door and called out loudly, but the house stood silent and hollow. I stepped back for a moment to contemplate my next move.

The front door moaned slightly.

"Raise your hands over your head and move over into the light where I can see you," came an order from inside.

The voice issuing the command was unmistakable. "Cowboy!" I said, turning around. As I stepped forward to greet my old friend I was somewhat taken back by the form in front of me. The voice may have been the same old Cowboy, but what I saw was a middle-aged, balding, bearded man, wearing light cotton slacks and an Hawaiian-style shirt stretching over a protruding bay window. I wondered if the changes in my own appearance were as noticeable to Cowboy.

"Hey, now. What kept you away so dang long?"

My greeting turned serious.

"Cowboy, I've got bad news. Co Hai's been arrested. And, Bo stepped on an old artillery round and was killed."

Cowboy's visage turned ashen for a moment. He quickly recovered his composure, having steeled himself long ago in preparation for hearing the worst.

"That is bad news. Yes, indeed. We'll have to see what we can do about Hai. Hey now, you're the first American visitor I've had in twenty-five years, and I've forgotten my manners. Forgive me if my English is a little rusty. I've been trying to stay in practice by singin' along with Frankie—do I sound like him? Come on inside and have some tea."

Cowboy escorted me into the sitting room and fetched the tea pot and a loaf of French bread, from which I readily tore off a big hunk.

"Jax. I cain't believe it's really you after all these years! I think about you boys all the time. Then one day, presto, here you are on my door step! We've got a lot of catchin' up to do. But, before we get off on somethin' else, Hai's welfare is my biggest concern right now. Where's she bein' held?"

"The Hall of Justice in Nha Trang. I guess Hai thinks you can help save her. She directed me out here to find you."

"You betcha I'm gonna help."

"Z came over from the States about a month ago. Father Han, Co Hai's priest friend, told me Z blew his cool at her hearing, so they threw him in jail, too."

"Z always had a thing for Hai."

"Father Han hired a good lawyer for her, but he's not helping much."

"That doesn't surprise me," said Cowboy. "Over the years I've seen the Communists do this time after time. They arrest someone for aidin' the United States, go through the motions of a kangaroo court, and then hang 'em. Her only hope is for us to break her out of there somehow."

"I thought of a plan while I was on the trail. It's risky, but it may be her only chance. The Team spent some time in the Hall of Justice thirty years ago, so I'm familiar with the layout of the building. The problem is getting all the way back to Nha Trang in time. It took me nearly a week to get out here, and her trial could take place any day now."

"You came the slow way. I can get us back to Nha Trang considerably faster. It's better to wait until tomorrow so we can travel in full daylight. So, before we get too wound up about releasin' her and Z from jail, let's get caught up with each other while we can."

"Okay. I don't want to lose sight of helping Co Hai, but I've got lots to ask you about. First off is most obvious. What have you been doing all these years, and how did you end up living like this? I was shocked when Z showed me a picture that proved you survived the chopper crash. Did Cap'n Buck escape from the crash, too?"

"Hey, now. You never knew about all those goings on, did you? I guess it starts with that crash in the jungle. That's been a while ago now, but it seems like yesterday."

Chapter XII

"**I** SHOULD HAVE KNOWN better than to stay over in Nha Trang that night. It was bad enough I had to take Buck and you boys down there to that inquiry to face Major Daniels. Nothin' chapped my butt more than knowin' what they were fixin' to do to Buck. There wasn't a finer commissioned officer than Buck, and they were gettin' ready to crucify him.

"After droppin' you boys off, my crew wanted to go downtown to unwind a bit. They had been cooped up for a while, so I gave in and let them stay over. I wasn't really in the mood to go partyin' with 'em. I was worryin' about you boys facin' the music the next day. I hung around the aviator's hooch at the airfield, had a couple of B's, and took in the evening flick. It was *Lion In Winter*, with Hepburn and O'Toole, about a king payin' a visit to his exiled wife. That was the last picture show I ever saw. After the flick I hit the sack early.

"The next thing you know, Chollie gave us a wake up call. Someone yelled that the Viet Cong had overrun the airstrip and were in the compound wire. I grabbed my '16 and ran over to a window. Sure enough, Chollie was runnin' wild all over the place outside. There weren't very many of us in there, but we holed up like the Alamo, battened down the hatches, and made a stand of it. Chollie was tryin' one thing or another all night long, but we managed to hold on.

"Chollie pulled back beyond the runway at dawn, and we were in a Mexican standoff with them all day. We kept callin' over to headquarters, requestin' them to send over some grunts to help run Chollie off, but they said they couldn't spare anybody, and to hang on. There we were, just a bunch of pilots who should have been up in the air sup-portin' the effort, and HQ left us stranded down there to defend ourselves. When I got to feelin' blue I asked myself: where is that rascal Buck and his boys? After all I've done for them!

"That went on all day and into the next night. After nightfall here comes Chollie again. Except this time there was a big explosion to Chollie's rear and lots of other rear action stuff goin' on, and I knew Buckie and you boys were out there givin' 'em hell. Finally an ARVN unit showed up to relieve us. I was one tired Huey pilot. 'Bout dawn you boys come stragglin' in. It was kinda funny 'cause we were expectin' a whole herd, and there was just the three of you.

"Everything was pretty well in tow by then, but they still told me I couldn't take off yet. I was goin' crazy sittin' on the ground. I looked over at Buck, and I could see by the appre-hension in his eyes the inquiry was hangin' heavy over his head. And I thought what does this guy have to do to get some respect around here?

"When the call came in about the heelo goin' down, Buck and I took one look at each other, and the next thing you know we were off and runnin' for my Huey. We were both exhausted and not exactly in our best racin' form, and we were gaspin' and gigglin'. First one of us would pull ahead, and then the other. We jumped on board and started windin' the engine out. We saw you and Z a-huffin' after us, but we shoved off without you 'cause this was our gig, and it was the one time when it wouldn't be right to let anyone else risk their lives on somethin' crazy like that. We lifted off and cleared the field without takin' any serious hits. It was the greatest feelin' of my life, risin' up out of the mist into the blue that morning. Buck and me never felt freer or more close. We were clownin' it up all the way out 'til we reached the objective.

"Then we went to work. The flames were still bright, and there were no signs of life. Buck got in the back where he could run back and forth to look out both side doors. He plugged in my co-pilot's helmet so we could talk to each other.

"'Hang on, Buckie. We'll give her a rip down low. She's comin' up on our left.'

"'Roger. I've got it in sight. Mac, we're taking ground fire! We've sustained three or four hits. Hold her steady for the pass. Okay, I got a glimpse of it. Will this thing still fly?'

"'No problem. What'd you see down there?'

"'There's a couple of bodies down there that the flames haven't gotten to yet. Can't tell if they're still alive. Also looked like some bodies in black PJ's. Were they carrying some prisoners?'

"'Beats me.'

"Mac, set her down next to the wreckage, and I'll go see if anyone's still breathing.'

"'Whoa, now, Buckie. That's a hot LZ down there. We might not be breathin' long ourselves if we do that.'

"'Come on, Mac. Those Americans down there may still be alive. That chopper's on fire and could go up any minute. We don't have time to do this any other way. I'll be your right door gunner and lay down suppressing fire as we go in. It'll only take a minute.'

"'Okay. But I'll be pissed if they shoot my baby out from under me. Oh, oh, rocket at eight o'clock!. Hey, you actually hit it—I can't believe it! Rocket at four o'clock! Dang it! WE'RE GOIN' DOWN. MAYDAY! MAYDAY! See ya, Buckie.'

"'You too, Mac.'

"Despite Buck's usin' the machine gun to explode the first rocket, they zapped us good with the second one. My tail was knocked out, and we were spinnin' down out of control. We spiraled down, down, down, and no matter what I did, I couldn't handle the stick. It was real frustratin' bein' so helpless.

"We plunged in right on top of the other crashed heelo, causin' one hellatious fire ball. I guess the big explosion underneath us was our savin' grace. It must have thrown both of us clear of the wreckage. That's all I can make of it. All I know is, when I woke up my head was propped up against a tree at the edge of the clearin'. I felt like I was watchin' a silent war movie. Everything kept fadin' in and out and gettin' brighter and dimmer. I watched the two wrecked Hueys pop and burn. I felt like I was a bodiless head watchin' that inferno.

"I saw black-clad figures walkin' around in the haze. I got excited to think there were some other life forms in this new world I was in. I thought of Buck and tried to turn my head to see if he was around. I saw his form restin' against the tree next to mine, which made me feel good. He wasn't movin', but they had gone to the trouble of draggin' him over next to me, which was a good sign.

"A black figure knelt down beside me. He jerked my dog tags off and started pullin' everything out of my pockets. A lot of my things he stuffed in his own knapsack. He untied my boots and pulled them off. He pulled the laces out and used them to tie my hands in front of me. Next, he carried my boots and dog tags back over to the burnin' wreckage and heaved them into the flames. When he walked away I saw an SKS rifle strapped across his back. I realized my caretaker was a Viet Cong, meanin' I was a prisoner! That was something I had dreaded throughout the War. To be in the hands of those little devils was the most horrible thing I could imagine. Now that it was happenin' to me for real I was in such a daze I couldn't feel the pain or horror of captivity yet. I was just sittin' there watchin' the events unfurl without mindin' one way or the other how things might turn out.

"I may have been oblivious to time, but my little friends in black were sure scurryin' around in a big hurry. They knew another rescue force would be on the way in a matter of minutes. Woozy though we were, they forced Buck and me to our feet and half-pushed and half-dragged us down the trail.

"The Army tells you the best chance for escape is soon after your capture, before they get you back to the rear to an organized retention camp. That advice is highly impractical when you're barefoot. I couldn't have made it three feet off the trail in that condition. I never realized how tender my feet were until that day. After a while, every root and rock we stepped on was sheer agony. I looked back and saw I was leavin' bloody footprints.

"Even though my mind was cloudy that first day, my inner survival instincts kept me goin' despite the painful feet. If you lagged behind they would jab you with a rifle butt or slap you to make you keep up. To avoid the negative reinforcement I staggered blindly ahead.

"That neither of us had any broken bones from the crash was a flat miracle. Any serious injuries and they would have shot us at the outset. But a captain and a Huey pilot in one fell swoop were a worthy prize, and since we were ambulatory they seemed willin' to take the trouble to move us to the rear.

"Later in the day when my head cleared, I started wonderin' about Buck. He was walkin' behind me, and they'd hit me if I tried to turn around and look, so all I could do was worry. I hadn't heard a peep out of him all day. Was he okay mentally, or some kind of walkin' zombie? I longed to turn around just once and look into his eyes. Then I'd know.

"There were eight of 'em movin' us along. Whenever they heard heelos overhead, they would bury themselves deep in the bushes, with two of them holdin' each of us down. At one of those times, Buck must have tried to escape, because I heard a scuffle behind me, and they started poundin' him over and over again. I tried to pull free to help him, but they slugged me a couple of times on the back and held me tight. I couldn't bear listenin' to the beatin' Buck was gettin'. One of the guards especially had a real mean streak. Every time after he hit Buck he'd whisper something in Vietnamese and say 'eh?' I can still hear it now.

"When we finally headed out again, I didn't know how Buck was able to get up and move. I could hear by his footsteps he was falterin' and they were proddin' him severely. When they stopped for lunch I gestured about givin' a drink of water to my friend. The cruel one laughed and said something in Vietnamese and came over and tried to take a whiz in my mouth. I kept my mouth shut, but some piss got up my nose, causin' me to gasp and sputter. That gave them a hoot.

"It was too dangerous for them to move us for long during the daytime. By mid-afternoon, once they thought they had put enough distance between us and the crash site, they led us down into a dense thicket. We rested there until dark. They gave us a small bowl of cold rice and a cup of water, which was like manna from heaven. I finally got my first chance to see how Buck was. Good ol' Buck. Somehow he was hangin' on. He even tried to give me a wink through his swollen, black 'n blue eyes. That made me feel real good. I got in a couple of hours of sleep, which I needed badly. It had been a rough three days for me. Even without the crash and captivity to cope with, I was pretty much a goner already

"After the nap I felt better. They had us on the move again as soon as it got dark. We marched along on the trail for most of the night. Before dawn we arrived at some sort of outpost. They stripped off our fatigues and made us put on black pajamas, which were way too small. Then they pushed us into bamboo animal cages barely big enough to sit in. Scrunched up like that, my legs went out on me real quick. The entire outpost was well-camouflaged so it couldn't be seen from the air. VC soldiers would come by and squat and stare at us or poke us with a stick or spit on us. We seemed to be a very special sideshow for them.

"We spent the day in our cages, with one bowl of rice and a couple of cups of water. I was feelin' pretty faint from hunger, and I didn't know if I would ever move my legs again. My back was killin' me from bein' hunched over. All there was to do in the cage was study the sores on your feet, which were twisted around right in front of you for easy examination. I could hardly breathe on account of the stench from the excrement and urine left by previous occupants of the cage. I wondered what had happened to those poor souls. Were they still toilin' in a prison camp somewhere, or had they met their final peace? Was it better to continue the struggle to live, or give up and go quickly? I had to fight off notions of futility which kept poppin' into my thought. I wished I could talk to Buck to bolster my spirits, but they wouldn't let us talk. When we tried, they would jab at us brutally through the cage with sticks and clubs. Buck kept persistin' in yellin' things over to me, so they finally went in and gagged him. His cage was several feet over from mine, and there were bushes in the way, so we couldn't see each other. The day moved slowly by, and then we spent another lousy night in the cages.

"That second night, I could hear our Phantoms layin' in an air strike about ten clicks away, down the valley. We found out later they had knocked out a bridge Chollie relied on to move his supplies across. When word reached our location, everybody seemed pretty shook up about it. They were ordered to repair the bridge and make it operational again, ASAP.

"At dusk on the third day of our captivity, they decided to move Buck and me over there to help rebuild the bridge. They dragged us out of our cages and left us layin' on the ground until the feelin' started comin' back into our legs. I wanted to just lay there, with my cheek jammed into the dust, and not move a muscle forever. They yanked us up and made us start marchin' again. We didn't know yet where they were takin' us. At first it was really painful, with spikes of pain shootin' through my feet. Since my feet were still somewhat numb, I staggered all over the place. When that problem finally went away, there was the old problem of walkin' barefoot again. After two days in the cage, the swelling was just startin' to go down, and now I was breakin' all the scabs open again.

"We got to the bridge a couple of hours before day-break. They put us right to work helpin' to clear some bombed-out timbers out of the way. Just before dawn we were pulled back out of the way, and everything was carefully concealed from air reconnaissance by tyin' branches from nearby trees together to camouflage the bridge from the air. They hid us in a low thicket for the day. Buck and I were tied up with our backs to neighborin' trees so at least we could see each other now. They also brought in four Montagnards and tied them up a little ways off from us. Some Montagnards were friendly to the VC, but these unfortunate fellas must have been non-sympathizers they had rounded up for forced labor. Chollie needed them to fell the trees and size the logs for use in replacin' the spans that had been destroyed.

"The next night the VC worked furiously to get the bridge functional again. They untied our hands so we could work, but each of us was connected securely to a guard with a rope tied around our waists. Some of the big timbers took every available person to heave ho and maneuver into position. There were a couple of VC honchos there who knew what they were doin'. Everything was organized and fell into place like clockwork. They had us busy all night long doin' the heavy liftin' and poundin' pillars in place with a sledge hammer. By mornin', one side of the bridge was passable to foot traffic, and a few foot convoys crossed over before daylight. Since we had at least another full night's work to finish the whole thing, they relegated us back to the thicket for the day. I was exhausted. Now I didn't have only my feet to worry about. I was achin' all over, and my hands were all blistered up. I had no idea how I'd have the strength to heft that hammer another night. The VC were beat, too, and even our guards were dozin' while on duty.

"I happened to wake up about mid-morning. Everything was quiet. Our guards were droopin'. I looked over at Buck, and he was alert and lookin' over where the Montagnards were tied up. I looked over that way, too. The four of them were wide awake and very attentive. I started to look away when I noticed a slight movement behind them. At first I thought it was some kind of wild animal, maybe a wild dog or mountain lion. When I studied the form more closely, I spotted some bushy hair. I recognized it as a person, a Montagnard person. I scanned the jungle and suddenly two or three other forms became perceptible to me. They were creepin' up very carefully to free their tribesmen. It was fascinatin' watchin' those guys operate. They moved so slow and so quiet. I'd be starin' right at one of them, and he'd disappear into the shadows of the jungle right before my eyes, reappearin' minutes later several feet away.

"They managed to get two of their men untied and were workin' on the third when the guard coverin' Buck woke up and looked over and saw what was goin' on. He wheeled around and raised his rifle to fire on them.

"'BO!' Buck shouted suddenly. Buck leaned over and kicked the guard just as he fired, causin' the rifle shot to miss its mark. Three other VC guards in the area jumped up and prepared to fire. But no other shots were fired. They all fell down to the ground simultaneously, lookin' like pin cushions. I looked beyond them to the thicket, and a wall of Montagnard warriors had stepped out of nowhere and were reloadin' their crossbows.

"The one shot fired by the guard attracted attention from the bulk of the VC, who were camped nearby. I could hear some voices and runnin'. The Montagnards quickly freed their other two men and began to vanish. In a second, only the one Buck had called out to was left. He stopped and looked over at Buck for a split second. Drawin' back his arm, he threw his knife at Buck before disappearin' into the jungle. I'll never forget seein' that knife flyin' through the air right toward Buck. With no time to free Buck, the warrior had opted to put his American ally out of his misery rather than subject him to the further horrors of Viet Cong captivity. I winced when I heard the thud the knife made as it hit its mark. But, to my relief I realized the knife hadn't hit Buck at all. The blade had stuck in the tree at Buck's side, just below his armpit. Buck had known all along the knife wasn't meant to hit him. He calmly covered up the handle with his arm before the VC guards came crashin' into the area. They became enraged when they saw the Montagnard slave workers had been freed and four of their men had been killed. They sent out patrols to track down the Montagnards. Bein' pumped up like that, they kicked us around some to vent their frustrations.

"I didn't know whether Buck would use the knife to try and make his escape that day or wait until the next day when the VC had calmed down. If he waited, I didn't know how he would conceal the knife until the next day. I should have known better than to worry about him stayin' around for another day, especially since we were the only two laborers left and they were bound to work us doubly hard on the next shift. I never even noticed Buck cuttin' himself loose. I kept watchin' him all day, and even though I was tired and physically whipped, I didn't dare be in a doze when he made his move.

"In the early afternoon, they changed their guards. Buck still waited. He waited a couple of hours until these guards were near the end of their shift and perhaps gettin' a bit careless. After a while the guard next to me got up and went back past the one closest to Buck to get himself a drink of water. The guard on Buck glanced up at his partner as he passed by. In that instant of distraction, swashh! Buck lunged out and slit the guard's throat with one motion, and then drove the knife into the back of the passing guard, mufflin' his mouth while wrenchin' him to the ground with his left hand. Watchin' Buck operate, I was in awe of how quick he was. The guy with the slashed throat started makin' this eerie 'uuuuuh' sound, and the other three guards in the area turned and saw what was happenin' over at our end. Buck didn't hesitate for a second. He had just hit the ground on his back with the stabbed VC on top of him. He reached around and grabbed the guy's rifle from around either side of his body, and with one shot a piece BLAM BLAM BLAM he hit each of those other guards dead on. That brought the whole camp down on us again. Like a cat Buck was out from under the dead VC, grabbin' his ammo bandolier and a second rifle. He sprang over to me, cuttin' my hands and body free from the tree. While I was gettin' up he whirled and BLAM BLAM BLAM dropped the three closest VC who were chargin' us. When he did that everyone else hit the deck and opened up on us, but we weren't there anymore, 'cause Buck had us low crawlin' out into the jungle. There were bullets ricochetin' everywhere, and I was scared silly, which made me low crawl faster and lower than ever. After their volley started to die down, Buck turned and fired several times back at them. I don't know if he was aimin' at anything or not, 'cause I wasn't lookin'. Buck immediately changed course and led us off at a ninety degree angle from our original direction. And a smart thing, too. 'Cause Chollie poured everything they had on our old course. And while they were busy doing that, we were able to get up into a crouched position and hightail it out of there like crazy.

"Those VC knew their stuff, and they weren't about to let us run off so easily. They soon picked up our trail and started houndin' us down. Buck tried everything in the book to shake them—swingin' over to a new trail, wadin' through a stream, backtrackin' and cuttin' off at nineties—but nothin' fooled them for long. They knew the terrain and where we were headin', and we didn't. Frankly, after a couple of hours I didn't know how much more of that I could take. I was ready for it to end when it did end. Finally they boxed us into a little draw in the dense jungle. They had us surrounded. Every which way we tried to go to get up out of there, they were closin' down on us. We divided up the remainin' ammo and got back-to-back to make our last stand.

"'See ya,' Buck whispered.

"'You too,' I answered.

"The Chollies on my side approached us first. We were well camouflaged and didn't move, so they didn't spot us right away. I waited until they were only about ten feet in front of me so I'd be sure to bring one down with each shot. At last I aimed my rifle and started to squeeze off a round. But before I could fire, there were several *ffwhht* sounds and the four VC who were bearin' down on me suddenly all fell forward with a surprised look on their faces. I looked down at them, and each of them had a couple of arrows stuck in his back. From out of nowhere, Bo appeared and motioned to me. I tapped Buck, and we slipped stealthily up to where Bo was only barely visible now. Like steppin' behind a stage prop, suddenly we were invisible, too. We followed Bo and his warriors away from the rest of the Viet Cong.

"One good thing about those Montagnards, unlike the VC they slept at night and traveled in the daytime like I was used to. When we stopped for the night, all they offered us for food was water and some kind of dried meat they carried with them. I gestured to Buck to ask him what kind of meat it was. He gestured back, Never mind! The next day I was still hungry but feelin' much better after some sleep. They had noticed how much trouble we were having walkin' barefoot, and overnight they had gone and snatched a couple of pair of Ho Chi Minh sandals, which they gave to us before we moved out. Man, did those sandals ever make a difference! We journeyed with them for two days until we reached their village. When I saw it, I breathed a big sigh of relief. We were free!

"The Montagnards let us hang around their village for a couple of weeks. I don't know if they really wanted us there, or if they didn't know how to tell us to leave. They remembered that Z had regarded Buck as his chief, which gave Buck a certain amount of status with them. I caught on with them pretty fast, too. It's a shame about Bo. You say he stepped on an old shell? He and I built up a trade over the years benefittin' both me and the tribe. To this day they are pretty much untouched by the outside world, except for my dealin's with them. They're still hunters and food gatherers. Back then, neither the VC or the Americans had recruited this particular tribe to assist with the war. They weren't the type to get involved.

"Buck and I were free to come and go anytime we pleased. Buck took me over to the Colonel's Cave a few times. Y'all had left some of your old tiger fatigues in there, so we were able to get back into LRRP clothes, at least. The downside was there weren't any boots, so we were stuck with Uncle Ho's sandals a while longer. The big thing we got from the cave, which became my savin' grace later, was the money. Buck still had most of the money stashed there that he had seized from Colonel Xi during their first encounter— some in MPC, some in greenbacks, and lots and lots of Vietnamese Piasters. I was shocked at how much there was. We took the MPC, the green backs, and some of the piasters and hid the rest again.

"Even then, Buck spent his time in the cave ponderin' those pictures of Xi. I gave him plenty of berth to brood, since I knew he had a lot to work through in his mind. In a matter of a month's time he had been dumped by his wife, and his career had gone down the tube. We knew good and well how it would be when Buck returned to the Brigade.

They'd congratulate him on his escape from the VC and then throw him in the American brig at LBJ, on account of those other charges made up against him.

"I myself was just bidin' my time. I was due to leave for the States in a few weeks, and I knew when we went back to the unit I wouldn't get to see much more flyin' anyway. Oh, every time I'd see a heelo flyin' in the distance I'd get the itch, but I knew it was about over.

"One day after Buck had stared at the pictures in the cave for a while he asked me a question that damned near knocked me on my butt.

"'Have you ever thought about us staying over here?'

"'You've been out in the sun too long, Buckie Boy.'

"'No, seriously. Let's face it, your flying days are over. Ex-Huey pilots are a dime a dozen back in the States now. You'll never touch another joy stick again once you get home. But if you stay over here, you could live like a king.'

"'Well, thanks for the rosy picture, Bwana Buck, but this isn't quite the royal life I had in mind. I'm not like you. I've still got my sister and some other family back in Texas. No offense.'

"'None taken.'

"That was the first time I'd thought of the idea of stayin' in Vietnam. It was an interestin' notion, considerin' the situation we were in. We were no doubt listed as Missin' In Action, and this gave us a great deal of flexibility about when we wanted to resurface. That is, if we wanted to resurface at all.

"Like I said, Buck spent most of his time thinkin' over and over again about all his encounters with Colonel Xi.

"'What's missing in our case, Mac?' he'd ask. 'What more do we have to prove?'

"'If what we saw is what we think we saw, those papers from the Colonel's safe and the pictures Z took are all we need. Colonel Xi is nailed.'

"'Maybe if we can catch him actually paying off an American.'

"'Look, how many times do I have to tell you? His accountin' records cover all of that. And, I sent the whole satchel with all the papers in it to the Embassy, care of Co Hai. We don't need to pull any more double-0-seven stuff to collect more evidence. It's all there.'

"'How do we know we can trust Co Hai to keep the information confidential and have it there waiting for us? She owes her allegiance to Spencer and the other high hats in the Embassy now.'

"'We can trust her, okay? I know her, and I know I can trust her, that's all.'

"'I don't know who to trust anymore, Mac. Everyone seems to be letting me down, lately.'

"'Listen, I'll make a deal with you. Let's go down to Saigon and see Co Hai. We'll get the papers and Z's pictures from her and study them. If there's not enough there to nail Xi, I'll stick around and help you get enough. If there is enough, we turn it in, get everything cleared up, and go home.'

"'Who are we going to turn the information over to?'

"'Spencer is bound to know some top brass who are far enough distant from this situation so they'll give us a fair hearin'.'

"I had to work on Buck a while, but I finally convinced him. We waved our farewells to Bo's tribe and set out for Saigon. Makin' our way through the jungle, even to reach a highway, took several days—through the mountains to the Song Ba River, then down it to Highway Seven and the coast. Buck picked our way carefully. He wanted to steer clear of both the Cong and friendly forces. We had decided to make this trip incognito, since Buck was subject to arrest, and I guess they could've even charged me with desertion. All I could think of, every flip-floppin' step of the way, was gettin' my hands on a pair of size eleven boots. When we finally found us some boots from a mama san on the strip at Tuy Hoa, it was the one and only time when I ever had the thrill of ecstasy from puttin' them *on*! I also partook of an ice-cold Coca-Cola, which was one of the last times I've indulged in that pleasure. Out here I avoid the temptations of crass commercialism."

I noticed one of the obvious evils Cowboy was avoiding was electricity. As the sun set outside we continued to sit in the parlor without light, and it was becoming more and more difficult to see. Oil lamps seemed to be the lighting medium of choice. If there was an electric generator, the decision to expend the fuel to operate it was saved for occasions more special than the arrival of a long overdue house guest.

There was little evidence Cowboy had invested much effort in making the house his own. Save for the parlor, all the rest of the rooms on the first floor were bare. Cowboy had dragged whatever furniture had been abandoned by the previous tenants into one room and supplemented it with shipping crates.

"From Cam Ranh Bay on in was easy," Cowboy continued. "We walked right through the main gate at Cam Ranh, had a haircut, shower, and shave, and got in line for the next flight to Tan Son Nhut.

"By the time we made it to Saigon, we had a plan to contact Co Hai at the Embassy without gettin' ourselves arrested. We headed straight for the quarters where Z had told us the civilian morticians were housed. We hung around there a while until Clifton, my old buddy from my R&R in Sydney, came trudgin' home after a hard day at the drain board. When I stepped out to greet him, he looked like he'd seen a ghost.

"'My God! Where did you come from?' he asked.

"'We got kind of tied up with Chollie out in the boonies for a while. Why?'

"'I shipped you home in a body bag a month ago!'

"'No kiddin'? What'd I look like?'

"'A boot, some ashes, and a few bones thrown in for good measure. You two better come on in my room.'

"Seein' as how I was probably his only acquaintance who was actually out wagin' war, Clifton had gotten in the habit of scannin' the manifest lists to make sure I was still kickin' out there. When he saw my name and then Buck's, he took it upon himself to handle our remains personally. All of this surprised the heck out of Buck and me. Here we thought we were still fugitives, and we found out we were ghosts! I started horsin' around with the humor of it all, but

Buck went straight to the bottom line: no one was lookin' for us anymore, or expectin' us to report anywhere, or even carryin' us on an MIA report. In the official eyes of the United States Army, we were KIA's. And at the time, that was a convenient place to be.

"Clifton went with us to Spencer's villa and got Mrs. Spencer to gently explain to Co Hai that we were still alive. When Hai looked over and spotted me, she took out runnin' across the street, dodgin' cars, to come to me. I spun her around in my arms, and we both shed tears of joy. I gotta admit, the fuss she made over me touched the ol' Cowboy deep inside. She told us you and Z had been to see her and had told her Buck and I were dead.

"Co Hai gave us the satchel and pictures, and we took them back to Clifton's room in the civilian barracks. Clifton let us sleep on the floor in his room for a few days. Buck spent the night pouring over every document using a Vietnamese dictionary to determine what every bit of it meant. He held out a few of the pictures Z had taken and some of the papers from the satchel. The rest of it we took to Spencer the next mornin'. Spencer was surprised at the size of Xi's operation and the extent of the evidence we had on the whole deal.

"For the next few hours, Buck paced the floor in Clifton's room going over everything in his mind while he waited for Spencer to react to the information. In the middle of the afternoon Buck decided we needed to go back to Spencer to explain a couple of points in the documentation that we had firsthand knowledge of. By then I knew it was a waste of time to try and talk Buck out of any notions he had about this Xi thing, so I put on my boots and we headed back to Spencer's villa.

"As we round the corner, who do we see gettin' in an ARVN jeep with the satchel and drivin' off, but Colonel Xi. In that late afternoon traffic he was too far ahead of us for us to chase after him.

"'So Spencer will know some top brass to give the satchel to, eh?' said Buck.

"Buck darted through traffic and knocked on the door to the villa until Spencer opened it.

"'So, you're dirty, too!' Buck said.

"Spencer stepped out into the courtyard and closed the door.

"'Rogers, you live in a black and white world, but I live in a gray one. Everybody's on the take over here. That's the way of life. The evidence in that satchel would have brought down the Thieu government and had half of Westmoreland's general staff arrested. We couldn't let that happen.'

"'And in the process, you collect a nice finder's fee from Xi to send your kids to private school in the States.'

"'You can think of me what you will. The fact remains that information like that could be very damaging to our country. If *Time Magazine* got wind of a story about coffin smuggling going on right under the nose of American authorities, the U.S. Army would never live it down. What's more, the thought that countless Vietnamese agents had been smuggled into the United States would cause panic among the public. There would be witch hunts in the new Vietnamese communities springing up in the States, and innocent people would be hurt. Do you want that to happen?'

"'We risk our lives to hand you the smuggling ring of the decade on a silver platter, and this is your attitude. No wonder we can't win this war. Our top leaders are only interested in maintaining the status quo.'

"'Come on, Rogers. That's unfair. A lot of us are doing all we can to end this war, but we have to be pragmatists and pick the battles we can win. It's not as though the information you gave us is going to go for naught. The coffin smuggling deal is over as of now, and tomorrow the police will begin rounding up smugglers and breaking up the ring.'

"'That's very noble of you. After you give Xi all night to destroy records and get himself and his leaders to safe havens, you'll see that third and fourth echelon operatives are picked up. You'll be known in your circles as Mr. Tough Guy on fighting corruption—the guy who's not afraid to wade right in and clean up messy situations.'

"Buck wheeled around and walked away, and I tagged along behind him. He went straight back to Clifton's room to brood. It didn't surprise me when I woke up in the night and Buck wasn't bunked out next to me. I got up and looked out in the corridor. Buck was sittin' on the floor at the end of the hallway, starin' blankly out the window into the darkness. I padded in my bare feet down to the end of the hall and eased down next to Buck. 'Mercy! I'd forgotten how hard a floor was!' I said. 'What I wouldn't do for a mattress right about now!'

"There was a long stretch of silence before he finally spoke.

"'I'm dead.'

"'Hey now, don't let all you did over here go down the tubes because Xi and a few higher ups are gettin' away. A lot of the operation will be broken up, and that's a good thing. There'll be less GI's compromised and less girls like Co Hai corrupted because of your efforts. You accomplished a lot, and you should be proud.'

"'I'm dead.'

"'Well, if you look at it that way, I am, too.'

"'No, you've got everything to live for, and I've got nothing.'

"'C'mon, now. You've got lots of people. All your high school buds. You've got me. You've got a whole great big ol' life just waitin' for you out there.'

"'Right now I'm dead. I can either stay dead, or come back to life again. If I decide to reappear, my career in the Army will be over. After blowing the whistle on all those field grade officers, there's no point hanging around in the Army pretending I'd have a viable career left. As soon as they could make it look like it was for some other reason, they'd rift me out. So, if I come back to life, I'll be discharged as Paul Rogers and sent home to Indiana, where I'll live unhappily ever after. I'll be denied doing what I've been trained to do and the only thing I know how to do. But, if I stay dead, everybody's happy. The Army's got an untidy scandal neatly closed, and I can put it all behind me and go wherever I want and be whoever I want to be.'

"'You can do all that as Paul Rogers.'

"'I can be Paul Rogers again anytime I want to be. All I'd have to do is wander into a VA hospital and explain who I am and let them check out my fingerprints and become the Associated Press' feature story of the week, and route myself back to Indiana that way. That's an option anytime I want to take it. But, I've got a chance to be really free, and I'll never have this chance again once I've passed on it.'

"'What are you sayin'?'

"'That I can stay dead and start all over again and be whoever I want to be.'

"'Are you talkin' stayin' here, or goin' Stateside, or to a third country?'

"'That's the beauty of it. I can go any of those places. For starters I thought I'd return to the States. Wherever Colonel Xi may go to lay low, he's got some serious connections in the U.S. If I happen to run across some of his operation Stateside I'll be in a position to deal with it.'

"'So, that's what this is all about. You're still tryin' to hunt down Colonel Xi. And, if he's convinced you're dead, he won't be lookin' over his shoulder for you.'

"'Not really. I'm serious about starting a new life. Any time I spend tracking down Xi's operation will be as a hobby.'

"'How're you goin' to get back to the States if you're dead?'

"'The way any respectable dead person would do it.'

"When Clifton woke up to get ready for work, we talked him into goin' along with Buck's plan. Clifton would get a green hospital jacket for Buck to wear, and Buck would walk into the warehouse with the other workers who were filin' in to begin their shift. Then durin' the mornin' coffee break Clifton would slip Buck into one of the transfer cases that Colonel Xi had modified for smugglin' humans into the States. Those special cases were still bein' kept in the mortuary as evidence even though the smugglin' ring had suspended operations the night before. Buck, lyin' in a coffin, would get a free ride to Travis Air Force Base the same way Colonel Xi's operation had smuggled so many others into the States.

"While we were waitin' on Clifton to arrange things, Buck and I said our good-byes.

"'You sure you're goin' to have plenty of food and water in that thing?' I asked.

"'Clifton is taking care of all that.'

"'Flashlight and batteries?'

"'Yes, don't worry.'

"'Two days from now you'll be at Travis.'

"'I guess so.'

"'What are you gonna call yourself?'

"'I haven't gotten that far with my plan yet.'

"'How will I get in touch with you?'

"'I've got your folks' address in Killeen. I'll send you a Christmas card sometime.'

"'Thanks a lot! What about Co Hai?'

"'If I need to contact her, I'll write her at the Embassy.'

"'Where do you think Xi will be headin'?'

"'He's probably still hiding somewhere in Vietnam, or heading for a third country nearby. That way he can continue to run the ring from this end.'

"'So, if you go back to the States, you'll never finish it with him.'

"'I'm sure he knows it was us that messed up his operation here. What needs to be done now is to uncover his infrastructure in the States.'

"Clifton brought a green jacket over, and Buck slipped it on. We shook hands for the last time.

"'Well, it's been grins,' I said.

"'See ya.'

"'You, too.'

"I followed along and watched him make it through the MP's at the main gate of the warehouse, and then I went back to Clifton's room to sweat it out until the end of Clifton's shift. I couldn't rest easy until Clifton told me Buck's transfer case had been loaded onto a C-130, and he was on his way. Just liftin' off from Tan Son Nhut was the big worry for me. I knew gettin' out of the case at Travis without bein' caught would be tricky. But that was a different world and out of my control. I had my own future to decide on.

"I realized there wasn't anything pressin' me into makin' a quick decision. Like Buck said, I had the rest of my life to turn myself in and be me again. Why hurry? I could do that any time. Like Buck, I decided to enjoy bein' dead for a while. I decided to go up to Pleiku and see how Co Hai's Mama San was doin' with her restaurant and just go from there.

"Well, one thing led to another, and I never left. This country sorta grows on you. I bummed around, mostly between Pleiku and Saigon, while the American forces were still here. For a while I flew a Huey for SOG. It was easy to stay on the loose back then. I could put on jungle fatigues and mingle almost anywhere, with everyone thinkin' I was just another GI in town for the day. I invested the money Buck had left at the cave in a little import business—native trinkets from the Montagnards, carved ivory or teakwood figurines from Cambodia, things like that. Nothin' big, but it more than meets my needs over here, where a buck goes a long way.

"After the collapse of the Thieu government things got hairy. The Communists didn't have any use for American stragglers. I've lived with the Montagnards. I've lived in abandoned bunkers—both ours and theirs. The last eight or nine years, I've managed to stay in this old lodge, more or less harassment-free. Oh, I've had to skedaddle out of here a few times when a search party came through, but they never stayed long or tore it down or anything like that, so I've always come back and set up shop again.

"Let me show you something."

Cowboy got up slowly and made his way to a corner table where he picked up an old guest book and blew the dust off it.

"The best I can figure from old pictures and such, this place was a huntin' lodge built by a French family by the name of Michelin, when their rubber plantations held sway here. Lookee here at this signature. He must have come here one time on a tiger hunt."

The faint brown scribbled handwriting read: "Theodore Roosevelt".

"Very nice. That's a real keepsake. Cowboy, have you ever crossed paths with Colonel Xi again?"

"Hey now, that's the ironic thing. After all that time Buck spent tryin' to track Colonel Xi down, Xi is the

Province Chief in Khanh Hoa Province now. That's the province Nha Trang is in. He's been the chief for years. He was in cahoots with the Communist regime for so long before they took over that they had no problem acceptin' him as one of their own. He goes from a colonel in the ARVN ranks to a province chief for the Communists. Isn't that the damnedest thing you ever heard of?"

"That is something! What about Cap'n Buck? Where does he live now?"

"He's mostly based in the States. He keeps a low profile. He's been my partner in finding retail outlets for the goods I send over. But he's kept on expandin' his end of the business—bringin' in imports from all over."

Cowboy looked at his watch. "Pardner, it's gettin' late, and we have work to do tomorrow. I'll show you to your bunk upstairs."

I followed Cowboy's candlelight, drifting upward, tracing L-shaped jogs through the darkness as we ascended the grand staircase and moved down the creaking hallway to the second floor bedrooms. Cowboy lit some candles for me and left me in my room. It was huge and would have been very majestic were in not for the lack of furniture. Its meager furnishings consisted of one plain table and an old Army cot shrouded in a mosquito net, which seemed lost in the shadowed emptiness of the large room. Sleep was a long time in coming.

In the night I awakened suddenly, my heart pounding rapidly. I detected Cowboy's faint footsteps out beyond the front hallway. I decided to venture forth into the darkness to see if he could use some company. Out on the front balcony I could make out Cowboy's shape in the darkness, leaning against the railing. As I joined him the mosquitoes began buzzing me immediately.

"You'd think there wouldn't be enough warm blood around here for these little suckers," I said, swatting at them.

"The westerly breeze will push them away soon enough," Cowboy said.

"Cowboy, there's one more thing I've been wondering about."

"Shoot."

"That time when you gave the Captain his nickname. What all went on out there that made you and Cap'n Buck become such close friends?"

There was a soft chuckle from deep in Cowboy's throat.

Chapter XIII

"**A**H. HOW WONDERFUL IT is to be young! You have no limits. Just blue sky. That fearless belief you can shape your destiny to whatever you wish it to be. Flight School's a breeze. There's not a thing you cain't make your bird do. Finally you get your first assignment, where they're actually entrustin' you to put a two million dollar flyin' machine through more paces than the designers ever imagined. All in the name of God and country. Who cares if it's a war zone, because you're invincible, indestructible. That's how I felt back then, when I first came to the Nam. All caught up in the dream. Lord knows I had no idea I'd never leave. There wasn't a place I wouldn't take a heelo, and there wasn't a mission I wouldn't attempt. And I wasn't the only one. There was a whole breed of us up there freewheelin' in the wild blue.

"I guess Buck and I both got over here sometime in early February of 1967, but I didn't meet him until a month or so later. Back then I was flyin' a Huey Cobra, which was a real kick. You could just about make it do anything your mind wanted it to do. Around Pleiku there were dense jungles and jagged mountains, with lots of enemy ground fire comin' up from anywhere, anytime.

"That particular day I had been busy flyin' several missions already. We were short on pilots, so I was flyin' her solo. In the early afternoon, I was on station over Highway Nineteen, west of Pleiku, ridin' herd over a convoy headin' out to resupply the Berets at Duc Co. I was beginnin' to think we were goin' to make it without incident when suddenly about ten clicks from the Camp all hell broke loose. I came in low, and I could see our boys jumpin' out of the deuce-and-a-halves and divin' for cover. I noticed puffs of smoke comin' from the jungle along the north side of the road, and I was able to get off a few bursts on my first pass. I came in from the southeast on my second run and laid down a good string of fire suppression. Sergeant Boogaloo, the leader of our Mech Infantry outfit, popped yellow smoke to mark a machine gun for me, and I launched a couple of 81 mm rockets on my third pass. The way Boogaloo got all excited, I guess I hit it. Meanwhile I had taken a few hits myself, and my stick got jammed. I could only turn toward the right. HQ ordered me back to Pleiku, but it was goin' to be ten minutes before they could get another gunship out there, and I didn't want to leave our boys without air cover while they were gettin' hammered like that. Chollie launched an RPG which hit the fuel tank of a deuce-and-a-half and, KAPOW! that baby went up in a ball of orange fire. Boogaloo was cryin' for me to knock out that rocket launcher, so I coaxed her around to the right and eased back on line. The enemy fire was like drivin' into a hail storm when I came in for the kill. I had the target in sight and was ready to squeeze off a 2.75 when I took a couple more hits and got bumped off target. Now, I really had to fight to control the stick. I held her down on target again, but I realized I'd have to fly right through that black smoke from the truck to deliver the finishin' blow. My instinct told me if I didn't pull out right then I wouldn't be able to clear the tree line, but I was so close, and these guys were countin' on me, so I held her steady, and when I came out of the smoke, I couldn't believe how close I was to the woods. For a split second I actually saw Chollie with his launcher, but I immediately launched two rockets of my own. When I realized I couldn't bank left and the tree line loomed high above me on my right, the pucker factor went way up. I slammed on the brakes and then banked right with all my might. I got her to spin back around, but that sharp turn at low altitude was all Chollie needed to finish me off. For a moment I reveled in the sound of my rockets puttin' a serious hurt on Mr. Chollie, but then I felt my fuse-lage rippin' apart from multiple small-arms fire. I wondered how much more the Cobra could take and still stay in the air. Somehow I managed to clear the tree line and head for the barn. I looked back and my tail was on fire, and I could-n't get any altitude. I knew I'd never make it all the way back to Base. I doubted if I could even make it back to the road for a crash landin'. Suddenly, I saw a patch of savanna to my front. I tried to hold 'er on course for the clearing, prayin' I'd make it over the trees. I skimmed the tops on the way down, and with no lift or holdin' power left, I plowed in pretty hard.

"I have no idea how long I was out. When I came to, it took a while for the cobwebs to clear and for me to figure out what I was doin' there. The Cobra was still smokin' on the back end. I checked my appendages to see if they still worked. I was able to successfully wiggle my toes from both feet and my right fingers. But nothin' happened with the left arm. I looked down, and there was a big wad of blood oozin' out from my flight suit under my arm. The impact of the crash had shoved my .45 and shoulder holster right up through my left armpit. Blood and guts were oozin' out. The thought of it made me feel woozy, and I had to rest for a minute to come to grips with it. I wondered why it wasn't hurtin' yet, and should I yank the holster out or would that just cause more bleedin'? Before I could do anything, I heard Vietnamese jabberin' and footsteps pushin' through the bush. All I could do at that point was play dead, so I dropped my head down and froze. Three or four Chollies approached the aircraft. They put out the fire in the back and walked all around, banging on it, and finally came up and shook my face. I was doin' my best to hold in and not move. They seemed to be arguin' about what to do with me. When they finally headed off again I knew they'd be back soon, so I struggled to wiggle myself out of the cockpit.

"After rollin' down to the ground, I scooted myself to my feet by pushin' myself off with my right arm and usin' the Cobra's fuselage to steady myself. I went to draw my .45, and for the first time the pain hit me. I closed my eyes and clenched my teeth and gave my pistol and holster one big jerk. I didn't know anything could hurt so bad. I tried to keep my arm squeezed tightly to my side to hold my blood in. I shucked the holster and held the .45 between my knees to peel some of my arm tissue off the action and jack a round into the chamber. The shock from all this made me very shaky. I knew I had to get out of there. I started staggerin' off through the breaks, but it was too late. Two VC appeared in front of me. Without hesitation, I blew them away with two shots, BOOM! BOOM! This was just an instinctive reaction for survival. With everything else goin' on, I never gave it a second thought.

"Naturally, those two gunshots alerted every enemy soldier within half a mile, and I could hear them shoutin' and thrashin' toward me from three directions. I started retreatin' toward the Cobra, but when I looked back a rifle butt smashed into my face. The next thing I saw was little red flashin' blobs, and I felt plant stobs prickin' into my face. I heard voices far away. When I tried to tune into them I realized they were standin' over me in a circle. I groaned, and they proceeded to ram me all over with their rifle butts. At this point I just laid there with kind of a detached view, not carin' really what they did to me. Finally I heard some shots fired, and then some thumps landin' around me. The Chollies who had been messin' with me had just had a rude comeuppance.

"Next I felt like I was floatin', but I could hear heavy breathin' and frantic footsteps and felt my legs draggin' effortlessly over the vegetation. My rescuer was tryin' to haul me out of there. Every now and then he laid me back down, and I could hear huffin' and puffin' next to my ear. Then I floated some more, and then more huffin' and puffin'. I was enjoyin' the ride and wonderin' where my rescuer was takin' me. Finally he laid down next to me and was mumblin' something to me. I listened real close to try to understand it. The voice sounded so serious and determined, so I knew the message must be important. I relaxed and opened up to it, and the mumbling focused into a murmur.

"'Be very still, now. Don't moan on me, please. Charlie'll be passing by us any time now.'

"I did what my rescuer said and tried not to make a sound.

"'They're tracking in on us from three sides,' he whispered. I'm going to have to use you as a decoy and leave you alone for a while. Hang in there. I'll be back. See ya.'

"I tried to whisper, 'You too,' back at the voice, but my mouth was too smashed up to shape the words. I felt good about helpin' my rescuer in whatever he was doin' by bein' his decoy, but I didn't know what a decoy was supposed to do to perform its role effectively. I heard a couple of crashes and rollin' sounds, and I got the idea my rescuer was chunkin' rocks at me. I tried to shout, 'Hey, is this any way to treat your decoy?' But all that came out was a loud groan. That set off thrashin' and shoutin' and gunfire, and I felt sorta proud, listenin' to all this ruckus around me set off by me bein' a decoy. There was silence, followed by footsteps runnin' toward me. My rescuer returned, and off we went floatin' across the savanna. I opened my eyes and looked back at where we'd been, which was closin' up behind us again, and we were still stoppin' every so often for more huffin' and puffin'. Finally, we faded into the shadows, and I thought the sun must be goin' down, but I looked around and saw we were now in the jungle, and this frightened me 'cause I couldn't see the sky anymore, but I sensed my rescuer was relieved now, so I tried to calm down and trust his judgment. And then I really was floatin' this time, and I realized my feet were danglin', and my rescuer was utterin' some faint grunts from the strain. He carried me for a while and then plopped me down. The undergrowth was so dense I couldn't move even if I had been able to.

"'Here's the situation,' he whispered. I listened attentively. 'They won't be able to track us in here. We're going to have to hold up here through the night. I don't have a radio to call for a Med-Evac. Let me take a look at your shoulder.'

"He started probin' under my arm, and pains started shootin' up my shoulder.

"'Man, you were really tryin' to conceal your .45, weren't you? A shoulder holster wasn't good enough for you!'

"He patched up my wounds the best he could out in the boonies. By now, everything was throbbin' so bad already that his pokin' around didn't make much difference. I opened my eyes and saw this round, determined face in tiger fatigues workin' over me.

"'Who are you?' I managed to ask.

"'I'm Paul Rogers from the LRRP Platoon. How about you?'

"'John Mac Smith.'

"'Pleased to meet you, Mr. Smith. Our LRRP Team heard the battle going on over by Highway Nineteen, and we started moving that way to see if we could help. I sensed we were being followed, so I sent my men on ahead while I set up a rear ambush on the trail. As expected, a VC squad came along behind us. I was just ready to pull the trigger on them when your chopper careened overhead and crashed out in the clearing.'

"'Why'd you bother draggin' me out of there?'

"'We don't leave Americans behind.'

"'More'n likely, I'll be dead by mornin' anyway.'

"'Then I'll see you get sent home. And if I don't make it, I'll go home alongside you. But, don't be thinking so nega-tively. You've made it this far. You're alive. The bleeding's stopped, and you're now in the Recovery Room, so to speak. After a night of healing, I'm expecting big things out of you in the morning.'

"He fed me and watered me and tended to me and whis-pered words of encouragement to me all through that horri-ble night. I couldn't sleep for pain. Off and on I would get chills or tremors. Sometimes I had a sinkin' sensation and felt like I was fallin' off the edge. Through it all he was reas-surin' me and tellin' me I could do it. It was the worst night of my life, but lookin' back, it was also one of the best, 'cause I had him now. It's only once in a blue moon that someone special like that comes into your life.

"We weren't out of the woods yet, not by a long shot. By daylight the cobwebs were clearin' up, although the head wounds were still sore as all get out and throbbin' away. My left arm was swollen up double, and I could barely move my fingers. Rogers told me I was goin' to have to get up and walk on my own, 'cause it was time to find out how much I'd learned during the Escape and Evasion course at Fort Gordon. We didn't have any choice but to hoof it out of there. Chollie would be expectin' this too, so it was goin' to be pretty tricky tryin' to slip through. To make it worse, his Team had been out a while and were due for extraction, so he was low on food and ammo. We shared his last LRRP ration for breakfast and started out.

"Let me tell you, after that first step, I wanted to lay down and die right there. The pain was so bad I didn't care what happened to me. He kept after me to take one step and then another one. Somehow, we kept movin' forward. After a while, I got to where I could get up a head of steam and do pretty well on the straight aways, but I was stumblin' all over the place on the up and down parts. What's more, every time a branch brushed my face or my arm, it took a half a minute for the pain to subside enough for me to go on.

"Well, it didn't take long for me to learn just how good you LRRP's were on the ground. Rogers won my respect in a hurry. He'd hear stuff way before I could and button us down deep in the brush before a squad of Chollies passed by. Around noon, I was just loosenin' up and gettin' the hang of it, when our luck ran out. Some Chollies caught up with us from behind and opened up on us. I'd taken a lot of hits in a Huey, but havin' those branches snappin' all around you was something else. Rogers returned fire and veered of in a different direction.

"Soon Rogers pulled me down again, pointin' ahead to an enemy unit comin' our way. He decided we'd make a frontal assault to try to break our way through their line. We got down real quiet like, and when they were almost on us, he stood up to wax them, but I could almost see him gulp, 'cause there were ten or twelve guys instead of the four or five he was lookin' for. He dropped two or three of them before one of them outflanked us and raised up to shoot him from his blind side. BLAM went my .45, and then I stared at it for a moment, askin' myself, 'Did I do that?'

"We broke contact and slipped back the other way, where we bumped into another VC group. They had us boxed in on three sides, and we soon found out where they were drivin' us to, 'cause we ran into a river. Rogers returned fire from the top of the bank, probably zapping a few more of them before he was down to his last magazine of ammo. All this time, we were the target of heavily concentrated fire. The VC didn't let up, and Rogers and I were finally forced to slide down the bank and wade up under the roots of a big overhangin' tree. They tried lobbin' Chicom canister-type grenades down at us, but Rogers would quickly kick them out into the water where they fizzled out. Next they started sloshin' out to get a shot at us from the flanks, and he fended off these intrusions until his ammo ran out. Finally he waded back under the tree where I was.

"'What do you think about the prospects of a POW camp?' he asked.

"'Not much.'

"'Me either.'

"I fished in my pocket and came up with a single .45 caliber round, which I inserted in the magazine and shoved back into my pistol with my good hand. 'I always save one back, for humane purposes only.'

"Rogers drew his k-bar from a scabbard strapped to his leg. 'See ya,' he said.

"'You, too.'

"When the next VC waded into view, Rogers leaped out at him, knockin' Chollie down in the water. I watched them splashin' and rollin' in the water until two more appeared and waded in toward me. I glanced down at the big dark hole in the end of my pistol, hangin' onto life until the last possible second. Suddenly, the two VC jumped a bit and got startled looks on their faces. They fell forward, almost at my feet, and I noticed one of them had a knife in his back, and the other one had some kind of axe stickin' out. I looked behind them, and here come two Americans, Z and the Moon Dog I learned later, burstin' up out of the water and splashin' in toward the bank. Meanwhile, you were layin' down suppressin' fire from the other side of the river. Rogers finished off his opponent and came staggerin' back.

"'Get a Med-Evac in here,' he said to the Moon Dog, who was carryin' the radio. 'We've got to get this pilot to a hospital fast.'

"'There's a clearing big enough about two hundred meters down stream, Captain,' said Z. 'You go on. I'll keep them busy.'

"I didn't see how we'd get to the clearin' through that barrage of enemy fire, but when we started to make a run for it, suddenly the whole bank behind us, where Chollie was, started explodin'. I looked up and saw two of my buddy Cobra pilots layin' in fire support for us. Mercy! That was the first time I'd been on the receivin' end of that. With their help we worked our way downstream. When we reached the clearin' the Moon Dog popped green smoke, Z arrived, and we pulled into a tight circle, waitin' for the extraction Huey to bank in.

"'What took you guys so long?' Rogers asked.

"I'll never forget how you answered that question, Jax.

"'You're getting better at covering your tracks, Sir. Z lost your trail twice during the night.'

"I got to thinkin' about how Rogers had managed to get the two of us through all those close shaves like he was a super human space guy or something.

"'YOU'RE BUCK ROGERS!' I shouted over the Huey's roar. 'THE REAL ONE!'

"I reckon the name 'Buck' kinda stuck with him after that.

"Well, you know the rest. I was laid up in the hospital for a few weeks, and Buck looked in on me every chance he got. We hit it off real good. When I got back to the unit they assigned me to regular Huey duty—no more hotshot stuff they thought. 'Course, I was able to invent a few new ways to use a Huey, too. And Buck and me, shoot. There wasn't anything one of us wouldn't do for the other."

Cowboy and I stood on the balcony for some time without speaking, reminiscing in our own way about Buck Rogers.

"What about you and Co Hai?" I asked. You're obviously very close. What's with that?"

"Well now, we have this special thing goin'. Twenty-odd years ago, after the collapse in '75, we spent a lot of time together, helpin' each other survive. After a while, we both realized that we meant a lot to each other. She's a beautiful, intelligent woman. She's always been the most excitin' thing in my life. I'd like her to stay out here with me, but she's got her work she's dedicated to, and I cain't very well move in with her there. I manage to visit her four or five times a year."

I could see Cowboy's silhouette plainly now against the glow of the reddening eastern sky. Beyond the stillness, there was a faint annoyance, a humming that interfered with the beauty of the dawn.

"What's that whirring noise?" I asked. "Don't tell me your generator finally kicked on!"

Cowboy cocked his ear and listened. "Heelos! Lots of 'em. They're comin' after us! We've got to get out of here!"

I raced to my room and grabbed my gear, meeting Cowboy at the upper landing and following him downstairs. The helicopters were louder now. I guessed they'd be over the house in two or three minutes. Cowboy led me around to the back kitchen hallway and then down into the wine cellar. He rotated one of the large shelving units ninety degrees, revealing a trap door leading still deeper into the ground. I jumped down into the hole while Cowboy held the flashlight.

Rockets began whistling in and exploding into the upper parts of the house, causing the cellar to shake. I shuddered from the sheer power of the impact, choking on the dust. Cowboy rotated the shelving and closed the trap door behind us. We could hear direct rocket hits again and again on the house. The tunnel trembled, causing dirt to jar loose with each explosion.

"They've never done this before," Cowboy said. "They've searched before, but left the house alone. The bastards are going to level 'er this time!"

"Where does this tunnel lead?" I asked.

"Out onto the side of the bluff, well away from the house. They'll never find us there. We'll be safe when we get out of here."

Ducking down we proceeded through the tunnel.

"Did you dig this?"

"Me? No way! I guess the Michelins had it done. I didn't know it was here for years. The Montagnards showed it to me. Some of the old-timers had helped dig it."

I followed Cowboy for some time, winding through the tunnel. I stooped to keep from bumping my head. My shoulders frequently brushed the sides. Although it seemed adequately vented and shored up with timbers, I was getting claustrophobic from the smell of stale earth. This was definitely an emergency exit only. At last we came to a wooden hatch covered with undergrowth. Cowboy and I struggled to push it open. Through the square of light the beauty and freshness of the early morning jungle burst in on us. Reaching the earth's surface again was like being reborn.

The tunnel opened out into some dense vegetation on the side of the mountain. Cowboy and I slid down to a trail. When we reached the trail, Cowboy stopped. "Okay, dump everything out of your pack."

A bit puzzled by this directive, I complied nonetheless. Once everything was spread out on the ground, Cowboy rummaged through my things, picking up and examining various items. Finally he held up my can of shaving cream and shook it.

"Did you buy this?" Cowboy asked.

"Yes. At least, it looks like the one I bought."

Cowboy took out his pocket knife and pried apart the bottom of the can. To my surprise, a radio locator beacon transmitter fell out of a compartment in the bottom.

"This is how they homed in on my house!"

"They must have switched their can for my regular one at the hotel. Sorry."

Cowboy placed the transmitter on the ground and smashed it to pieces with a rock.

"They'll think the rockets knocked it out of commission," he said.

Cowboy led the way as we headed northeast on the trail, winding down around the side of the mountain. We crossed a saddle and made our way up to the top of the next ridge. In about an hour we arrived atop a small clearing. The ground felt unusually hard and flat under my feet. I scraped through the weeds with my boot and realized we were standing on some old steel planking material.

"This is an old abandoned fire base of the First Cav," Cowboy said. "Be careful to stay in the old perimeter or use the path we came in on. There's all kinds of uncharted mines around this place. Now follow me."

Cowboy went to one overgrown corner of the old fire base and peeled back the vines and undergrowth, revealing a ladder leading down into the ground. I gazed warily into the cavern before going in. There in the dim light were two steel doors facing each other. Two CONEXes had been buried in the ground to serve as the Operations Center for the fire base. They were badly rusted, but still intact. Using both hands I swung open the creaking doors of the large steel cubes.

"Hep yourself to anything you might need," Cowboy called down from above.

The containers were filled with a hodgepodge of military clothing, equipment, and weapons. It was like walking into a combined Army surplus store and armory. I became engrossed in finding the right size fatigues and boots, strapping on LBE, and working the actions of various American and Russian-made weapons. I was able to outfit myself with all the weaponry we might need for the mission ahead.

"You've got quite a cache down there," I said as I climbed back up to ground level.

"It's not hard to get a good stockpile when you know where to look, and you're the only one out collectin'," Cowboy said.

"There's still the question of transportation," I said. "We've got all the equipment and ordnance we need to pay the Hall of Justice a visit, but no wheels to get there."

Cowboy led me to the other side of the clearing. There was a large, camouflaged canopy suspended over a home-rigged canvas covering. Cowboy went to a crank fastened to a tree and wound the suspension ropes back. This slowly opened the canopy and camouflage net, revealing through the subdued light a Huey helicopter, as if hatched out of a shell.

"Care for lunch in Nha Trang?" Cowboy said.

"Where'd you get that?"

"During the collapse of the ARVN army in '75, they were yours for the pickin'."

"Will it still run?"

"Shoot, yeah. I use it all the time for my business. Of course, parts are getting harder to come by."

"How do you get fuel for it?"

"The Americans had fuel stored in underground tanks at dozens of LZ's all over Vietnam. Most of them I'd flown into at one time or another and was familiar with. Chollie located some of them, but not all. They're all overgrown now, like this one, but I know where they are. I mounted that pump on the side of the Huey to pump fuel out of the ground. I've got enough fuel at various places around the country to keep me goin' for another hundred years."

Cowboy swung into his pilot's seat and started cranking up the big jet engine. I slid into one of the door gunner's seats on the side of the helicopter. I put on a flight helmet so I could talk to Cowboy during the flight. The floor swayed from side to side under my feet as the ground shrunk beneath us. It felt like old times to watch the jungle whizzing by below us.

About ten minutes later I spotted trouble. Leaning to the right and looking up I saw a black, waspish silhouette against the sky, heading our way.

"We've got company at two o'clock." I said.

"Hang on," said Cowboy.

He banked the aircraft sharply to the right so that the floor was almost standing vertical. I looked back again and saw two more wasps joining the chase. They were the old, 1960's style Soviet MI-8 helicopters. They opened fire on us.

"Incoming! Three o'clock," I said.

Two rounds of hostile fire ripped through the fuselage. Cowboy dropped the chopper down over the mountain away from our pursuers and took it down as low as possible, winding his way through the valleys at treetop level, heading in a westerly direction.

"Where are you going?" I asked.

"We'll let them chase us into Cambodian air space. Make it look like we're poachers."

We zigzagged our way between the mountains for about thirty minutes.

"Welcome to Cambodia!" Cowboy said.

Cowboy rolled left and right, looking back to see what the Vietnamese government choppers were going to do. After a while the dots began to recede and finally disappeared.

"Thank goodness they didn't scramble their jet fighters," I said.

"They never do. On a radar blip we're just another ivory runner."

"What's our plan now?"

"See that black cloud up there? That's our ticket to Nha Trang. The monsoon'll roll right across Vietnam, and we're going up to 5,000 and go right along with it. They'll never find us in that storm bank. Close the doors—it's goin' to get a little chilly and bumpy."

I spent the next hour-and-a-half hanging on to my seat while the helicopter lurched in all directions. My back and head slammed repeatedly against the wall of the cabin behind me. The only view outside was dark gray mist. It was as if a gigantic monster had the chopper in its grasp and was shaking it vehemently.

At last we descended through the rain below the clouds into a blur of rice paddies. We landed in a clearing hidden in a grove of trees a few miles from Nha Trang.

Chapter XIV

COWBOY AND I WENT directly to the Cathedral to get an update from Father Han. He took us around to the back of the Cathedral to a gardener's storage shed. We went inside, and Father Han closed and locked the door behind us. Then a man stepped out of the shadows.

"Cap'n Buck!" I said.

Cowboy stepped over to greet Cap'n Buck. "Hey now, you rascal, this was even big enough to draw you back to the Nam! How'd you get the word?"

"Father Han cabled me. It's sure good to see you guys. Mac, would you look at yourself? Jax is still solid as a rock, but you've been sipping too many mint juleps."

"Mint juleps I wish! I spend all my time scramblin' around tryin' to fill those ivory orders you keep sendin' me."

"Before we celebrate a full reunion, sounds like we've got to round up two more members of the Team," said Cap'n Buck.

With Cap'n Buck's appearance, I suddenly saw a whole different side to the situation. "Hold everything. Colonel Xi may be behind all this. Cowboy told me he's the Province Chief here. He's probably known about Co Hai for years. Why did he pick this as the time to arrest her? She may be a decoy to get to Buck."

"Hey now," said Cowboy. "Let's not let our imagination run away with us. Co Hai is in deep trouble. That's what we've got to focus on."

"Yes, Co Hai is in trouble. But, why now? Colonel Xi is putting the pressure on her. He may have even coerced her into requesting Z to help her so he could get Z behind bars, too. When you're closing a noose, Z is too cagey to leave on the loose. Then someone tricks Father Han into cabling us to get over here ASAP. I'm sure Father Han thinks the instructions to send the cablegrams came from Hai and Z, but who knows? They slipped a homing device into my gear and used it to trace Cowboy's location and blow up his home, believing Cowboy and I were eliminated in the process. Those are pretty sophisticated countermeasures. This is exactly the way Colonel Xi works, and we always get lured right into his traps. It looks like this whole thing is Xi's plan to destroy Cap'n Buck. If we try to break Hai and Z out of jail it will be pure suicide."

"We've got to try and rescue Co Hai somehow," said Cowboy.

"What else can we do?" asked Cap'n Buck.

"I formulated a plan to try to surprise the guards and make a rooftop escape," I said. "But if we're walking into an ambush, a rescue attempt would be just what they want."

"No, we want to avoid an encounter that could turn violent if we can," said Buck. "Xi may assume the two of you are dead, which may work to our advantage. Maybe I can reason with Xi to give up on this vendetta."

"Fat chance," said Cowboy.

"It's the only real option we have. I need to set up a meeting with Xi and try to persuade him."

After all those years, Xi had finally trumped Cap'n Buck. He had no choice but to go after Co Hai and Z, even though he knew there would be no way out. Cap'n Buck did have one bargaining chip. Before turning Xi's documents over to Mr. Spencer during the War, Cap'n Buck had held back some items of personal interest to Colonel Xi. These included two passbooks for unlisted accounts at Swiss banks. By now these accounts were worth tens of millions, and there was no way Xi could get his hands on the money without the passbooks. The other information Cap'n Buck had was documentation that Xi, in playing both sides against the other, had bilked the National Liberation Front as well as the Americans. Even though these events happened more than thirty years ago, Xi's position in the

Communist regime could be compromised if they knew he had swindled them in the past for his own personal gain.

Cap'n Buck contacted Xi and made a deal to turn the documents over to Xi in exchange for the release of Hai and Z, to include a legally binding affidavit exonerating them from all past crimes against the State. After the exchange Cap'n Buck had Xi's personal assurance that Hai and Z would be allowed to drive away from the area unharmed and leave the country by normal means of customs clearance and public transportation. The exchange was to take place at 6:00 am the next morning in the street in front of the Hall of Justice. Cap'n Buck was to drive there alone in a regular sedan, and Xi was to be alone when he met Cap'n Buck. Cap'n Buck knew full well that Xi would have the area surrounded by sharpshooters. The odds of the three of them getting away from there alive were slim, but it was the only chance they had.

As agreed, the next morning Cap'n Buck arrived by car at the area near the Hall of Justice at 6:00 am. He was stopped at a roadblock set up two blocks from the Hall. Both Cap'n Buck and the car were thoroughly searched to assure that no weapons were on board. Then Cap'n Buck was allowed to proceed down the deserted street to the front of the building. Cap'n Buck got out of the car, leaving the car door open. He waited on the driver's side of the car, which was nearest to the Hall of Justice. In a few minutes the large iron front door to the Hall opened, and Xi appeared. He walked methodically down the stone steps to the street level, stopping about ten feet from Cap'n Buck.

"So, Rogers, we finally meet," said Xi.

"Yes. If only it had been thirty years ago. How long have you been back in Vietnam? Your position as Province Chief gives you a clever cover for your operations. When your smuggling ring was exposed during the War, I heard you fled to Hong Kong and continued your smuggling operations there, eventually establishing yourself as a partner with the underworld Triads."

"A partner? No. We share many common goals. And they are a useful conduit for our commerce. Meanwhile you were living in California, having dedicated yourself to interdicting our enterprises. All these years you have been staging one-man commando raids up and down the West Coast against our trucks and ships. Your tenacity has been very annoying to my associates."

"I'm sure the Triads favor someone like you who has no qualms about working both sides of the fence for your own profit, through involvement in what you like to think of as high-level smuggling, but what amounts to common drug running. You're really nothing more than a two-bit dope pusher."

"You must not separate my business ventures from my commitment to my homeland. They are really one and the same. While my country sees it as advantageous at this time in history to hold out the olive branch to the West so that our economy may once again regain the strength it must have to suck the life out of Capitalism, on the other hand our struggle for victory goes on in American by tying a rubber tube around the arms of those of influence—the politicians, doctors, and educators, and yes the youth of your country—filling their willing, outstretched veins with the numbness all of you as a nation seek deep inside. No, we won't have to bury you. Instead, you will put yourselves to sleep!"

"Let's give it up, Colonel. We're just a couple of old soldiers who can't turn loose of the past. I'm tired of this, and you surely must be, too. There's no sense involving Hai and Chandler in our feud." Buck reached in his pocket and pulled out a packet of papers. "Here's what you want. There's enough here to make you a rich man all over again. And you can destroy the evidence of your past double deeds. These are the originals, and I made no copies."

Xi reached for them, and Buck immediately whipped out a cigarette lighter and lit a flame just below the papers. "No. You don't get these until you hand Hai and Chandler over. Alone."

Xi considered the situation and then waved toward the Hall. In a few moments Hai and Z were pushed out the door. Hai was very wobbly, and Z helped to steady her. They were both handcuffed. Step by step they descended the stairs. Xi signaled them to stop at his side.

"I want to see the papers exonerating them. Let Co Hai read them to make sure they're legitimate."

Hai looked them over and nodded her head that they were in order.

"Okay. Slowly walk Co Hai and Chandler over to me. When you get here, you hand me their papers and I'll hand you yours. Then back away from the car and signal your goons to let our car pass."

After Xi received custody of the documents from Buck, he pulled out a gun. "I do not need my goons," Xi cackled. "I will have the pleasure of doing this myself. Too bad your pilot friend and your other sidekick met with an accident yesterday morning. The three of you have no one to defend you now. Every time I set a trap for you, you always walk right into the middle of it. That is your one flaw, Rogers. You will always place yourself at grave personal risk when something you believe in is at stake."

"Before you pull that trigger you need to decide whether you want to die in the process. Look down beside you."

I slid the manhole cover to one side and aimed a sawed-off shotgun at Xi from inside the manhole. In that moment when Xi realized I had the drop on him, Z stepped over and jerked the pistol out of Xi's hand. I then popped three canisters of smoke and rolled them out in the street to screen our movements from Xi's men on the rooftops.

"Maybe our sidekicks didn't die out there on the mountain yesterday after all, Colonel," said Cap'n Buck. "Now, get down that manhole. We have no problem with leaving you dead in the street if you don't cooperate."

Hidden by the smoke, Xi was forced at gunpoint to go down the manhole into the sewer main. Co Hai, Z, and Buck quickly followed him down. I climbed back up and pulled the cover over the hole. I had rigged some metal bands on the under side of the manhole cover, and I wedged some blocks of wood in them to prevent the cover from being pulled off from the street side. During the night I had blocked shut every manhole cover within four blocks of the

Hall of Justice. While Xi's men ran from manhole to man-hole trying to get down to us, we followed the sewer mains for several blocks before surfacing in a secluded alley where Cowboy had a car waiting. Cowboy also had a handcuffs key, which we used to free Hai and Z from their shackles and to snap a pair of cufflinks on Xi's wrists.

Cowboy's helicopter was ready to go, and we took off immediately. We landed briefly at an LZ west of Kontum to refuel. From there we took the long hop across Laos to an airstrip near Ubon Ratchathani, Thailand. Cowboy's repu-tation in Thailand seemed to precede him. The owner of the air field greeted him and set about to refuel the helicopter while Cowboy let the propeller wind down to a stop.

"Looks like you've been here before," I said.

"Thailand has a good connection with the West," Cow-boy answered. "I pick up specialty items here. Occasionally, I bring some export goods out this way, too."

"As well as some of Co Hai's clients, I'll bet!"

"Hey now," Cowboy said with a wink. "There's always a few real deservin' folks, with the government sittin' on their paperwork, that need to go on and get out of Vietnam pretty quick like!"

"What are we going to do with Xi?" I asked.

"The Thai authorities will be very interested in him," Cowboy said. "It seems he hasn't been payin' the duty on the goods he takes out of Thailand. They've been wantin' to get their hands on him for a long time."

The next day the freight train destined for Bangkok was due to pass through, which was our ticket back to civilization.

"It looks like we've got a long and bumpy train ride ahead of us," I said. "But, I'm looking forward to discovering the mysteries of Bangkok with all of you."

Cowboy glanced at Co Hai and Cap'n Buck. "We'll be leavin' you and Z here," said Cowboy.

"I'll be staying with Cowboy for a while," said Cap'n Buck. "I want to hang around and see how Xi's trial turns out, and I want to check out this end of the business while I'm here, too."

"We have not finished our work here," said Co Hai.

"I don't know if I'd trust that pardon paper they gave you," I said. "You'd better come back with us."

"Don't you worry about us," said Cowboy. "Hai and I have lived in Vietnam under the Commies for a long time, and we know how to get along. They're lots of places to lay low if you know where to look. Hai's still got her work to do, and I've got mine."

"Aw, I judge you'll need some help getting re-situated," Z said, arching his eyebrow.

"Oh, no. Not you, too! C'mon, Z," I pleaded good-naturedly. "Don't run out on me now."

Z looked at Co Hai.

"You know you will always be welcome here," said Co Hai. "It is your decision."

"Vietnam is my real home, too. I know that now," said Z.

A strange feeling of isolation welled up in me as I realized I'd be traveling back to the United States alone. However, I knew Z had never really left Vietnam, and he belonged there.

Z ended up establishing a thriving hunting and guide service. Now that Vietnam is open to American travelers there's a demand for guides. Most of Z's clients are vets like himself who are impelled, one last time, to return to the place where they lost their innocence.

Before my train left I went over to the airstrip to see my friends off.

"Hey now," said Cowboy as he began to wind out the helicopter's jet engine. "Don't you wait thirty years for the next visit. And, don't you go sneakin' up on me next time, neither!"

The helicopter cleared the tree line and began gaining altitude. Cap'n Buck stood in the door of the chopper. I saluted him, and he returned my salute. They rose higher and higher, until eventually even the speck of the helicopter disappeared into the wild blue.

Chapter XV

WHATEVER THE LONG RANGE Recon Platoon meant to me, I realize I only knew a small part of what the total Vietnam War was about. It was really a conglomeration of many little wars. Every story was different. Whether you were a Marine at Khe Sanh, a grunt in the Highlands, Mechanized Infantry in the Delta, an MP in Saigon, an Air Force Forward Observer or jet jockey, a nurse at the 6th Evac Hospital at Cam Ranh Bay, a swabbie on a Navy patrol boat in the Mekong, flying a Dust Off chopper, manning an artillery fire base, a Green Beret at a Special Forces Camp, or a MACV adviser with an ARVN unit, whatever phase of the war you supported, your environment, the people you worked with and your enemy encounters were all unique. It was all part of a macrocosmic, unending process.

While each participant was doing his or her best to stay in one piece, and at the same time not let fellow soldiers down while engaging in that painfully slow, daily personal countdown from 365 to zero, there was a 15 year-old kid in a Little League game in Marked Tree, Arkansas, who had only the vaguest notion of what Vietnam was all about who would be wading through a rice paddy in full combat gear three years hence; there were hundreds of thousands of people employed back home making F-4's, and guided rockets, and bombs, and M-16's, and bullets, and hand grenades, and Huey helicopters, and helmets, and C-rations; there were punks standing before a judge being given the choice: enlist for Vietnam or go to jail; there were

Seals at Coronado, and Jar Heads at Le Jeune, and paratroopers at Bragg, all running in the sand along the beach,
pushing their bodies to the limits every day, getting ready
for their chance; there were mothers and girl friends saying
their last tearful good-byes. All of these elements were constantly funneled into the hopper, night and day, from all
over the country, transported by plane or ship to Vietnam.
At the other end, there were the freedom flights home for the
lucky, and months of rehab or a body bag for those less fortunate; again, there were mothers and girl friends crying
tears of joy or sorrow; and, finally, the pilgrimages to the
Wall for those who could, to trace the names, with no sense
of redemption, of all those who came home too soon.